Captivity

LANDER HAWES

To Alan,
I hope you get a
lot out of the book!

Lander

UNTHANK BOOKS

First published in 2012
By Unthank Books
www.unthankbooks.com

Printed and bound in Great Britain by Lightning Source, Milton Keynes

A CIP record for this book is available from the British Library

Any resemblance to persons fictional or real who are living, dead or
undead is purely coincidental.

ISBN 978-0-9564223-7-8

Cover design by Ian Nettleton and Dan Nyman

Cover image © Ian Nettleton 2011

To Sarah and Penny

Chapter One

When I want to remember my life with Hannah, my life before training with Jakub and acting in a Hollywood movie, the Oscar nominated, star packed, action flick that propelled me to fame; I look through the photographs of us together. These are in a charred photo album on a table in my Canary Wharf flat and I keep delaying buying a new album to replace it. Perhaps I should as visitors always notice the album and so I have to explain to them how it got burnt. Recent dinner guests have advised arranging a few books or magazines on the table to distract visitors from staring, and some have questioned why I just don't store and display the photos electronically. But I like the bulk and heft of the album, and its isolation in the centre of the table, its shape a reproduction of the broader surface.

Usually I find myself mulling over it in the early evening, perhaps twice a week, in that period of time when the day's work is finished, and the evening hasn't properly begun; the hour or ninety minute long interlude before the television can be guiltlessly turned on, and a recipe book consulted. I say try as this time is also when Jeff, my immediate neighbour and the international megastar tennis player, likes to come round and berate me, or impose himself in a friendly manner which is endearing but verges on the irritating. For instance, last Tuesday there was the knock on the door. I answered, clutching a bottle of lager, opening the door with the other hand and raising the bottle hand up to rest on the frame.

'Hi.'

'Josh, what's up?'

Jeff then strode in, loose and confident, looking curiously about, as if this was the first viewing of some luxury suite he'd taken for the night. He's shorter than me, but has a stocky frame and broad forearms; the result of years of tennis training.

'Dude, take a look at this facial hair.'

He was carrying a laptop under his arm, which he put down onto the living room table and opened up. Then he noticed the open photo album on the low table in front of the sofa.

'You looking at those again? C'mon, we've talked about this.'

The photo album was open at a photo of Hannah and me on holiday in Greece, sitting outside a café laughing because of the waiter's way of pronouncing cheese as he took the picture; we're suntanned and Hannah's wearing a printed petal dress. The early evening sun glows on the paving stones and plaster walls, a soft orange and pink that seems to have been absorbed by and be emanating from the bare legs of women and the car tyres and chairs behind us. Hannah and I look like we've been swimming all day and we had, snorkelling in the aquamarine water over seaweed clad rocks that appeared much darker from the cliffs above than the surrounding bright Mediterranean. The photo doesn't suggest the arguments about money we were having around that time, it doesn't reveal the escalating frequency of her half serious sarcasms, the sour remarks and asides which were steadily increasing during the holiday and worsening in tone.

'Do you want to pay for this Josh? Ooh pardon me, I forgot, you're a struggling actor.'

Or:

'Perhaps I should get this, again.'

Or:

'Why don't you just lie and pretend you've been mugged?'

I walked across and picked the album up, and bought it over to where Jeff had set down his laptop. It was typical of Jeff to have bought a gadget round, a prop to provide the centrepiece for conversation. There was a gallery of photos on the screen, a portfolio he had downloaded from the website of a celebrity hairdressing salon.

'Hey, check this one out.'

Jeff leant forward and tapped the keyboard, clicking the gallery back a few panels. It displayed a photo of a male model with long sideburns, each of which tapered to a point, almost touching the corners of the man's mouth.

Jeff looked round to assess my reaction.

'I'm thinking Sherlock Holmes but I'm also thinking werewolf,' he said.

I ignored the screen and sipped from my bottle.

'Beer?'

Jeff began fiddling with a 360 degree multi-angle option that rotated the model's head.

'Yeah. Guueer, in fact no, it's a non alcohol night.'

'How about a juice?'

'Ok. Hit me.'

I carried the photo album over to the kitchen and laid it down, open, on the counter. Then I poured Jeff a cranberry juice and pulled the tray of ice cubes out from the top of the fridge and slapped the tray onto the marble counter. When I'd put the album down I'd turned over a few pages, and as I lifted the tray to bash it again I glanced at the revealed photo. This was one taken at a wedding. I'm almost certain it was in Suffolk but Hannah and I went to plenty of weddings at that time and my memories of them have merged. We're in the garden of a country house hotel alongside another couple; it shows two ordinary men next to their attractive and well presented girlfriends. The men seem uncomfortable in their formal outfits, a little self-conscious, as if they feel uneasy wearing black ties. The women, on the other hand, are happy in their make-up and deep coloured dresses; Hannah's is purple and it suits the dappled browns and oranges of the leaves of the oak trees behind us; it must have rained just before because everything is so wet and gleaming. I'm holding a glass of red wine and I remember that it was Hannah's and she'd given it to me so she could adjust her hair before the picture was taken. We'd quarrelled on the drive there, over all our future plans whose realisation was fading into impossibility.

'I thought we might have got married this summer,' Hannah had said.

I winced.

'I mean we have been engaged for two years now.'

'Well I did think that walk on part was going to lead into something more permanent, and I was waiting for them to propose a contract, and then they didn't,' I said.

'It can't go on like this, Josh.'

5

'People stay engaged for years.'

'No. Dicks stay engaged for years. I mean how do you think I feel when we go to all these weddings and there are people moving on with their lives and we're just doing the same old thing?'

'I suppose it's not nice.'

'It makes me feel shit.'

Then I smacked the tray of ice cubes down for a third time and almost all of the cubes detached and skittered across the marble counter. I gathered a handful into my cupped left hand, the sweeping way a high roller slides together amassed chips with his forearm, and funnelled them into Jeff's drink.

'Honestly man, which of these? I mean do I risk the moustache?'

Jeff was half facing me, his right hand indicating the laptop screen, which showed two panels, one featuring a moustache and goatee combination, and the other a goatee. The photos were close ups; giving the models a dominating and impersonal quality, a resemblance to civic statues.

'You'll look like Drax.'

'Who?'

'Hugo Drax. He's the Bond villain in Moonraker.'

'Can I've that drink?'

I walked round the counter and handed Jeff the juice. He took a considerable swig, managing to maintain eye contact with me for most of it, until the final removal of the glass from his lips; then he swallowed and glanced down for a second, before looking back up.

'You say some weird shit. You know how big moustaches are in Latin America? You know how everyone from Salvador down loves motherfucking tennis? Do you have any idea what this could do for my fan base?'

'Does Castro watch tennis?'

'Oh fuck off.'

He stepped over and put his glass down on the counter behind me. Then, frowning, he swivelled the photo album round, looked at the photo, and turned the page.

'Why don't you just stick with the jackets?'

Recently Jeff had started wearing tweed jackets at all times, on the advice of a public image consultant.

'The jackets are good, I mean I like the jackets, but there's always more, there's always another level, you know.'

He was staring at the photo on the next page.

'What about the jackets and the facial hair, I'm not sure, will that work?' I asked.

'What?'

'You know, as a combination.'

'Is this Paris?'

He tilted the album up and showed me the photo.

'Yes.'

It had been taken on our city break there, standing on the bridge over the Seine. Hannah and I are wearing woollen hats and scarves and our faces are pressed together like the faces of brothers and sisters photographed in mid-winter in snow-laden fields behind farms and rural houses. It was cold enough for our cheeks to be flushed pink and behind us the river looked dark and empty like the deep water of a lake. Hannah had won the holiday in a competition her mobile phone company had organised; they'd paid for everything.

Jeff laid the album back down on the counter, and leant over it, examining the photograph more closely.

'Maybe I've stayed in that hotel in the background,' he said.

'You know moustaches and those tweed jackets won't work. You'll look like something out of Madame Tussauds.'

Jeff folded the album almost closed, keeping one hand inside to mark the page, and then began stroking his thumb over a burnt patch on the front cover. He looked over his shoulder at me.

'I'm in Madame Tussauds, next to goddamn Becker. Becker.'

'And?'

'McEnroe. Agassi. That's who I should be next to. Why don't they put the Americans together?'

Then he began picking at the burnt patch with a fingernail.

'You know this is more a scorch mark than anything.'

So, in terms of interruptions, last Tuesday was more or less typical. Whenever Jeff comes round, he refocuses events on himself. Tonight though, he's in Australia, and so I can mooch about the flat, snacking on a bag of peanuts, and sit for a while on the sofa, the photo album open and supported by a cushion on my knees.

One of my favourite photos was taken in the kitchen of our new build home on the estate, the house Hannah and I lived in for three years. It was her twenty sixth birthday party and she's seated at the table with some colleagues. There are cup cakes decorated with candles in front of her and she's grinning prior to blowing them out. The two girls each side of Hannah are leaning close so as to be included in the picture and it's clear all three know how photogenic they are. Hannah's wearing a black dress and she's still tanned from our holiday six weeks before.

One of the reasons I like this photo is because it presents our life as sociable and enviable. A stranger might look at it and assume that we were accustomed to both hosting and being invited to parties. It's possible that this stranger might even feel jealous, believing us to be living a perfect sort of life made up of a rich network of friends and acquaintances; a fuller life that this stranger might feel eludes him or herself. The photo allows me to briefly persuade myself that our lives then were diverting and eventful.

In contrast I remember those years as barren. During that time I was a fitfully employed actor and often at home during the day. Usually I went up to London once or twice a week to go to auditions, to see a play or meet another actor or a director. But largely I struggled to fill my days or maintain any kind of optimistic momentum. In recollection a few things characterise that time. There were the long train journeys to Waterloo, journeys made in mid morning amid a handful of other passengers, journeys in which I stared from the window at grey skies and listened to the monotonous rhythm of the wheels and clicking undercarriage of the train.

Then there was the estate. At first it appeared to be a desirable place to live with its new houses and new cars and aspirant owner occupiers. In the months after we moved in I found satisfaction by watching a young family cycle off together in their matching Lycra outfits, from saying hello to the regular dog walkers who passed along the path towards the wood behind the estate or from discussing the weather or the council with one or other of my immediate neighbours. Early on I enjoyed these interactions and felt uplifted by my place amongst this discernible community.

But eventually these charms began to fade. I started to notice the silence during the day, when virtually all the residents were at work or school. Then the estate felt abandoned and unpopulated, as if all the real people had left some time ago. In these deserted mornings I would empty the dustbin or visit the newsagents, conscious more than anything of the noise of my own footsteps and the blank windows that I passed. During each walk I had an urge to glance up at one or more of them, an urge that was prompted by the sense that I was being watched, or by an impression of movement at a window. There was never anyone there.

The move onto the estate, and the inevitable acquiring of a mortgage, had been planned to coincide with an upward gear shift in my career. Unfortunately the drama I'd been cast in was indefinitely postponed a fortnight before the start of shooting, and so I was forced back to auditioning for minor, one-off roles; irregular work which hardly paid at all, and yielded few enduring contacts. The resulting financial tension began to wear Hannah's patience.

'I would quite like to have bought a new car, I mean with all the driving that I have to do. All the charging up and down motorways is knackering my Golf.'

These arguments often happened as she was leaving for work, as I was helping her to go, assisting in a way that was placatory and desultory, generally token errands naively intended to make up for my having no chunks of money to buy the shopping at the supermarket every other trip, or split the cost of the house insurance or help replace the shabby carpeting in the spare room. So I'd be there, carrying her bags or files or boxes out to her car, flapping about in my dressing gown while boiling the kettle or toasting the toast. It didn't help that she was more clearheaded than me in the morning.

'If you don't get anything this week, what are you going to do?'

I was at the rear of her car, in dressing gown and slippers, cradling a heavy box.

'I'll get something. The agency's calling me this afternoon.'

She opened the back passenger door, and I half knelt and shunted the box in.

'But I'm saying if you don't.'

'Don't worry, I'll call later and tell you what they said.'

I stood and then followed her round the car, and watched and waited while she settled in and strapped on her seatbelt.

'I might be too busy.'

'I'll try anyway.'

And then she would drive away, me becoming, in those months, concerned over the varying speed of her departing acceleration, as if she began starting off faster and faster each morning; the difference between leaving and escaping becoming less and less clear.

And so my day by day presence on the estate wore on, largely unrelieved by continuous days or weeks of work. Increasingly, I began to feel deprived of privacy. Not that any of the neighbours were deliberately intrusive, or that any of the views into our house were very invasive. More that the instincts which alerted me to being watched were kept constantly aroused, that without keeping the blinds closed at all times it was impossible to say for certain whether I was being observed or not, as I passed between the rooms of our house.

Equally there were the moments when I glanced out through a window and noticed another resident on the inner side of their window, preoccupied and unselfconscious, going about their household affairs. Each of these accidental viewings caused me to feel that I had broken a convention of politeness and worse, done something sinister. Such instances stockpiled, and I started to feel irritated by the inhabitants and the layout of the estate.

These sightings unsettled me in other ways. Everyone I saw appeared as incomplete; as a torso crossing before a window or as an indistinct floating that would turn out to be a duvet being folded or a curtain being adjusted. These blurred motions seemed the actions of ghosts, agitated phantoms banished only by the arrival of evening and conversation and the watching of television. The flurries of movement were muted; as if involving the concealment of noise; as if the houses were sites of acts committed in silence, deeds of pursuit and evasion, or of stealth and secrecy.

Generally the conversations that I had, in these solitary days, were with disoriented furniture delivery men, or postal company employees with an oversized and undeliverable package, or white vans circling round and round. Our front room faced the road that any vehicle making a circuit of the estate had to pass along, and so I'd often go out and wave down the ones that were on their second or third lap.

'Hello mate,' I'd say.

'Do you know where number 68 is?' the driver would ask, from his cab.

'No. I don't think there is one,'

'Oh.'

'There's access to four different estates off the mini roundabout back there.'

'Oh yeah. All this is a bit new for the Tom-Tom, and the map says…'

Conversations that were repetitive and contradicted each other; which revealed the drivers' confusions between half memorised routes and between almost identical layouts of different housing estates; conversations that left me feeling like a man stranded by a roadside, unclear as to my exact location, doubting my estimations of distance, mistrustful of all my bearings.

By the end of the first year the days had become ordeals. When as a matter of circumstance I spent the day at home, I'd crave Hannah's return in the late afternoon or evening. As she came in the door, usually carrying a bag or bags, bringing with her the lingering traces of the energies of her day, as if shreds of conversation and email successes and networking elations were snagged in her hair and clinging to her coat, I'd feel a sense of deep relief at being rescued from another eight hours of tolerating my own disorientation.

Each day like this led me to feel that I'd drifted further into a state of captivity, succumbed more to a numbed condition of complicated origin. It's true that I was separated from the necessary bustle of work, and being immersed in silence for too long is notoriously unhealthy. But I never felt fully satisfied by such explanations. For some reason I felt myself to be a witness, as if my trudging walks around the estate and speechless journeys to London were excursions into a widespread desolation that only became visible during the working day; in that time when the things which make the landscape amenable to people are either absent or switched off.

Hannah did her best to alleviate my deterioration. She insisted on our going out for dinner during the worst patches, to gastro pubs where I sat, propped between the chair and the table, nodding, trying to be receptive to all her entreaties and propositions, and usually revealing my mood by being pathetically bitter and spiteful.

'You just need to keep working as hard as you are.'

'Yeah I know.'

I was chewing a mouthful of pea and mint purée.

'There's always a constant pressure with these things.'

'It's true.'

'Do you want a dessert?'

'I'm starting to bring out the professional in you, you know that.'

She sipped her glass of Sauvignon.

'This does you good, you're at the house too much.'

'I'm just becoming another of your 'projects', aren't I?'

She stared at me, then looked at her plate and shook her head.

'Oh my god Josh, I can't believe you.'

'I think I want an espresso.'

'Do you have any idea of the kind of week I've had?'

'No I don't. Do you want anything?'

This moodiness lifted when my acting career began to pick up. After a year of chasing parts in London I was offered an interesting role in a play that led to other minor parts in weekly television serials and radio plays. Suddenly I was working two or three days a week and preoccupied with memorising lines and arriving punctually and precisely inhabiting the characters I played.

My return to work reinforced my sense that estate life asked so little of me that my inner resources were atrophying. Perversely, that solitary first year had made me into a better actor because I now understood that acting was a way of sustaining an emotional range. Without it I was certain to gradually withdraw from myself until only a core of functional humanity remained; the estate seemed to oversee this process of reduction.

I suppose that our married routine intensified the humdrum tone of those years. Hannah worked in a laboratory that specialised in veterinary science. It was a job that required her to work late and drive long distances as she was in a response team for outbreaks of animal disease. There were always samples to be collected and analysed, a time-consuming, exact and laborious process.

Then there were Hannah's half marathons and triathlons. At the time I had no strong feelings about exercise. I was a timid gym user, only going every couple of weeks and never progressing beyond a short run and experimentation with the cardio-vascular machines. I never thought it worthwhile buying suitable clothes, and went wearing Bermuda shorts and whatever t-shirt was to hand. The gym was no more than a diversion for me, something to pass the time when the day would otherwise drift by. After a while I began to resent my visits; perhaps it was the décor, the monotone greys and rubber blacks and metallic reflections, but I began to view the gym as another neutral space, another void in which people seemed to be suspended; running without moving forward or being inexorably shaped by intense pressure and weighted force.

Hannah, on the other hand, was devoted to a regime of training. She rose three times a week and ran for three or four miles. One evening a week she went swimming and in the summer evenings she liked to cycle.

These disciplines extended to the weekends as well and I spent hours reading newspaper supplements in gym cafés and driving to rendezvous points to collect her and the bike.

One of her favourite meeting spots were the sugar-beet pads in nearby farmland; these concrete platforms were where she stretched and did sit-ups and press-ups. I often sat in the car waiting for an hour, staring out at the featureless mass of corn or the serrated brown rows of tractor-dug soil. There was always a tangible sense of vast agricultural processes at work, of industrial capacity measurements and consumptions presiding over the malleable state of the earth.

To tell the story of how the photo album got burnt, which is also the story of making the blockbuster film, I should start at the time when Hannah and I had been living on the estate for almost three years. By then my acting had settled into a routine of soap opera appearances and TV drama walk-ons and regular stage-work. The story of how the album got burnt is simple; the story of why is more complicated, and that's what will take time.

It's a story with complications and delicacies and nuances that Jeff has consistently failed to understand.

'Just fucking tell me what happened,' he said on one of the occasions when his bemused interest in the photo album was matched only by my reticence about it. This was on a boring Sunday afternoon when, hung-over, he'd lurched over to mine in his white dressing gown, and had installed himself on my sofa, with big hair, holding a Virgin Mary.

'There was a house fire.'

'Man, I know there was a fucking house fire. How else would the thing have got burnt?'

'I can't tell you what happened. I've sworn not to speak about it.'

'Sweet Jesus. Did you burn the place down? I mean what kind of house was it? Did you hate it that much? I've seen those Brit estates. They're small. I mean boxy. In the US even the drug addicts have bigger houses than that. Who would blame you? Not me.'

'Jeff just swivel on it. The album's just part of my old life, you need to respect that.'

Jeff drained the dregs from his glass and lay back on the sofa.

'You asshole, you enjoy this, don't you? You enjoy leading me on.'

On a shelf here, in the Canary Wharf flat, there is a boxed DVD set of the TV drama I was working on at the time of the fire. I own two other copies of this box set; one of these is in my New York apartment, the other is in a safety deposit box in a private London bank. There are a few other items in the safety deposit box, stored to inform the public of the truth of certain events. This story will be put there too, if I feel satisfied with its accuracy.

In a moment I'm planning to watch the TV drama again. But right now I have to collect a parcel. It's with a receptionist in the lobby downstairs, and he called up earlier to remind me to come for it this evening. This package contains half a dozen film scripts from my agent, which a courier dropped off this morning; these deliveries from the agency usually don't fit in my post box on the ground floor; so the staff cache them under the lobby desk.

When I exit the lift downstairs, Joe, the elderly Nigerian, is behind the desk and in conversation with one of the cleaners. She's holding a mop and is standing next to a blue rectangular bucket on wheels. When he sees me he holds his palm to her.

'Go away. Get back on the television. You are confusing me,' he shouts.

I take a deep breath.

'Hi Joe.'

'You know it's here,' he says.

'Oh OK.'

He bends down and pushes boxes around under the desk.

'Are you alright then Joe?'

He answers from under the desk, and then straightens, putting the parcel onto the counter.

'Am I alright? That is a question.'

'Have you got the pen?'

'It's there.'

'Oh.'

Then Joe turns to his colleague.

'This man is on the television.'

She smiles and tries to talk. She moves her lips as if it strains her, as if she finds it uncomfortable.

'Not very often,' I say.

'More than me,' Joe says.

'The famous man,' the woman says.

'And he needs a wife,' Joe says.

They both laugh and I smile, mildly embarrassed, and also aware that these exchanges never happen professionally and smoothly, with a minimum expenditure of time and energy by both parties. As always, my celebrity powers have no influence in the reception, and there's never the fretful scurrying that my presence usually induces in domestic staff and retail assistants and waiters.

Since moving into the building I've noticed other residents having similar chats with the staff. These, however, are usually entered into with gusto by the residents, are heartily engaged in and relished by them.

'Oh hello Joe. How are you? How's Fatima? Really? Marvellous.'

Or:

'Did you see the game? I was there. Yes. The hospitality box. Wasn't it a fantastic goal?'

It's possible that many of these people have a similar routine to mine; a routine that can deprive a person of opportunities for personal contact. They are almost all well dressed City professionals and European businessman, and I suspect that they too spend too much time alone: in hotel rooms, sitting in their flats which perhaps resemble hotel rooms, waiting in airports and meeting in offices with colleagues, very few of whom they know well. A life which can give a person a sense of knowing the world only through glass screens: taxi windows, laptops, twenty four hour news channels in gyms and hotel rooms, aeroplane windows and the windows of first class train carriages. In such a life a little pleasant banter must be something to savour.

I wonder if Joe and the others look forward to these chats. After all their work is dull, as they sit facing the plate glass that fronts the building most of the day or night. Surely there are periods of hours, particularly at night, when almost nothing happens. One shift begins at five in the morning, and it must be repetitive to observe the day starting in the street outside each time: to watch the thickening of the traffic and pedestrians, to note the newspaper delivery vans and the supermarket grocery lorries, to recognise the regular passers-by and notice when one of them is late or absent. Perhaps Joe and the others like the chats for the same reason as the residents; because they provide a moment of engagement in the otherwise predictable spectacle of their day.

As I re-enter the flat the intercom buzzes. I press the button to listen and talk.

'Mr Haddon? Joe here. The family is outside. I thought you should know.'

'Thank-you Joe. Much appreciated.'

'See you later Mr Haddon.'

'See you Joe.'

The family is our code word for the paparazzi. By our, I mean Jeff, me and the reception staff. The term was coined by Jeff, during one of his exasperated rants about the paparazzi. I remember we were both crouching down behind the reception desk at the time, talking with our faces inches apart. Outside, in the street, three or four men, wearing waterproof jackets with cameras on straps around their necks, were loitering.

'These situations always make me feel like a rare bird,' I said.

'What kind of word is paparazzi anyhow? Isn't it Italian? Like pizza.'

'It's definitely Italian. It's a photographer's name in a film by Fellini.'

'Whatever. It's similar to an Italian word. Mafia. The mafia.'

I nodded. On reflection there were parallels to being a paparazzi and a mafia target: the sense of being pursued by a sinister and pervasive organisation, of being under threat from countless and anonymous foot soldiers, of the constant fear of betrayal by those with mixed loyalties.

'You know you're right.'

'It's like we're enemies of the family.'

'We need to make a run for it Jeff. Have you seen Butch Cassidy and the Sundance Kid?'

'No man. But I've got a tennis ball in my pocket.'

'OK. On the count of three...'

Now, in the flat, I leave the package on the kitchen counter and pour myself a juice. After having a piss I put on the DVD of the TV series and sit back on the sofa. The idea had been to create a historical drama with a greater than usual sense of realism, to avoid that toy soldier feel that characterises so many of the epics and classic films and serials.

I remember most of that period of shooting as a series of moments of intense action. Particular instances are embedded in my mind, and together they form a collage of cannons and saddles and shouting men. For instance when our cavalry line surged over the brow of the hill, and clods of earth torn up by the horse's front hooves struck and muddied my linen breeches.

On watching the DVD a person might assume that the filming went smoothly, that we were all professionals, competent in horse handling and dueling and the use of antique armaments. The footage is a mix of coordinated set pieces and detailed minor action. In the opening battle, lines of cavalry converge whilst the camera focuses in on a smaller scene; an infantryman stuffs wadding into a cart-mounted cannon and another fumbles with a flask of gunpowder as the sound of hooves grow louder.

In truth the shoot was at best a crudely managed affair, at worst a disorganized caper that verged on causing serious injury. Only a few of the actors could handle horses well, and the others had mostly exaggerated their experience. The muskets and pistols used gunpowder, and the many firings half deafened, half blinded and scorched the actors. Also it rained constantly, causing us some of the problems that genuine armies had in the past. Horses slipped over trapping or throwing their riders, heavy equipment such as carts and cannon slid down even the gentlest slopes or became bogged in thick mud. Rescue attempts using tow ropes on four wheel drive vehicles were useless, as the ground was too sodden for the tyres to find purchase. So for every minute of footage filmed there was an hour of lines of actors hauling on ropes and stable hands soothing frantic horses.

Watching the drama now, as a viewer, I feel a rush of adrenaline. The drawn swords and contorted faces and cannon-smoke present a life that is the opposite to mine. I'm unlikely to ever watch men die or to experience what it feels like to save a life one moment and kill the next. Nor am I ever likely to know that full self possession that seems to animate these men in the rawness of battle. There are emotional extremes here too, vast measures of defeat and victory that wholly encompass the characters; these are terrains of feeling that are unmapped to me. I'll never know the residual emotions that remain in a person after these experiences, the stirrings and surges that must persist.

In fact it's possible to see this drama as a kind of photographic negative of my existence; its appeal being that it includes everything my life doesn't. There is romantic love here and self sacrifice, heroism and determined purpose, a drama laced together with grand emotions; by comparison, my expressions of affection and hate are disinterested and insipid gestures.

And what makes my confusion more intense is my role in it. There I am being pulled from a horse and wrestling in the dirt before clubbing my assailant with a musket handle. But I remember this as a passing discomfort, like a tackle in a football match; like the viewer I feel essentially unchanged by my participation.

I showed this episode to Jeff once. We sat at opposite ends of the sofa, in profile to each other. Jeff slumped, massaging his knees with his fingertips, bored and distracted, still preoccupied by his day's practice.

'You know something?'

'What's that?'

I looked sideways at him, making reluctant eye contact, fearing what was to come.

'I love watching Brits getting the shit kicked out of them. Even in this, when it's Brits on Brits, it's still good.'

'What?'

He turned to face me.

'Yeah I know. It's bad. But there you go. I can't help it. Look this is a confession. You're the first British guy I've been friends with.'

I shook my head slowly.

'I can't believe you. You know really, you're a terrible cunt.'

Jeff extended his left arm and hand, gesturing with the palm face down.

'Hey Josh. Easy there. That's not a nice word.'

'No you don't understand. It's a very particular expression with a very particular meaning.'

'Explain yourself man. Politeness dictates.'

'Ok, well…'

My day today, like most days, has been mundane; I spent the morning in the gym and the afternoon browsing on the internet and sending emails. Soon I'll cook a meal and maybe telephone my brother. The challenge I face is how to use days like this properly, how to respond to them in a way that is committed, in a way that does justice to their possibilities or that counters the comfortably yielded to nothingness that seems to seep into and gradually fill them.

Despite my recent celebrity and my relocation to Canary Wharf, the feel of the days here seem to resemble the days on the estate. For instance the landline in this flat is a private number known only to my family, who call in the evening or at the weekend and rarely during the day. In spite of this the phone rings most mornings or afternoons with companies calling to offer me double glazing or satellite TV or home insurance.

These calls are identical to the ones I answered in our house on the estate. They have the same unreal quality. At first I wonder if it's my phone ringing. Then there is a moment when I assume the sound is a neighbour's phone, or a mobile in the corridor outside. When I finally answer I respond to the questions politely but negatively, and presently the call is concluded with a minimum of fuss.

In the early days of living on the estate my treatment of these callers was different. I was inclined to seize the handset angrily and inform the salesperson that I was busy; often I'd hang up during their polite and elaborate greeting. But in time the persistence of the calls disabled my aggressive response. They became, like the weather or television programs, so much a part of the fabric of experience that reacting to them seemed ridiculous; the easiest solution was passive submission to the role they invited me to play.

It was during the filming of the TV drama that I first worked with Jakub. He was a consultant to the production, a choreographer for the combat scenes. After his first few days on the set he became a prominent and much discussed personality. When the actors dressed in the costume tent in the mornings, someone usually described Jakub's most recent violation of social conventions. On the day before he and I were introduced, the day before the fire, I saw him be typically wayward.

I was mounted on a horse on the top of a slope, alongside another mounted actor. We'd just finished another attempt at shooting a scene where our cavalry charge some infantry and horsemen. The take had failed again as their horsemen hadn't engaged us in the planned place or at the right moment. Once more the fighting had started too close to the tree-line and our cavalry had swept on into the woods where the low lying branches and uneven footing had created dangerous conditions. The other actor and I had ridden back to our starting position, and were watching the confused scene below. There were riders remounting their horses near other horses whinnying and thrashing in the mud, while infantry untangled their rifle straps and themselves from the bushes they'd pressed into to avoid injury.

Jakub appeared on a rally motorbike heading across the grass towards all this confusion. The bike wove and skidded on the wet ground.

'Here we go,' the actor next to me said.

There were strict rules on the set about where vehicles could go. In the main marquee was a blown up aerial photograph of the entire site. This was marked with shaded patches with a key in the lower right corner. Each patch was where various types of vehicles could go or where only horses and men were allowed. Otherwise there would be footage of the seventeenth century fields marked by tyre tracks. Jakub was crossing a patch 'off-limits to all vehicles'.

Every actor had been issued with a microphone to receive instructions from the director. Mine was on a cord around my neck and I reached under my shirt and turned it on.

'Jakub, get off that bike,' I heard the director say.

'I'm showing them.'

'You're on the grass, get off the bike.'

Then Jakub reached the muddy track and the tree-line, dismounted and approached some actors near a cannon. He began talking and he jabbed his clipboard at them for emphasis. Behind, the director was jogging slowly towards him along the track. The director stopped close by and bent down a moment, pausing for breath; then he began gesturing and talking, his greying hair shaking against the collar of his waterproof jacket. Jakub started to reply and moved and slapped the cannon with the clipboard to underline a point. The cannon fired, accidentally triggered, engulfing both men and the actors in smoke.

This was the kind of behaviour that Jakub had a reputation for, nothing criminal or really vicious, just a persistent determination to shape the filming that led to a few eccentric decisions, and the occasional accident.

I must have seen this first episode on the DVD a dozen times. My leather sofa is very comfortable, and the flat is so high up that it's perfectly quiet. Just recently I've been going through the back catalogue of a director who wants to cast me, and this has meant spending afternoon after afternoon with his films. These are mainly ones I've seen more than once before, as most are well known Hollywood productions, but I was happy to watch them again.

The daytime viewing of films has always been work to me. When we lived on the estate I spent much of my empty time watching films. These were bought on trips to London, when following my audition or a meeting I might visit the DVD shop at the British Film Institute. Here was a vast array that I liked to linger over, reading the backs of the boxes and choosing two or three. Over time I evolved strategies to make inroads into all this cinematic history; for instance following the careers of famous actors by buying films from every stage of their working lives or buying the obscure early work of influential directors.

I developed obsessions with particular directors that lasted for months. Herzog, for instance, helped me through the difficult second winter on the estate. His film about the Bavarian village, using hypnotized actors, hypnotized me. Over the following spring I watched most of the Charlie Chaplin silent comedies, and at times my laughter rang out in a house that was otherwise silent save for the whirr and click of the freezer and central heating.

I usually lost all sense of time during these viewings. With the blinds drawn I tended not to take much notice of the passing day. On the more extreme occasions Hannah would arrive home to find me on the sofa beneath a blanket, peering guiltily up at her. At these moments I must have seemed no more than a grub forming a cocoon; a larvae spinning a protective casing, nurtured by the incubating energies of the television screen.

Chapter Two

It's evening now, and when I stroll across the flat to see the view and then wander over to the black marble counter in the kitchen area, I can only think how insulated this flat is. So little sound penetrates the thick glass that the landscape outside might be on volume control, and, besides Jeff, there's usually no chance of an unexpected knock on the door, or an outbreak of disruptive music or noise. The third resident in this corridor is a German financier but he doesn't live here permanently. Any visitors must enter through the lobby downstairs, where Joe or Stan have to authorize them.

Theoretically, this building is a sanctuary of calm and civility; a utopian and Starship Enterprise style affair characterized by deference in the corridors, a taste for short business-like greetings, and a tangible sense of purpose and resolve in the lifts. In reality, however, this ideal is constantly punctured, usually in my case by Jeff. There was the night, for example, when we ended up drunk on the roof, squabbling right at its edge. We'd been drinking whisky at mine, since returning from a nightclub in Mayfair. This incident started as we were seated opposite each other, at the lounge table.

'So what man, what is the most valuable thing here?' Jeff asked.

I stared at him woozily for a moment.

'It's probably that painting.'

'Bullshit.'

Jeff stood up, leaning heavily forward onto the table.

'What?'

'It's not,' he said, slowly shaking his head from side to side.

'Yeah right. It's your watch. Silly fucking me.'

'The watch is classy, but it isn't that.'

He was leaning knuckle down onto the table, looking around. I pointed to a slender assemblage of copper rods and glass cubes in a corner.

'It's not the figurine.'

Jeff waggled a forefinger at me.

'No I know what it is. It's your burnt photo album; the one from your old life.'

He stood up and walked over to the sofa.

'Where is it?'

The album was in its usual place in the middle of the low table.

'It's there.'

He climbed over the back of the sofa, picked up the album, turned round, and then stepped back up to stand on the sofa. He opened the album up and began turning the thick, card pages.

'Umm, I don't think I've seen these ones.'

Then he put one foot onto the top of the sofa, and it tipped over backwards towards me, delivering Jeff, still in a standing position, to the floor.

'Jesus Christ be careful,' I said.

'Don't worry Josh, you can afford it.'

I stood up.

'Jeff, just put the album back.'

He snapped it closed.

'I say why don't we take this little conversation, to the roof?'

He pivoted, ran to the door, yanked it open and charged out.

'Jesus.'

In a flash I was chasing, just in time to see Jeff, at full sprint, his head tilted back, rounding the nearest corner. There was a crash as he threw open the utility door that accesses the stairs to the roof, and momentarily I was bounding up these concrete steps. They led out to the lower section, which is a verandah area of wooden pillars with trellises between, and pavilion like roofing. There are terracotta troughs, half full of soil, where climbing plants are grown in the summer.

'Hey, tough guy.'

Jeff waved at me. He was sitting at a table at the far end, one knee propped up on the other, the photo album resting on his horizontal calf.

'It's nice up here, isn't it?' I called out.

'The view's great.'

I was approaching him, steadily, making no sudden moves. Jeff had picked up the photo album and was holding it close to his face, near and then further away, inspecting a detail.

'You know how value is measured Josh?'

I was about fifteen metres away.

'No. Enlighten me.'

'By what someone will do to protect something, by the risks they'll take.'

He stood up, and gripping each side of the album with both hands, raised it above his head.

'Jeff, what are you doing?'

I stepped a pace closer, and he stepped one pace back.

'No closer, man. That's a long drop.'

'Jeff, if you throw that, I swear to God I'll...'

'Burn me out?'

'What?'

'C'mon, was it the insurance money? I bet it was the insurance money?'

'Sorry?'

'Don't tell me that you wanted to kill her.'

'Christ Jeff. Is that what you think? Is that what this is all about?'

'Yeah. Of course it's what I think. What do you expect people to think? It's what everyone fucking thinks.'

He dropped his arms, letting the album fall to the front of his crotch.

'I can't believe you're denying it. I mean, I'm your best friend.'

'Of course I didn't burn my own house down, you gigantic cock.'

So without Jeff around I am able to begin preparing my dinner in peace: I can listen to Radio Four, a pastime he considers ridiculous; I can cook the simple British food he considers tasteless and unfashionable.

And I can drink mug after mug of tea, a habit which induces a kind of goggle-eyed apprehension in him.

The contents of the fridge here are much the same as they were in our fridge on the estate. It's easy to imagine that the diet of a famous actor includes foods usually associated with the very rich. But there's no caviar in my fridge, nor truffles, nor rare vintage champagne. Instead when I kneel down in front of the door I see stacked packages of steaks and chops, a row of cartons of smoothies and fruit juice, and the bright red and orange peppers and bags of spinach and potatoes clustered together on the lower shelf.

During our life on the estate I tended to cook the evening meals. Hannah's late arrivals made this practical; she usually returned after six and then sat at the table in the kitchen. From there I'd listen to whatever she had to tell me, and now and again I'd have an anecdote or a story for her. But generally I'd be the one listening and moving around the kitchen: filling the kettle and boiling it, chopping the asparagus or broccoli stems, peeling the potatoes, prodding the chicken breasts in their bowl of marinade and maybe reheating the carrot or cream of mushroom soup that I'd prepared and blended earlier.

Most days I'd have taken some time to think about, prepare and then buy ingredients if our stocks were low. This process used to begin with me appraising the contents of the fridge, then continue with my flicking through some cook books to remind myself which herbs or vegetable should be used, and end in a farm shop or a supermarket, or with a freezer bag of meat defrosting in a plastic bowl on the kitchen counter.

Because I was at home so much this was easy. More than that, the process of cooking helped to use my spare hours; frequently it provided my only daily objective. Cooking involved visiting places that I would otherwise have no reason to go to: delicatessens, farm shops, speciality food shops and market stalls. I browsed for anchovies, yellow courgettes and fresh parsley, asked for Savoy cabbages and found jars of chili jam or bars of spiced dark chocolate.

Each excursion ended with me unpacking my bounty onto the kitchen counter to decide how to use or store it. And I suppose I began to find solace in these bright spices and bloody meat and muddy vegetables. Amid the daytime silence of the estate, a silence that I could hear my own breath in, they seemed the tokens of a raw life that lay distant from my car bound routines and net of obligations. At last, I felt, here was something real. So the meals became less a recommended mix of proteins and vitamins and carbohydrates than an antidote to the sterility of what I felt to be lying around me. Of course celebrity chefs were starting to be popular then and played their part in affecting my attitude. But in the main I found a genesis in the rolling of dough or the pummeling of meat, as if each were an orb of primordial fire that I was kneading into shape. Whenever I cooked a meal for Hannah I imagined myself as providing her with the essential substance of the earth; that I was nourishing us both with a core matter that existed in abundance – only very far from our lives.

The knife set I have here in the flat is very different to the assortment of kitchen knives I had on the estate. Now I have a rack of Japanese Tojiro Senkou knives that stand in a wooden block on the counter. When I slide one out it is reassuringly heavy and the blade is thicker than the supermarket-bought knives I used to own. The Japanese knife feels densely made and its steel seems immovably fused with the Micarta laminate handle.

The blade passes easily through the leeks and asparagus stems. It takes the merest pressure, no more than a tilting forward onto the knife, to press the steel through to the chopping board. When I've finished preparing the food, when I've dropped the vegetables into a pot of boiling water and slid the marinated chicken into the oven, I might go and watch more of the drama series while everything cooks.

In this series, there are significant differences in my appearance between the opening episode and the later ones. In the first I am plump and healthy, a self assured and obstinate young officer. In the later episodes I am a different person: hollow-eyed and distracted, frowning and squinting whenever anyone talks to me. A viewer might attribute this change to my acting skills, assuming that I was playing the role of a young man in the process of being traumatized by the experience of warfare. In fact the reason I looked so ill and tired for those weeks was because of a frightening event and its aftermath; a terrifying experience one night three years ago. As it was our lives were disrupted for several months.

In fact I remember doing the cooking that fateful evening three years ago, a few hours after seeing Jakub accidentally set off the cannon and argue with the director. During the journey home I had the usual sense of being channeled through a maze: the grey walls of the warehouses on the retail estates; the steeply angled embankments flanking the motorway; the pressing rush of vehicles; all these combined to make the traffic seem almost biological, a cellular but automatic flow; as if Britain were a mechanical organism I was in microscopic service to.

The drive from the TV shoot took forty five minutes and when I went inside Hannah was in the kitchen. I called to her as I wiped my feet.

'Hi. Are you ok?'

'Not too bad. Your sweatshirts are upstairs.'

I walked around the living room, putting my bag on the table and laying my jacket over the corner of the sofa. Then I went into the kitchen.

'Why are you in here, it's my turn?' I asked.

'I didn't think you were coming back in time.'

'You should have called.'

'I did,' she said.

'Oh. Oops.'

I went over and kissed her. I tucked her fringe up behind one of her ears and rubbed her back through her striped blue jumper. Then I rested my chin on her head. Hannah always made me think of Scotland or Cornwall or Ireland, and a milieu of camping holidays and trekking adventures and coastal walks. She had an oxygenated quality, something that originated in her white teeth and clear complexion and green eyes.

'Is that new?' I asked.

'No I've had it for ages.'

I spent half an hour cooking supper, white fish baked with chorizo and tomatoes. Hannah lay on the sofa and watched the news while I clanked around. Then we ate at the kitchen table.

'Work's getting busier at the moment,' she said.

'Why?'

'Apparently there's an equine virus near Oxford. We've been told to go and take samples.'

'Is that serious?'

'Probably yes.'

'Will you wear a white coat?'

'Jesus Christ Josh,' she said.

'Sorry.'

We watched TV after eating. I eased my arm behind her neck, and she leant on my shoulder. There was a drama on, and I knew one of the actresses.

'I know you know her,' Hannah said.

We went to bed around ten thirty. I massaged Hannah's shoulders for a while and then we slept. Later I was the first to consciousness, smelling smoke and noticing it seeping under our bedroom door. I shook Hannah awake and we hurried downstairs. The fire was already fierce there, flames leaning menacingly out of sight, disco lighting the walls into dull orange and mottled shadow. Hannah tried to close the kitchen door, but the fumes were too dense. She recoiled, pressing her right hand to her mouth and clutching the other to her stomach. The smoke was tumbling and pouring along the hall ceiling, and I coughed as I unchained the front door.

Chapter Three

In the event of a night time fire here in Canary Wharf I'm not sure I'd survive. A kitchen fire would generate enough smoke to make crossing the living area impossible. If the leather furniture in the living area ignited, perhaps due to ash dropped from a guest's cigarette, the intense heat would trap me in the bedroom. A blaze in any of the neighbouring flats would fill the corridor and stairways with smoke, making them impassable. The exit stairs are built around the outside of the central lift shaft, and if a fire reached there, no-one remaining in the building could hope to escape, unless they made it to the roof.

Jeff has oxygen equipment in case of a fire. He has goggles and a mask connected to a back mounted cylindrical tank, like a New York fireman. Incredibly he has an axe as well, to clear obstacles with, or so he claims. Once I was descending the stairs and met him ascending wearing this gear and holding the axe.

At first I thought he was a genuine fireman. My second thought was that he was a burglar; then I realised who it was.

'Jeff are you alright?' I asked.

'You know these stairs?' he asked me.

'Only to walk down.'

He was breathing heavily, gasping for breath.

'You don't use the lift?'

'Not always.'

'Oh.'

He bent down and put his hands on his knees.

'Most people just have fire extinguishers,' I said.

'There are almost three hundred steps,' he said.

Since then I've tried not to burn toast in case he smells the smoke, assumes the worst and tries to break my door down. But a serious fire seems unlikely. I don't smoke cigarettes which eliminates what I assume is the most common cause of domestic fires. The building is less than ten years old, so the wiring is presumably in reasonable condition, which eliminates electrical fires, surely the other common cause.

As a cook I've put out a few pan fires. The proper frying of steak was one of the first cooking skills I taught myself on the estate. This involves heating a fair quantity of oil to smoking point and, in the early days of learning the procedure, I often just dropped the steaks in or flipped them too vigorously, in each case splashing oil out of the pan to be ignited by the gas flame below. These fires were easily extinguished with a damp tea towel. The effect was never more than a scorched pan and a few blackened kitchen tiles. But still, every time it happened I had a few moments of panic, a few seconds of shocked reaction at the suddenness of the fire and the gusto and rampant energy of the flames.

Now, in the flat, I have a fire extinguisher and a fireproof blanket, both fixed to the side of the kitchen counter, each in their metallic case. I doubt that I'll ever have to use either as my cooking techniques are flawless now. These days I'm more likely to crash my car than ignite a steak. I suppose I keep the extinguisher and the blanket there because you could say that watching my house burn down has made me wary.

Prior to ours I'd only seen one structural fire first hand. This was when a garage along the road from my parent's house burnt down. My brother and I saw the smoke from the windows and ran out to investigate. We joined the other locals gathered on the street and together watched the building burn. In less than ten minutes it had collapsed. I remember two things clearly: the almost immediate melting of the first floor girders and the garage owner on his knees beating the road with his fists.

My initial reaction to our house fire was emotional. There was the hasty departure through the front door, then a minute or two when I smashed through a window with a plant pot and managed to retrieve a few drawers and a small filing cabinet from the lounge. After hurling out the first items I blundered around inside while Hannah urged me on from the verge.

'Get the photos,' she shouted.

The photo albums were in a low drawer and, one under each arm, I edged out of the window and toppled onto the grass, scattering our possessions about. There were tears and mucus all over my face.

'Christ,' Hannah said.

I turned over, hyperventilating.

'God Josh.'

And then the immense heat pressed us back. At this stage my instincts began to subside. Hannah and I became part of a slack faced crowd retreating to the far edge of the cul-de-sac. A small audience formed, and I watched the fire with them, frowning and conscious of a dumb heaviness to my expression, a lead-browed incomprehension which flattened my cheeks and mouth. I was clutching a rug that I'd tried to wrap a drawer in, and considering my baggy jeans and naked torso, I must have resembled a toddler clutching a comfort blanket.

The scene had a cinematic quality: the people silhouetted in the flickering light, the smoke and fire bulging around the house, the flashing arrival of a police car and a fire engine. Then there were the shouts of the firemen fading in and out, this varying of volume matched by their movements, which seemed to slow and then speed up, as if responding to some remote control.

Neighbours were talking to me but I didn't answer. Instead I watched their urgent and insistent faces with a concerned but detached interest. Later I discovered that this reaction is a first stage of shock, a mental slowdown in response to trauma, a disorientated sleepiness that affects mountaineers in blizzards and sailors capsized at sea.

There were now three or four hoses being directed at the flames. The firemen were cradling and hauling on the hoses; the canvas tubes twisting and stiffening, forced to tautness by the inner pressure of the water; the men shuffling and huddling as they kept control. A circle of spray sprung from one nozzle and its crew crouched, their soaked jackets as gleaming as celluloid, behind this vapour shield.

'Keep it going,' one man shouted.

Some of the firemen must have been volunteers. I recognised the manager of the garage and a regular from the pub near the hotel. It was odd to see these docile husbands and fathers so resolute and yelling instructions. They seemed more inclined to watering gardens than burning houses, to decorating rather than dousing these new-build homes.

My stupefied condition meant I barely reacted. My legs stood immoveable and each turn of my head felt prolonged. My voice, had I spoken, would have been a dumb moan. Oddly, my dominant hope was that Hannah wouldn't see me like this. When I was peering around it was to locate her, so as to avoid or at least ready myself for one of her curt remarks. This confusion of priorities, I later discovered, is, along with the sense of disorientation I experienced, another initial symptom of shock.

My concern was that my unfocused state would irritate her. I recognised this condition and feared that Hannah would recognise it as well. It seemed a condition familiar from our life together, a condition I was prone to and one she found irritating.

It tended to arise when we were shopping, usually towards the end of a long morning of walking around town or of visiting different retail estates. It would start with a lessening in my field of vision and a sense that my face had begun to droop. The end of my eyebrows would feel as if they were slanting and tipping downwards, a kind of tense contraction of my cheeks and mouth set in, and then a powerful diminishing of my ability to concentrate, accompanied by a headache, arose.

I suppose it was a fatigue caused by exposure to too many shop fronts and windows, to too many vivid banners and advertising posters, to too many brightly lit displays of products. Their visual display had an overloading effect. But there was more than this to it. Amid all the manufactured excitement of the adverts and the clothes and books and computer games, I felt curiously inactive. It was as if all these things stimulated me but provided no way to alleviate what they aroused.

It was this conflict, between activated instincts and a lack of opportunity for action, which affected me at the house fire. Part of me wanted to run at the house or grab a hose from a fireman and charge in. The other part knew that it was time to stand back and leave the matter to the professionals. I suppose my deadened sleepiness was caused by the breaking down of extra adrenaline and hormones.

A hand grabbed my arm and I looked round at a paramedic.

'If you'll come sir.'

He led me over to the ambulance and I sat in its open back doors. Even from forty metres or so I could feel the heat from the fire.

'I'm OK,' I said.

Then he was pressing an oxygen mask to my mouth and a red blanket was draped across my shoulders. There were others being tended to on the grass nearby: a fireman who had tried to enter the house was being given oxygen too; another was a neighbour who was suffering from shock, she was breathing heavily, propped on her elbows with her legs splayed out in front of her; the final person was Hannah.

She was standing with her back to me, facing the blaze, clutching her left forearm. Alongside, a female paramedic was kneeling down, searching through the medical supplies in a bag. Then she sprayed some liquid onto Hannah's arm; they exchanged tiny smiles as the paramedic began rolling a bandage around the burn.

There were similarities between Hannah and the female paramedic. Hannah had a capacity for busy concentration, a certain readiness with prompt athletic responses that must be a necessity for emergency work. I was used to these manifesting on our holidays and bank holiday weekend excursions: when hill walking she'd be organised with maps, she'd remember the sun cream and always know which stream to drink safely from; when sailing she'd be brisk with the ropes, squinting up and releasing the sail or adjusting the canvas with taut jerks.

When we'd met I'd been attracted by this side of her. At university I took to visiting her drunk, clutching a pint, or immediately after jogging, sweating and flushed. I'd stand roused in the threshold of her room, with its line of shoes and row of books, waiting while she completed trivial details: folding her glasses away or finishing some notes. Then she'd swivel around, excited by my role as an intruder.

In the part of London I live in now, close to Canary Wharf, I often see women who resemble her. They jog past, their hair kept back by headbands, wearing fluorescent plastic jackets and blue or black Lycra leggings, with a slowly intensifying pinkness on their faces; that gradual as opposed to sudden flushing, which, when it occurs under the duress of exercise, distinguishes the fit from the unfit. Presumably they are the employees of investment banks or accountancy firms or management consultancies; careers that Hannah may have pursued, had she not become a research vet.

The fire was extinguished close to dawn. By then the facade of the house had slumped in, the rubble covering the front garden. The disorderly sprawl of the fallen walls resembled corroded pyramids. Everyone was grey and smudged, newly rendered by the ash and dust. It was as if freshly made clay figures tottered about, exploring and unsteady.

The bystanders and firemen had become daubed with bold stripes and circles, as though freshly initiated and bearing the primitive markings.

Some of the biggest losses were our clothes and shoes. We lost the brown coat I'd bought during our holiday in south west Ireland, one of the stupendous bargains of my life. We'd lost Hannah's collections of jeans and leather boots and cut off jackets. We'd lost my chunky woollen sweaters, the ones I'd amassed choosily over four or five years, choosily because I wanted to be warm between November and February but also to avoid the poacher look. There were her formal grey trousers and black jacket tops and thin v-neck sweaters that she wore at work when she wasn't in the laboratory. We lost the cowboy boots that my brother had bought back from America for me, the boots that I'd never worn because of the way they made my buttocks stick out. Gone forever were my short sleeved shirts and high collared Lee T-shirts and two suits, my supermarket and department store boxer shorts and black socks, our expensive weather proof jackets from camping shops and my silk or silk and polyester combination ties in bronze and silver and gold. We lost the coat hangers and the shoe laces and the beach towels and the spare duvets and the gloves and the scarves and the dirty laundry and the wicker laundry basket the laundry was in.

We had lost all our electronic products: the 48 inch screen television that I'd had specially listed on our home insurance, Hannah's i-phone, the Sony DVD player that I often forgot to turn off at night, the X-Box I usually played with when my brother came over, the radio stereo, the digital cameras and both our laptops.

We lost all the flat pack Swedish furniture. There was the wardrobe that had taken me a month on and off to assemble, a month during which I'd joked to Hannah that we might need to take the roof off the house and the ceiling off the room, just to be able to maneuver this cumbersome object more freely. There were the two bookshelves laden with play scripts and DVD's and my odd novels and Hannah's classic novels that always seemed about to tip over forwards so I'd wedged folded cardboard under their fronts. Then there were the rugs and mats and their molted strands of fluff that had to be hoovered up, the folding plastic chairs and plastic storage crates, the trolley filing cabinet that held our certificates and school photographs and passports and PAYE forms and insurance details and bank statements, the CD rack full of CDs, the table with the metal legs and the office furniture swivel chair that had broken the second time I sat on it. There was the mattress from my mother and the bed frame the removal men had put up and the bedspreads and sheets and pillowcases we'd bought in the late summer and January sales. There were the simple light wood picture frames that, like almost everything else, had odd sounding names in Swedish, or were just from HomeBase.

When now, here in Canary Wharf, I pause the DVD and go over to the kitchen and take the foil wrapped chicken from the oven and the leeks and asparagus out of one pot of boiling water and tip the lemon rice into a colander from another, I think over how visible the effect the fire had was on me. When I've put the plate onto a tray and returned to the sofa, I am confronted by the paused image of my face in close up. It's surprising how flabby I am, how much my jaw line is obscured by fat swelling my chin and throat. There is a few days stubble growth, which with the puffy weight creates a picture of a man who is at the sharp end of circumstances, who is not in as much control as he would like.

Now, I am lean and muscular, and it took just three months of training with Jakub, in preparation for the film, to alter my physique. These days I'm not as strong as I became then but I'm still very athletic. If I tense the muscles in my leg I can feel their coordinated flex, from the ankle to the thigh, and if I forced my hands together I could bend this aluminum TV dinner tray into a U shape. Over the last two years I've often caused concern when slamming car doors, although I'm sure I haven't caused proper damage. I have to be careful now when leaning forward onto tables, several times I've misjudged it and tipped them in my direction, sliding pints of lager or plates of food or books and papers onto the floor. Whenever I see my mother she expresses surprise, and lifts her glasses to her eyes.

'Look at you,' she says.

Now, when I have a cold or flu, nobody really believes me. It as if, in their eyes, I have passed into another condition of being, a condition in which the laws that govern most lives have less effect. It as if they feel vaguely threatened, as if I can't be trusted not to spring across the room and strike at a head or neck in a crippling way. There are other consequences; when I watch sports on television I find myself assessing the athletes: noticing the development or otherwise of particular muscle groups, evaluating their powers of balance and the fluency of their reactions.

After eating, I leave the flat to go for a cigarette. I put on my leather jacket, and pat my pockets to check I have my phone, and a pen to sign autographs. Going down in the lift I try to whistle, in the way I think is customary for people when alone in lifts, but produce only a faltering note, like a child's novice efforts at the flute, and so settle on putting my hands in my trouser pockets and fidgeting with my feet.

I'm halfway across the lobby, staring at Joe's back and deciding whether to talk to him, when I hear a shout.

'Josh.'

Suzie, Jeff's girlfriend, has just come through the main entrance and is approaching; she is waving and smiling exuberantly, as if we were family.

'Oh hi Suzie, how are you?'

I stoop and kiss her on the cheeks and then we face each other, her smiling in a way that is difficult to ignore, that is almost difficult to look at, her coat thrown open, her ample and globular breasts thrust towards me.

'I'm fine, fine. Oh the office. Busy, god.'

She smiles again.

'How are you?'

She rises up and kisses me on the cheek, at the same time she squeezes my hand.

'Not bad. You know. I've been reading some scripts.'

'I could see into your flat from the street outside, your TV is massive you know.'

The flat is on a corner of the building and two of the walls are glass windows that are sheer from floor to ceiling; the TV is visible from many points outside, such as the square in front of the entrance. There are places in the street, and from the nearby hotel and offices, from which the whole screen can be seen.

'Did you see any photographers outside?'

'No, I don't think so.'

I glance over her head, through the windows.

'Maybe it's getting too dark for them.'

Suzie flicks her hair back and stares at me.

'Are you, er, around, over the next few days?'

Our mutual eye contact, which so far has been meandering and cursory, locks on.

'Yeah, should be.'

'I was planning on staying at Jeff's. I'm having the bathroom redone at my place.'

I nod slowly, analysing this piece of information, almost instantly concluding that the bathroom excuse is bullshit, and that she's expecting sex, maybe even sex that's extreme and metropolitan; the kind which requires accessories.

'Oh right.'

'New tiles and shower cabinet.'

'Nice.'

We gaze at each other, without speaking. I'm staring at the pliant skin of her face; noting its tinted hint of a permanent tan in waiting, its resistant firmness and porno buttock plasticity.

'I've got to meet my sister later,' she says, eventually.

I'm trying to stop myself imagining her naked, or even her naked except for high heels, on her hands and knees, face scrunched into the pillows on my bed; but it's very difficult.

'Well, um, I'll be in the gym in the morning, didn't Jeff get you a membership?'

'Oh. Oh right. No yes he did. I might see you there, then.'

She smiles again, enthusiastically.

'OK. See you tomorrow.'

'See you.'

Over by the main entrance I stand, waiting for a group of men who have been hauling luggage out of a taxi to finish coming in, and I watch Suzie's reflection in the window, as she is waiting for the lift. She has her back to me, and so I stare at her reflection fully, without disguise or secrecy. The problem of Suzie has been growing over the last couple of months, and it seems clear that the unspoken matters between us will be resolved in the next few days.

There is the matter of the distance that has been opening up between her and Jeff, and the further problem of the way that I caught her looking at me, one night two weeks ago, when the two of them had come round for dinner. They were sitting on the sofa, and Jeff was on his mobile, having one of the aggressive conversations that he so often has, with a journalist perhaps or a financial advisor, or one of the employees of his agent, or even maybe with a relation of his ex-wife's; the relations who seem dedicated to creating innovative and breath-takingly imaginative legal predicaments for Jeff to try to escape from. These are conversations that anyone who spends time around him quickly tires of, and which Jeff uses as an excuse to disregard his intimates, as a way of blocking out social minutiae and pleasantries and small talk.

'What do you mean I can't? That's ridiculous. Do you have any idea how much money is involved here? Let me talk to Richard. No Richard. Do you know who he is? You should goddamn know who he is. What....'

Jeff had turned sideways on the sofa, so his back was to Suzie, and had put a forefinger in his ear, and was frowning and staring at the cushions. As I was chopping celery I glanced over, and saw that Suzie was using this pocket of distraction to stare at me, in a way that managed to be warm and expressive and curious, and which both admitted her exasperation with the noisy man beside her, and was a declaration of her unmet needs.

Outside I walk across the street, feeling around in my jacket pocket for the cigarette pack and lighter. Also I check around for paparazzi, hoping that none are around, and that nobody has taken a photo of Suzie and I talking in the atrium of the building. If Jeff were to see a photo of us together, in a British tabloid on sale in Australia, things might become complicated. When smoking my evening cigarette I often stand in a recess between two buildings, to the front and left of mine. After flicking the wheel on the lighter a couple of times, I light up. From here I can gaze into the different flats, including my own. At this angle I can see the upper half of my television, part of my ceiling and the rear of an easy chair; Suzie is right, my television does look huge.

Sometimes, when I'm in the flat, I notice people outside glancing up towards it. Once I saw two women in the news agency office staring and laughing; it took me a moment to realise they were reacting to the programme that was on. Perhaps the office employees like to try to guess what I'm watching, possibly it's a game they play. With the flat's lights off, or when only one or two lamps are on, the TV screen is the dominant source of light. If I stand by the curtains I'm shadowed to anyone outside. From there, I have a view of the responses to it of any passers-by: the abrupt upward flick of the head, the momentary slowing of a stride, or the frown of incomprehension and its clearing. For a second it is as if they've glimpsed some crime or catastrophe. When they realize it is only the television, they move swiftly on.

Taking a long drag, I see the lights come on in Jeff's flat. I imagine Suzie moving around: putting on the kettle, perhaps staring at the inevitable patches of unwashed clothes and strewn papers and maybe even finding, God forbid, an unrefrigerated dairy product in the kitchen, and feeling a prickle of irritation.

Jeff's television screen is out of sight from the street, and besides he rarely draws up his blinds. However I know his viewing habits are shameful, monstrous even. His television is the size of a bed propped on end, and he keeps it on for days at a time. His schedule involves regular long haul international flights, and these leave him in a jet lagged and insomniac condition. It's possible he has come to depend on the low murmur of his colossal TV to sleep, and so he dozes slumped on a sofa, the bluish light flaring on his inert face.

Presently I re-enter the lobby and take the lift up.

When I walk in the flat I turn the TV on. Then I make a cup of tea and stand watching the evening news while the mug cools. The volume is high, but nobody will be disturbed. The flats are soundproofed, and besides no noise of mine could drown out the city din. The problem of disturbance is more one of silence and equality; usually my personal noise creates a private enclave among the civic clamour, without which the general shrieks and clanks and grinds would prevail. Often the only indications of the city are these vibrations which shudder through the frame of the building, usually when a lorry reverses into the alley behind the tower or when a road nearby is being dug up for maintenance.

After drinking the tea I clear away the cooking pots and pans, tip the vegetable ends into the recycling bin, rinse cold water over my plate and empty the dishwasher. The machine is nearly full and almost all the crockery in it was bought by us in the month after the house fire.

I didn't return to the TV shoot until three days after the fire. By then the managing agent for the estate had rented us a similar house nearby. On the morning after the fire, once the emergency services had left, we drove up to my brother's flat in Ealing, and stayed for three days. Once there we slept for a few hours and then I went shopping while Hannah made telephone calls. Then on the second day we drove to the estate to meet an insurance company agent. He was late and so we had time to walk around and inspect the remains of our house.

The council had begun the clean up and demolished the standing walls. Nearby were two heaped skips and a parked bulldozer. The area where the house had been was an ashen mound fenced off with red and white tape. The wreckage was congealed and glutinous, embedded with fragments of cement and tar crystals. The debris seemed to have returned to its mineral origins; the tar was coal black and the fractures on the visible tiles were in layers like sediments. These gleamed with the wet shine of drenched rock.

The destruction was of a kind usually found on a larger scale; our house had become a compact chunk of devastation. It was like a civic artwork on the theme of catastrophic events. The jagged heaps of blackened bricks resembled photographs I'd seen of London in the Blitz or of Berlin after the Allied assault. There was a sense that a substantial process of leveling had taken place; and that the widespread clearing of the ground might permit another use.

I went to the TV shoot that morning to sign the contract for the film role, the film that has made me wealthy enough to buy this flat in Canary Wharf. This film project had long been a pipe dream for the director of the TV series. He, or rather his production company, had previously optioned the film rights on a historical novel that had won a prize about six or seven years before. It was a novel that I had been vaguely aware of while at university, one of those popular books that'd achieved international success.

I remember copies stacked in the entrances of the bookshops in Stansted airport when, as a student, I flew to Spain to watch a football match. Over the summer of my second university year, almost every sister of a friend, family house guest and friendly cousin either had a copy or wanted one. In each train concourse crowd I waited in there'd been a smattering of clutched editions. Even now I'd recognize the cover spine if the novel was on a bookshop shelf I was glancing over.

Usually I'm not so interested in novels and novelists. I suppose writing is an occupation I never really think about. For me, writers are grouped with electricity pylon engineers and board game inventors and thieves that steal rare eggs from the rare nests of rare birds of prey. It's only on seeing a documentary or on reading a magazine article about them that I speculate over the arrangements and motivations that are distinctive to their lives.

The novel was called *The End of the Ocean*. The title referred to the Atlantic, and the voyaging of the main characters from the east coast of Scotland to the east coast of America. The story was set in the eighteenth century, when the colonial powers governed a proportion of the territory, and the plot followed a mercenary who was an exiled son of a noble Scottish family. I read some of it over a Christmas holiday, and thought then it would make a good film.

At the time of the fire I'd known the director of the TV series for close to two years. He'd produced a radio play that he'd cast me in, and since then our working relationship had flourished. He always had several projects on the go at different stages of realization; after the radio play, he cast me in a two part drama that BBC2 had him direct, and then he offered me a role in the TV series.

What I didn't know was that he was gradually amassing the cast and crew to film *The End of the Ocean*. During the making of the movie he told me, over a restaurant meal, that he'd cast me on the radio because he wanted to assess my potential. In those former years the director had worked hard to secure a lead actor from Hollywood, and he'd had the script drafted and redrafted by script writers there.

So most of us involved in the film had worked with the director prior to it. In fact it was clear he, by employing us on his projects, had ensured our career stability for this purpose. By the time the funding was agreed by the Hollywood studio, he knew dozens of people ideal for *The End of the Ocean*.

Chapter Four

'Hi. Could I just have the black coffee and a pastry? And a glass of tap water?' I ask.

After my morning workout I usually have my proper breakfast in the gym café. This tends to be scrambled or poached eggs. These days I never eat meat before midday, nor do I eat much in the time after waking; just a piece of fruit and a smoothie after getting up. The gym is in a building close to my flat, and there're plenty of regulars in it who live and work nearby. While I'm waiting for my order Suzie comes in.

Suzie's wearing a grey tracksuit, quite baggy, which is partially unzipped at the front. She looks paler and more frail than she does in her working clothes. She stands at the counter peering into the open kitchen door behind the till, which is where the serving staff have vanished into; she's frowning and seems to be on tiptoes but she isn't: Suzie often seems to be on tiptoes. I can tell that she wants to be assertive in order to attract some service; I think she wants to call through to the kitchen. I know that as she puts her clenched fist to her face and bites a finger she's wondering how loudly she should call out.

'Suzie,' I call over.

'Josh, god.'

She walks over smiling and winding her way around the chairs and small round tables. She clutches her arms to her sides and grins and I think she looks sexy in this unprepared, morning state. One might have expected a famous tennis player like Jeff to be dating a glamorous actress or model. Instead he's been sleeping with Suzie, his divorce lawyer, for about six months now. She stands for a moment by the table and runs her hair through her hands.

'Look what I almost missed,' she says, and smiles then sits down and begins fiddling around with her chair, and edging it back to allow more leg room, then fussing around with the leg of her tracksuit, which needs to be tucked in or tied up, I can't really see which. Suzie's not wearing any make-up but then she's not entirely unselfconscious either; she's aware and enjoying the way my gaze is wandering over her face and neck; possibly she is making a slight effort to look unconcerned. She lifts her right leg up, above the level of the table, to further adjust the tracksuit and the movement is erotic, it is the same movement as if her leg were bare and she were pulling on a stocking, or one of those smaller, feminine socks.

'The coffee's good here,' I say.

'Is it? I hope so,' she replies, turning her head slightly to reply. Suzie has a charming habit of closing her eyes a little when she speaks, and this has the effect of making any conversation with her like an exchange of confidences, as if we were whispering together on the fringes of a crowded room.

The door of the kitchen opens and Suzie turns around and sees the employee, who's just left the kitchen carrying a tray with my order on it. Together we watch the girl weave between the tables towards us. Then she rests the tray down on the edge of the table and slides it gently over.

'Thanks.'

'Can I have some toast, and an espresso?' Suzie asks.

The girl is still looking down and adjusting the position of the tray.

'White or brown bread?' the girl asks.

'One white bit and one brown.'

'Oh alright then.'

The girl squints as if remembering.

'And an orange juice.'

The waitress smiles and walks off and Suzie watches her back as she goes. Then Suzie rests her chin in her hand and watches as I start to eat. A strand of her hair slips down, hanging in front of her face, and Suzie blows at it, to stop the hair tickling her nose.

'I should cook for you tonight,' she says.

A statement which makes me want to blow my first mouthful of breakfast out onto the table, and stand up and utter a pompous expression of incredulous surprise. Instead I sprinkle some pepper on my scrambled eggs.

'What do you want to cook?'

She doesn't immediately reply, as she is watching me take a mouthful.

'I've got an idea. Something we'll both enjoy.'

Her face and her voice are both still sleepy. Her face is unchanged since waking on the pillow in the early morning, soft from the rest of sleep, not yet exercised by the drills and stretches of her daylight worries and demands. Suzie's voice is cracked, slightly hoarse; an early morning voice not yet capable of anger, or forceful words; a voice that needs to pick up speed, one that is looking to join the highway of the day, and for which the hours of rising and breakfast are a slip road.

'Have you been back to Jeff's since the other night?' I asked.

'No.'

On Thursday last week Suzie had arrived late to stay in Jeff's flat but had somehow forgotten her keys; she claimed that she'd left them in another handbag. She'd knocked on my door and had ended up sleeping on my sofa bed. If I hadn't had the flu we might have slept together.

'Are you busy today?' she asked.

She leans back, and the tracksuit top is flattened; underneath she's only wearing a bra. The exposed skin over her collar bone is freckled, and the moles are pebble brown. There is a parallel between the fullness of her lips and the prominence of her collar bone; a shared quality that is ample and generous but also rough hewn, capable of bearing crude treatment.

'I'm preparing for an audition next week.'

Suzie is an associate partner in a London law firm, and has a life that is remarkably organised in some ways, but disturbingly chaotic in others. She owns a flat in Putney which overlooks the Thames, but hardly spends any time there. She eats at home a handful of times in a month. She is forever calling Jeff at unsuitable times of night or from unusual locations: Irish racecourses or Scottish castles or African capitals. She goes through periods of time when she is too thin and agitated, and I have worried about her before.

And the truth is I could've slept with her if not for the flu. My flat seems to have a powerful effect on some people; perhaps it's the décor or the view, but whatever it is it's mesmerizing. The interior was decorated by a consultancy that designs TV and film sets and advertising shoots. Their recreations of luxury homes and billionaire's flats and playboys' bachelor pads appear in blockbuster films, on the back covers of lifestyle magazines and on television adverts for beauty products or vodka.

The company furnished my flat using their exclusive suppliers. The curtains come from New York and the undulating folds of their hems rest lightly on the carpet like a duchess's ball gown on a polished ballroom floor. The shelf unit, a zigzag of drawers and book shelves and cupboards that diagonally crosses one wall, is from a London company run by a designer who permits Selfridges to stock his cheaper lines. The leather sofas seemed inexplicably familiar until I recognised them in an MTV hip hop video on a television in the gym, and then a week later saw a girl on one in a lingerie advert on a billboard. The coffee table in front of the sofa, the one with the burnt photo album on it, looks like it should be strewn with lines of cocaine and stacks of dollars and playing cards arranged into poker hands, alongside the knives and knuckledusters and black revolvers of the players.

Suzie's coffee has arrived, and she's sipping at it.

'You know you remind me of an ex-boyfriend.'

'Why?'

She shrugs.

'The way you put pepper on everything.'

'I love pepper.'

'So did he.'

She puts her coffee down and starts unpeeling a single portion carton of margarine.

In the days after signing the film contract I had to return to the TV shoot to act in another scene. It was a difficult time as Hannah and I were still shaken by the house fire. But I disliked being in that starkly empty house, and wanted work to provide a distraction. The destruction of our belongings had been virtually absolute, which in some respects simplified the situation. Being in that new house was like being in rented villas and apartments in France and Spain; we started with minimal kitchen equipment and cleaning products, but a couple of expensive trips to the supermarket supplied us with these fundamentals. The particular scene I had to shoot involved Royalist troops chasing the rebels. The objective was to shoot a melee on and around a bridge in the woods, and then film a pursuit amongst the trees there; Jakub was to be the choreographer.

On the drive there that morning I was overcome by the after-shocks of the fire. The pedals felt jerky and I had to concentrate to change the gears and at roundabouts. Then I began sweating and felt nauseous and so pulled over into a lay-by. I sat for twenty minutes, breathing deeply and staring out at the passing cars, feeling envious of the drivers, of their finding a daily renewal of harmony as they drove, of their ability to kindle reassurance from the familiar motion of the gear sticks and pedals. I was struggling with a fragmentation of my driving ability, a disruption of a long standing and casual mastery. It made me uneasy.

After eventually arriving I changed quickly and jogged down to the edge of the woods, feeling relieved to be there, seeing this set, like most I'd worked on, as a refuge. Even as a schoolboy actor the stage had been my sanctuary. I used to love the months of rehearsal time, the empty spacious halls we practiced in, the sense of avoiding the trampling life of the school. Acting has always lifted my mood like this.

The others were waiting in a group near the tree line. It seemed that Jakub and the director had just finished their morning talk. There were a few nods of greeting from the actors as I arrived. The director was talking into his headset, giving the impression that we were waiting for permission to leave. Jakub was standing behind the director and I watched him as we waited.

Jakub's neck was sinewy and corded, wound around with visible arteries, firm bindings the muscles bulged against. Pink flush mottled his cheeks; a rosiness that spread beneath his sideburns; the alchemy of his sculpted chest and the windy countryside. The neat style of his moustache and beard was military or police; it had a hint of Indian or Pakistani baton wielding officers or of Spanish soldiers under Franco or Italian soldiers under Mussolini. There, in his boots and combat trousers, posed with the swaying and unruly foliage behind, Jakub seemed a disciple of stern and rigorous disciplines.

He glanced at his watch and at the director before glancing at us. This glance was a professional appraisal, the kind that a sergeant might direct at army recruits. Standing there I felt very anonymous, just one member of this rabble he was regarding. For me it was one of those knock-kneed moments, like standing in line in PE at school, the gulping moment of waiting to be chosen by one or another team captain, as two different sides are assembled.

Those moments when your sportier, stronger classmates are picked first, and you stand and wait, silently begging to be pointed at, terrified more than anything of being the last, or of being among the last. Those last standing near you, frail of limb and jutting of hair and elbow, perhaps even visibly trembling, often with thick glasses, and almost certainly in ill fitting and inappropriate PE clothes. The boys who are wearing black socks instead of white; who have shorts that threaten to expose their genitals; whose footwear is inexpensive and undignified; who are wearing T-shirts that appear to have shrunk in the wash, or appear never to have been washed, or appear to have been borrowed from their sister, their mother, or even an elderly aunt.

Those moments, whose feelings surprise you when they reoccur in adult life, when you again feel knock-kneed and shaky, or unselected and cast out. Those moments: during a talk with a bank employee, or in a job interview, or with an imperious and difficult girlfriend; when all the trappings of adulthood seem to disappear, when all the accumulated substance of the years offers scant support.

'OK. No more bullshit,' the director said.

'Run with me,' Jakub said.

We followed him along a path that was slippery with sodden fallen leaves. Mud splashed up onto our gartered socks and breeches. The loudest sound was hoarse breathing.

'Run with your heads up.'

After ten minutes we arrived at the bridge; a panting and flushed mob, clutching at our legs or heads. I was reminded of schoolboy games in woodland, out of the view of parents or teachers. A danger comes with this kind of isolation, a lessening of the usual rules. At the bridge Jakub started the training session with a demonstration in which he made an actor pretend to attack him.

'Go at my face. Bring the sword on the right,' Jakub said.

Jakub swiveled and as their swords met his face was behind the blades. His left foot stepped well back and he parried the other sword out of the actor's grasp; it flipped high and splashed into the pebble stream below. This happened in a swirl of limbs and torso; the seamless motions of cricket bowling or figure ice skating. The move made my body feel restricted and imprecise, my limbs clumsy and dozily cooperative.

'Now you practice.'

Jakub kept a steady vigilance from the glade of the trees. When he moved he reminded me of the early photographs of Olivier, those agile limbs and tilted postures. Also of Charlie Chaplin's physicality, the bandy mischievous legs, the lively arms likely to twitch up and humiliate the body.

When he instructed us to take a break he approached me to talk.

'You're Josh?'

'Yeah hi.'

He nodded.

'How are you feeling?'

'Knackered.'

My hands were resting on the top of my head and I was taking deep breaths.

'OK. You are going to be in the film?'

'Yeah that's right.'

'I'm training you.'

He smiled a little and turned his head to one side.

'Oh right. It's in the contract isn't it?'

'Yes.'

He looked at me more closely.

'We should probably have a chat I suppose.'

'You find me this week.'

'Sure yeah easily. No problem.'

Now, three years later, there's part of me that regrets not backing away and refusing then, or at least insisting on another trainer. But there's another part that feels grateful to Jakub for my success in the film role. In fact I'd forgotten the contract clause that required me to be in "appropriate physical condition" or some similar phrase. I'd read this paragraph quickly and assumed it was to ensure I wasn't obese at the start of filming. The possibility of being required to have a personal trainer hadn't occurred to me.

Here in the gym there are clients who have personal trainers; usually gym employees. They stand by the cardio-vascular machines mumbling encouragement to their exercising client, or tick boxes on clipboards while observing sit ups and stretches. They seem a little forlorn and I always assume they once aspired to careers as professional sportsmen. There've been a few occasions in the gym when a professional sportsman has come in, and each time the gym staff and personal trainers tend to gather round and consult them. The sportsmen are always brawny and bullish and energized, and beside them the gym staff appear adolescent and lacklustre.

Of course when I started using the gym the staff recognised me. But they were always deferential and gently inquisitive, without any of the sense of entitlement and expectation that seems to motivate them in the presence of a visiting sportsman.

'Hello sir,' they say to me.

Jeff also uses this gym, and around him the staff abandon all pretence of self control. I've seen receptionists carry his bag from the front desk to the changing room, and Jeff told me once that the staff will often stand in groups of two or three in the doorway to the shower, quizzing him as he lathers his naked hairy body. Many of his gym sessions end in an impromptu lecture, as he, out of breath and streaming with sweat, demonstrates some rare calf stretch or abdominals exercise to a semi-circle of attentive gym folk. They assume that he possesses an infinite quantity of athletic knowledge; however I know that he doesn't.

'What's this book?' I once asked in his flat.

I picked up an exercise manual from his sofa.

'Oh man I read it before I go to the gym.'

'Really? Why?'

'Just so I've something to say.'

'Oh yeah?'

He passed me a coffee.

'You wouldn't believe it. Every time. Every time I'm in that place they've got some question for me. They have to have their dues.'

'Don't you know all this already?'

I flicked through the pages, which showed profile and frontal photos of men and women stretching.

'It's the penalty of fame. They all expect you to know. And to want to tell them. It's worse in tennis clubs. I can't even go into those anymore.'

He shook his head and sipped his coffee.

'Whooee,' he said.

Every now and again Jeff and I carry out a mischievous rendezvous in the gym. On these occasions I arrive first, and endure the usual reactions to a visiting celebrity. The receptionist glares as if he suspects we may have met, a customer leaving through the turnstile looks round frowning whilst exiting the main entrance door, and on ascending the stairs I receive bold stares from those descending. Twenty minutes later, by which time I am cycling or lifting dumb bells, Jeff arrives. For him it is much worse. Anyone standing nearby asks for an autograph, and many within sight immediately make mobile calls, presumably to inform their loved ones of the proximity of a celebrity. At times Jeff has seen gym employees running toward the swimming pool in their desperation to tell their lifesaving colleagues what is happening.

Then, when Jeff enters the training area, the fun begins. The staff and the other customers are already unnerved by my presence. There have been discreet consultations between the customers and attendants, there have been whispered queries and answering nods and brief explanations. Whenever I have glanced up, at least one person has glanced away, not quite blushing but almost. But when Jeff strides in, all forearms and body hair and panties off now American smile, the hysteria becomes palpable. Jaws really drop as people realise there are two celebrities present; bulky weight lifters stand frowning and looking from Jeff to me. If customers occupy any machines adjacent to either of us they do so hesitantly, making rapid flurries of intrepid sidelong glances.

Jeff and I have a routine that we enact. At first he and I ignore each other, but eventually we convene in the free weights area. Then I find a pretext to ask him a question, something like:

'Are you still using that bench?'

To which Jeff might reply:

'No dude, feel free.'

Due to the mirrors that line the wall by the free weights area, we have a clear view of the whole exercise studio. At this point the reflected scene is a tableau of voyeurism: the desk staff are frozen in mid action, stiffly facing us, their mouths pink dark holed little circles. One of them is holding a pen and was in the process of writing a name onto a list on a clipboard. There is a bald man on a rowing machine staring, his lips floppily apart, about to lose his rhythm in surprise. A younger blond man is standing nearby recovering his breath, concentrating fiercely, staring forward instead of at us, succeeding in his act of self control. By the bikes there is a girl with a pony tail who has just spotted us: she is half bent down, her eyes are wide open as if she has been startled, or as if she is wondering if she is being filmed, as if she fears she is accidentally trespassing on a film set.

The next part of our routine is when Jeff speaks to me, which sets into motion our overt and public mutual recognition.

'Don't I know you from somewhere?'

'I'm an actor.'

'Oh.'

'Aren't you that tournament busting tennis player?'

'That's right. I'm Jeff Brazer.'

'Hi. Josh Haddon.'

We shake hands.

'Good to meet you man.'

At the moment we shake hands the faces of those watching are a sight. Their contorted expressions are of a kind more usual among spectators close by the net at football matches, in that instant when a goal is nearly scored, when a player lunges with his head at the ball and the keeper leaps high and sideways, arcing his body and flinging out his arm. As Jeff and I begin to smile and chat the collective exhalation from our audience is almost audible. For them the overwhelming moment has passed, and now that the celebrities are conversing cheerfully normal life can once more be resumed.

On reflection what is most interesting about this scenario isn't this initial amazed reaction. More, it is the people's own later feelings about the situation, once the routines of their normal day are underway and their emotions have subsided. What troubles them isn't the oddness of what they saw, but rather the way their response has revealed a lack in their powers of reaction.

Later, as each of these people are drinking a coffee, perhaps with colleagues, describing or remembering the unusual scene they witnessed that morning, what is felt most acutely is self dissatisfaction. They recall the failings of their limbs and mouths and brains: the stupefied expression on their faces, the glazed look in their eyes, the docility of their arms and legs. And this is a rare sensation for each of these people, who are no doubt husbands and wives and fathers and mothers and also working professionals of various kinds. None are at all accustomed to this feeling of being unmanned.

And the feeling lingers because their timid reaction in the gym challenges their assumptions about how they would react in other surprising circumstances. A gap has opened up, and on one side is the knowledge of what they will do in a situation and on the other is what they believe or imagine themselves as able to do. Probably it is difficult for these people to gauge the size of their gap, and knowing that it's there haunts them a little.

After filming this pursuit scene I visited the set for two days each week over the next month, which the director agreed to rearrange the story to permit. He invented a serious battlefield injury for my character, and then, in the next two episodes, had other characters discussing the process of my recovery.

So I spent the other days of those weeks rebuilding our domestic life. These were days of form filling and negotiations with the utility companies. Hannah and I faced a ceaseless accumulation of direct debit forms, letters from the town hall and county council, banking reminders and department store catalogues. Our letter box became a flapping valve to this flow of municipal information. The stack of paper on the kitchen table endlessly divided and increased. All our documents had to be replaced, involving phone calls and follow up letters or letters and follow up phone calls.

That month I hired a van for bringing furniture from the nearby retail estates. I toured the warehouses, comparing prices and enquiring about stock availability. Then each evening Hannah and I browsed through catalogues. The next day I'd track down our choice and drive it home myself. Gradually the rooms of the house filled with chairs and cushions and lamps and tables and bookshelves. Rugs were laid out and curtains were hung; the wire clasp of lampshades were slotted onto bare bulbs; the string that backed the frames of prints was balanced onto nails; the TV was set carefully onto its plinth in the living room and its channels were programmed; the new Hoover was plugged in and turned on and the force of its suction was tested. Pot plants were positioned in corners; the ironing board was slid underneath the bed; the new dustbin was fitted with a black plastic bag and the washing machine rotated its first load.

Late one afternoon we rendezvoused at a bathroom supplier where Hannah and I murmured and measured, pondering the mirrors and opening and closing shower cabinets. We debated quietly, deferential visitors amongst the engraved slabs of porcelain, the prominent and tended chunks of ceramic. We spent time in whispered conferral by a disconnected bath, planning the intricate ritual of removal and final internment.

In that month I came to feel the strain of relentless decorating decisions.

'Do you think it's nice there?'

She'd moved a tall and slender lamp from one corner to another.

'It's better. Now it's out of the way of the light switches.'

'Yes but don't you think the room's gloomier now?'

'I don't know.'

'God.'

'Try putting this one on the table.'

'I did that last night.'

'Oh.'

But gradually our new domestic life began to form. There was the evening when I brought home boxes of new cutlery and glasses, the ones I now use in the flat. When Hannah first saw them she made a face and sipped some more wine. Later she sat cross legged on the living room floor and peeled away the folds of grey paper and bubble wrap from the glasses; each piece nestled and shone in the open cladding of these materials. She plucked each glass out and set them on the table; they glittered in crystal rows there, a chime sounding when one touched another.

'I like them actually,' she said.

Then Hannah cleaned the new cutlery. She filled then carried the washing up bowl from the kitchen sink, balancing the heavy tub unsteadily in its tipping and sloshing. At the living room table she wiped and massaged each piece with the blue cloth, turning them in her hands, her hair swaying into fullness with each tilt of her head. Then she placed the knives and forks and spoons onto a tea towel. Here, in their neat lines, they made reflective flashes; the opening strokes in the writing of a domestic alphabet.

Now, in the gym café in Canary Wharf, I'm putting down my knife and fork, and wiping my lips with a napkin. Suzie is chewing her last piece of toast, and has the cup of espresso in her hand, and as soon as the toast is swallowed she knocks back the last of the coffee. Then she wipes at her lap to sweep any crumbs onto the floor.

'Josh, I should go and get on. I'll be late otherwise.'

'I'll see you later.'

After a while, when I re-enter the lobby of my building, it is too crowded for me to wave at or talk to the receptionists. There are two maintenance men in blue boiler suits holding tool boxes waiting near the desk while a resident in an ankle length brown coat with luggage stacked around her feet and legs is talking to whoever is behind the desk. There is a mix of noises: the whining motor of a hoover, the clackety clack of shoe heels and soles on the marble surfaced floor, the cushioned shunt of the lift doors opening and closing, the guttural talk of a man into a mobile phone.

It is the noise of a day in full progress, a day when pipes will get mended and windows will get cleaned and carpets in corridors will be hoovered and pot plants will get watered and tunes will be whistled and almost everyone will have the kind of unencumbered working day that each has hoped for after waking in the morning. The kind when none of the potential distractions or time consuming colleague visitations and meetings actually occur and instead all tasks get whittled away at in peace and whatever is the maximum available level of quiet.

Amid this bustle I go unnoticed up to my flat and unlock the door and drop my gym rucksack onto the floor and then pour myself a tall glass of tap water. For a moment I stand appreciating the view, which is of glistening glass and steel buildings, the cityscape reflecting the pale sun, before sitting at the dinner table which is strewn with film scripts. These are at varying stages of being read, and I've used theatre tickets and shop receipts and pieces of tissue paper as page markers. There are red and black biros on the table too, with which I scribble on the scripts. On Friday, or maybe early next week, I'll meet my agent to compare opinions, so it's important for me to read each one and make notes.

This is how I spend three or four hours a day at the moment, from late morning to late afternoon, shuffling through these piles of paper, occasionally standing to walk around and ease my legs and back, sometimes going to refill my glass of water or juice or diluted concentrate. The dinner table is close to the window, so the light is strong, and gazing at the view helps, at times, to refresh my eyes and mind.

My lunch might be a carrot soup made by boiling the carrots in two pints of water with added chicken stock and then blending. Or a potato baked in the microwave and smothered with mashed tuna and mayonnaise. Recently I've been trying salads, TV chef concoctions of red onion and sliced chili and grated ginger, and I eat these with Ryvita and oatcake biscuits and humus or taramasalata.

After lunch I always have a half hour break, and for a while this involved leaving the building and strolling around the block, or walking to and fro on the old quayside nearby. Recently though, I've been spending my lunch break differently. A month ago Jeff came here for dinner, and was surprised to find I had no computer games console. What further amazed him was that I'd only once played the computer game of *The End of the Ocean*.

'Are you nuts?' he said.

So a few days later he returned with a games console and the game. Since then I've played it for a while each day, out of curiosity and to help pass the time. The game was released close to the opening date of the film, and apparently there was a TV advert for it. As a rule, I'm not averse to computer games. I suppose I prefer ones that involve sport, usually soccer or American football. During university weekends I often competed with my housemates in digitised leagues.

In the game a player chooses from several different avatars, one of which is the character I played. Then the player has to guide the character through landscapes and scenarios that are loosely similar to the film. There are prisons to be escaped from, battlefields to be crossed and boats that must be guided down fast flowing and pirate infested rivers. The character gradually amasses a selection of weapons, and treasure and food can also be found in the virtual landscape.

I find the game unsettling. Firstly because the avatar modeled on my character resembles me; the programmers must have used facial mapping software on the film footage. Then there is the 360 degree rotation; the character can turn to face the player, whereupon the unseeing eyes of this digital representation stare blindly out towards my own. At these moments the avatar seems trapped, as if he wants to escape the game, as if he might start bashing his fists in desperation upon the interior of the screen.

Often I have to stand to hold the controls and play, as my legs become numb from being crossed on the floor. In this standing position it is difficult not to mimic the character's actions, not to lean or turn slightly as the character does, not to pivot or swivel like him when in combat. All this serves to create a sense that his reality is close to my own, that I am also, in some sense, confined within an artificial world.

The more that I've played the game, and become familiar with its pace and action, spending hours swinging swords and leaping from barrel to barrel in rivers and shooting crossbows at stockade guards and stealing horses from Indian encampments, the more I've found a certain pleasure in its repetitions. During game combat, for example, the responses of my character have a formulaic pattern. There is the initial use of ranged missile weapons, then fighting with axes or swords or spears. The controls allow me to programme offensive or defensive manoeuvres, which mean that, during combat, there is only minimal twiddling and pressing of the buttons required. In general, the process of this planned attack overwhelms each opponent. There is a lulling quality, something calming, in the predictability of the moves and counter-moves of the fighting.

A similar pleasure can be found when travelling around in the game. It reproduces historical versions of several American states, so the game contains vast landscapes, and all journeys happen in real time. Therefore it is possible, within this virtual universe, to walk or run distances between towns and cities that are intended to be traveled by train, horse or horse drawn carriage, paddle steamer or even hot-air balloon.

Now, after only a few weeks of play, I choose to run these distances. When the character advances like this, across the scrolling grassy plains or sparse woodland or cultivated fields or meadows and orchards, a pleasant rhythm emerges. Opponents tend to attack at regular intervals, the character finds and collects food and treasure at regular intervals, and the features of the landscape themselves repeat cyclically, identical configurations of bushes and trees and fence posts rising up in their turn and then passing by the running figure.

This, like the game combat, has a distinctive, soothing effect. There is a security to this virtual experience, a sense of safety that perhaps emerges from the known quality of the game, from the knowledge of what elements or components might be encountered. A person's expectations are fulfilled, and their assumptions about what can or cannot happen are confirmed. It provides the player with the enclosed reality of the playground, and the expressions that form upon my face when I play, and the sounds my mouth utters, are infantile ones.

'Yes!' I shout, when a tricky scenario is overcome.

During play my reflection is often visible in the screen, and the drama of the action causes me to suffer the performance of my puffed cheeks, my pouting lips, my protruding eyes and my contorting jaw. There are twitches and grunts, and spasmodic lunges and gulping intakes of breath. It is when I find myself on my knees, in defeat, my face averted from the dying character on the screen, my trembling hand clutching the control gizmo at eye level; as if presenting it as a token offering to an angry deity; as if secretly pleading that a parent or guardian will pluck it from my aching fingers, that I usually just get back to work.

In the rest of each afternoon nothing much happens. My script reading often relocates to the sofa or to an easy chair. I make a mug of tea or coffee and consider whether to sugar it. I almost always do and then the inner argument is over one white spoonful or two. For snacks I try to limit myself to Ryvita or an apple or a banana but often this point of resolve is abandoned, and a discrete plate of shortbread or chocolate biscuits ends up beside me.

In this atmosphere any sounds become acutely noticeable: the crackle on turning a page; the tap of a pen or my fingers on the table, the scrape of my shoes on the wooden floor; the voices that swell from the street outside or the spaces of the building; voices diluted by the currents of air above the terrain of the city and by the concrete frame of the building; assents and dissents that are fading and diffusing into noise, into calls and outcries dispersing aloft towards the nearest altitudes.

Outside the weather has turned, and rain is flailing against the windows, the droplets on the panes being forced into channels by the pressure of the wind and the quantity of the water. Beyond, the towers of the City are becoming obscured by the advancing lines of falling rain. The rivulets trickling down in front of me resemble the sliding of rain across a windscreen when a car is being driven at high speed in a downpour. In the flat, for a moment, there is an illusion of acceleration, a sense that the entire building or only this floor is being propelled forward, and a further illusion that here, before this window, I am gazing from the control room of a flying machine. This thought, of course, is quickly banished, and I feel prompted to return to my reading.

Chapter Five

The police visited Hannah and I in the third week of our living in the new house. Two stout men in uniform came to the door one Saturday morning, and I invited them inside and put on the kettle while Hannah wiped down the living room table.

'I'm Detective Davies,' the larger man said.

These two officers took off their hats and Detective Davies put down a laptop bag and thanked us gratefully and then both checked the carpet around their feet for any tiny cubes of mud, or tiny links of mud in segments that may have detached from between the treads on their boot soles.

I tried to think who might have died, which relative of parent of Hannah's had suffered a slamming crash on the motorway, or if my father was now in hospital after a heart attack, the possibility of which had been growing incrementally for years. A heart attack that had long seemed inevitable, considering the fatty sediments that had been gradually depositing in his arteries, building up from the soft cheeses and pork pies and plates of bacon and eggs, and his other unhealthy favoured dishes.

Hannah's face had a tight, drawn quality, an uncommon expression on her. She was wiping at the jam residues and butter smears too briskly, using the task as an opportunity to evade eye contact with the men; sponging the crumbs too delicately into the curved palm of the yellow glove on her hand; spending too long wringing the sponge and rinsing it under the tap in the kitchen sink. Perhaps she was wondering if her father had fell or slipped during one of his yachting trips, and was now lying concussed or broken limbed in an intensive care ward. Perhaps she was wondering what could have happened to her mother, trying to imagine the circumstances of a gardening or domestic accident severe enough to require this police involvement.

'There's a fair amount to get through,' the detective said.

'Just the milk thanks,' the other said.

The larger man opened up the laptop and guided us through some PowerPoint slides.

'What these graphs show is the results of the analysis that was done on the remains of your previous house. This line along here indicates the quantity of combusted accelerant present in the overall sample. As is clear it's quite high.'

'Oh,' Hannah said.

'Now either you had a container of petrol or diesel in the house or even a can of WD40 that went up or someone slung some petrol in there and started that fire.'

'What?' I said.

'I know now in these next graphs there's a close, detailed sampling of the entire area of the premises. So from this and this you see that the fire ignited in the rear, and indoors as the ground directly bordering the rear showed no traces in the least.'

'Christ.'

'Were you in habit of keeping any flammable substances in your kitchen? Did you even store a toolbox there?' the other policeman asked.

'No.'

'That narrows it down then,' he said.

'I'm going to need to sample the petrol from your cars,' the detective said.

'Are we suspects?' I asked.

'No. But we'll need all your insurance details.'

'Did you see anything strange outside on the night of the fire?' the other asked.

'I don't remember anything? Do you Josh?'

'No.'

'The thing is we'd have been in here watching TV anyway.'

'Right,' the detective said.

'And there's no view from the sofa into the kitchen.'

'The kitchen door would've been closed. There's a draught otherwise, isn't there Josh?'

'Yeah.'

'Have there been any incidents on the estate that you remember? Any vandalism or burglary? Even anything really minor?' the policeman asked.

'I don't think so. It's quiet.'

'Do you think there's anyone with a reason to try to kill you?' the detective asked.

'Kill us?'

'We're treating this as attempted murder,' the detective said.

'No. Why would anyone want to do a thing like that?'

'Hannah is a research vet,' I said.

'Sir?'

'There are those animal rights people aren't there?'

'We can follow that up,' the other policeman said.

'Our lab's never been targeted before.'

'Could you write the company name and address down here madam?'

The police stayed for another hour. Hannah and I both wrote informal statements in which we tried to remember who we'd seen on the day of the fire and where we'd been and exactly when. The detective showed us photographs of the vicinity of the old house, images of the neighbouring houses and the woodland where people walked their dogs, and I told him who lived in which house and how friendly we were with them.

'It's not possible that the spilled petrol came from before the fire? Maybe it soaked into the concrete during the building work or something,' Hannah asked before they left.

'We'll have to talk to our forensic boys about that.'

Hannah and I washed up the glasses together after they'd gone.

'God, how weird,' I said.

Their visit was the third time in my life that I'd spoken at length to a policeman. Once, when I was a student, I was stopped for speeding near Victoria Station, and as it was late at night I was questioned over possession of drugs. On another occasion I was a passenger in a friend's car that was involved in a crash on the M25, and then the police took my statement.

Here, in this block of flats, policemen are unknown. The alternating howl of their vehicle sirens is one of the common sounds outside, muted though into the background by the concrete walls and the dense glass. The insistent and urgent sound seems alien when heard in this building, this sound with its high rising and falling, a sound like an angry and confronting voice suddenly rising to envelop its listener, this approaching and then receding sound with the rhythms of a threatened person making a denial, a sound ascending through a crescendo, as of a voice speaking under duress, to ward off violence, to persuade and convince its listener of its sincerity: denying and pleading, denying and pleading, denying and pleading.

And the echoing siren, vocal in its shape of high emotion, seems at odds in this building with its guarded acknowledgements in corridors when residents chance to meet upon returning from or leaving for the airport or the opera or a restaurant table or an office, standing in their expensive influential person's coats, stepping aside for each other, holding lifts, sometimes reverential or deferring in their mutual greetings. The repeating sound from outside is abrasive and has no place in the spacious flats where it's easy to imagine that the finest ingredients are refrigerated and opera is listened to; among the living rooms where exhaled cigar smoke might be idly watched as it hangs and drifts in slowly whirling coils; and where men or women in silk dressing gowns might make international calls.

Usually I finish script reading around five o'clock or so. By then I'm approaching a headache, a fuzziness of tired eyes that never dissipates quickly, and stops me watching television or reading anything until it's subsided. Consequently the hours between five and seven become fragmented, a time of errands and telephone calls and the ticking off of items from to-do lists.

In this period I'll shop at the supermarket, load or unload the dishwasher, open my mail, hoover the floor or wash down the fixtures in the bathroom. There is a laundry room in the basement and I'll heft bags of damp clothes down there, and sit on the wooden bench, the kind of wooden bench with a slatted top side that many laundries seem to have, to gaze as my clothes revolve and drop and turn over in one of the formidable drying machines. I could pay someone to do my laundry, but then that would allow domestic services to enter my life, and who knows where that trajectory would end.

Jeff and I had a conversation about this once.

'Dude never get a butler.'

'Never?'

'For sure never. You wouldn't believe the fucking headaches.'

He was standing in his kitchen with a frying pan while I was at the counter with a smoothie.

'I had this guy once, a Latino. One night he took off with my Porsche and all my trophies.'

'No.'

'Yeah. Son of a bitch.'

'Christ.'

'The servants man. They're there fucking on your bed while you're out, putting up cameras in your bathroom, stealing your clothes and giving them to their grandparents. I mean nothing is beyond those people man.'

'Well that sounds terrible.'

'It's like you try and do anything and they're falling out of the cupboards, literally.'

'I wouldn't know.'

Jeff glanced up at me from where he was mixing flour and eggs in a bowl.

'You've got to be careful with your money. You're rich now. The people that show up when you've got money. The servants are the advance guard of the army of fucking asshole eaters out there. You know one of the guys on the circuit, an Australian, he had his dogs kidnapped. Turned out it was the gardener.'

'What?'

'That kind of shit happens all the time. I swear the citizens are just lining up to try it on.'

'I don't think I'm after domestic help.'

'No man but it's the thin end of the wedge. Like the valet service here. Don't use them. Make your own arrangements. You know I dry my underwear on the radiator right there?'

'Oh?'

'Yeah. I can see those shorts from my bed at night. They aren't on eBay.'

So having taken Jeff's advice I do all my own laundry and cleaning and ironing. I don't pay anyone to do anything in the flat, and so far touch wood, I've had no problems.

It's usually around six thirty when I've finished my errands, and then the evening lies before me, with all its myriad possibilities. Now that I'm a famous actor, I have an ample supply of invitations. Up to five of these arrive in the post each day, forwarded on from my agent, and I have a divided folder to store them. One slot is for film launches and previews and premieres and private screenings, and I usually attend these. Another is for the opening nights of bars and nightclubs and restaurants, but I don't often go to them. The overflowing slot is for party or dinner invitations, sometimes from film or TV actors or producers or directors, or from wealthy strangers who are perhaps just interested to meet me; on occasion I reply to them. The final slot is where I keep any proposals I receive, which often have a comedy value, bizarre propositions that I laugh over, that I show to Jeff to amuse him when he visits. There have been investment requests from foreign dentists, offers of supporting roles in zoo safety films and invitations to lead the chanting at solstice rituals.

I could go to more of these evening events. I'm conscious though of a need to preserve a certain mystery about myself. Perhaps if I attend too often the hosts will soon lose interest and begin slightly to despise me, as I will become another known quantity; as intimately known to them as everyone else in their social universes, as predictable and avoidable; the items of interest or novelty in my conversation quickly memorized; the inclinations in my joking and humour soon assessed and approved or disapproved of; my tendency to lie or tell the truth or repeat myself noted, my likes and dislikes considered and perhaps discussed with another mutual friend or acquaintance.

Later, when I'm slumped on the sofa, watching the news, there's a tap on the door.

'Hi,' Suzie says when I open it. She's wearing dark blue jeans and a black tracksuit top over a white t-shirt, and has a cardboard box with two lettuces in it, and a rectangular silver foil packet, and a bottle of oil and other bits and pieces. She watches me searchingly, with some hesitancy, as if I might have changed my mind and decided to refuse her entry; as if I might be about to declare why it's wrong for us to be alone together. Instead I concentrate on the box.

'That's a lot of stuff. I could have come to Jeff's.'

She hands the box to me, and I walk slowly over to the counter, supporting it against my stomach with my left forearm around its front, picking over the contents with my right hand.

'Mmm, coffee beans.'

74

Then I put the box on the counter, and start taking the jars and bags out and onto the surface; Suzie comes to stand beside me.

'Do you have a steamer?'

'Sure, there's a pan in the cupboard by the oven.'

She goes into the kitchen and squats down and pushes her hair back behind her right ear, and reaches into the cupboard. Before long she's slicing up courgettes and mixing ingredients for the sauce while I'm uncorking a bottle of Chablis. And I'm thinking that she's doing all this too unconsciously, that she's being too servile and too automatic over these domestic tasks, and I'm thinking that Jeff has noticed this too and perhaps hasn't said anything or tried to rebalance the situation, and has just let her proceed and clean up and empty his dishwasher and wipe his counters and mop his floors. And then I notice that the sleeves of her tracksuit top are too long and that she's having to tug them back, and that the left one is rolled, which gives an impression that she is wearing hand-me-down clothes, which adds to her aura of Suzie cuteness.

A cuteness which is very different from Japanese animation cuteness, or babies in nappy advert cuteness, or even the sexy cuteness of lingerie adverts in magazines. It's a cuteness that originates in the undefended way she glances up at me as she's slicing, as if she isn't prepared to find me staring at her, as if she hadn't expected that a bit.

'I'm tired,' she says.

'Do you want me to do that?'

'No it's not that, it's just I'm saying.'

Suzie turns round and sweeps the courgette ends into the recycling bin. Then she goes to the sink and rinses the chopping board and I see that she's removed her boots; she must have slipped them off at the door.

'What have you done today?' she asks, from over her shoulder, as she wipes the chopping board down with a sponge.

I walk across the living room and stand by the reading table.

'Look.'

She comes over to the counter side of the kitchen.

We both stare at the table, which is covered with laid open scripts, with loose pages from scripts where I've removed the corner staple and with stacks of pages from scripts whose paperclip or rubber band has been mislaid.

'I was reading.'

'Me too, not film scripts though.'

I walk back across to the kitchen, and have to reach over her to take two wine glasses out of one of the cupboards. Then I pour the Chablis.

'Here.'

'Thanks.'

'Cheers.'

'Cheers.'

'That's nice.'

'I'd always imagined you in a courtroom, addressing the judge, convincing the jurors, you know.'

She puts the glass down on the counter.

'No. I spend most of my time reading reports. And advising business clients of their legal options, or the legal implications of something they want to do.'

'Do you wear glasses?'

'Yes Josh I do.'

'Oh.'

We're standing very close together now, which I think I'm enjoying, and Suzie's staring at me as if she isn't sure what I'm going to do, or what she's going to do, and I'm realising that she's still attractive close up, and I like the way her eyes are goggling; it is a playful feeling, as if we're hiding in a confined space together.

'I need to go to the loo,' she says.

'Right.'

I step back and allow her to pass. While she's gone I turn on the TV. There's a famous sitcom on one of the satellite channels. I've seen this episode so often that I can almost say the lines with the actors. As I watch I think of my habit of imitating the mannerisms of one or two of the characters; imitations I make conscious and jokingly, half in expectation of having the imitation recognised and acknowledged by the person I'm talking to, always implicitly or tacitly; and then having this become an act of complicity between us, like a secret.

Suzie comes back in; she's unrolling the sleeves of her tracksuit top. For a moment we watch the TV together.

'I know this one. I love this bit,' she says.

'It's really funny.'

'They went out in real life you know.'

Presently we're eating dinner, and the fish baked with thyme is delicious, and so are the lemon drizzled courgettes, and the lentils aren't bad, but they're a little hard, verging on the gravelly. Whenever Suzie takes a sip of the wine, which she does too often for me not to notice, often having to stare up at me to acknowledge she's listening, as she takes another gulp, I find myself staring at her lips, which are full and fleshed out, ornaments as much as her eyes on her partially Mediterranean face, a face that is quick to tan and slow to whiten. These lips are tactile and mobile, the kind that are photogenic; and as she is drinking they almost seem unwieldy, making her appear to be smirking, as if they are difficult to control.

'I was at work until two the other night.'

'Again?'

In her law firm there is an aggressive but undiscussed code of working hours endurance; leaving at nine o'clock is taken as weakness, midnight is more acceptable, and ordering a taxi in the small hours marks out a committed employee. To prove their unflagging attendance her colleagues seek to out-do each other in sending e-mails from the office during the night. On one moonlit occasion Suzie was physically prevented from leaving her floor; two men, both keen on rowing machines and spin classes, blocked the doorway to the lift, and flaring their nostrils like hospital matrons, recited to her the penalties for disobedience.

'It'll be like that tomorrow night.'

'What about in the mornings?'

'It's up to me. It's just those billable hours.'

'What's your boss up to, you know the one you're always telling Jeff about?'

'Oh God, well…

The conversation goes on like this, and towards the end of the meal we've both become drunker and more tired; we've almost finished another bottle of Chablis. Suzie's made a mousse for dessert, layered in red and white, and has served it with strawberries, the whole ensemble dusted in icing sugar. Suzie has taken off her tracksuit, and she's wearing a white sleeveless T-shirt underneath, and when she raises her arm to drink, her deltoids dimple at the shoulder joint; a notch forms there, a depression I could snag my finger in.

'Have you ever been papped here?'

'Yeah. A few times in the early days.'

'I know Jeff was.'

Suzie is right, Jeff was papped here, and apparently more than papped. In fact apparently he's been subjected to the entire tabloid arsenal: fake sheiks, fake sheiks with hidden microphones, fake sheiks with hidden cameras, fake sheiks with hidden microphones and cameras, fake cameras with hidden sheiks, reporters pretending to be strippers, reporters pretending to be autograph hunters who were pretending to be strippers, cameramen pretending to be delivering pizzas, camera-men with cameras disguised as pizzas, reporters with false moustaches pretending to be corrupt sports officials, reporters in pork-pie hats pretending to be bookies trying to persuade Jeff to drop a set or a game, reporters disguised as other reporters asking him to buy photos to prevent them being sold to other tabloids. Fortunately all this happened before I moved in, but at times there must have been a fancy dress crowd in the lobby.

One of my first bonding moments with Jeff involved the paparazzi. He came round with a celebrity magazine one morning.

'Dude have you seen these photos of yourself?'

I was in my dressing gown holding a cup of coffee.

'No I don't think so.'

He folded the magazine over and showed the photo to me. It was of my agent and I kissing on the cheek, the two of us by an idling taxi on the street outside.

'Yeah. Are you happy about that?'

'She came over to clarify a couple of things.'

Jeff tightened his hold on the magazine.

'Are you cool with this spying going on? Is this what you want?'

'It's only a photo Jeff.'

'You know they have these at the back?'

He flicked through the rest of the pages.

'That's from a premiere.'

'The paparazzi are circling dude. They're closing in.'

I looked at him and shrugged and swigged my coffee.

'These things happen.'

'Or not man. Or not. I'm taking you out later. I'm putting a pancake in me and then I'll be back. You're not busy or on appointments today?'

'Not especially.'

'No baby we're busy. You get me? We're busy.'

'Where are we going to go?'

'It's a surprise dude. You'll see.'

So by 11 o'clock Jeff and I were on an escalator in a Marks and Spencers, ascending towards the menswear department.

'This is the best place for this stuff,' Jeff said.

'It's M and S, Jeff. It's where elderly ladies buy tights.'

'No man I've looked around.'

The menswear floor wasn't busy, and an employee eyed us nervously as Jeff started rummaging through a rack of white t-shirts on hangers.

'That's your size.'

He lifted a t-shirt out and pressed the hanger to my collarbone.

'Perfect.'

'Why?'

'Because we're buying your anti paparazzi gear. All this stuff, it's your ticket to a life of freedom. Check out these blue caps.'

'Oh right.'

'If you wear the same things every day, nobody wants your photo.'

'Is that what celebs do?'

'You're one of us now. Here, try this hooded top.'

'I'd rather not.'

'Take it.'

After the meal, when I've cleared away the dishes and wiped the table, Suzie and I are sitting facing each other. Suzie has green tea while I'm drinking an espresso. We're making small talk about the government cuts, and both of us are feeling the force and potential of attraction; a tension that makes us restless and too quiet and even expectant of the other. An emotion that is making Suzie reluctant to meet my eye, which is causing her to fidget, that is making her cross and uncross her arms, that is beginning to give our conversation the dynamics of a faltering job interview, with her making meandering statements that tail off into silence.

Gradually our conversation seems to lessen, seems inadequate to the altering emotional temperature of the room. And for both of us, being that much older, and that much more wary of our impulses, there is more denial, more to resist, more struggle to undergo in the recognition of our feelings; so prepared as we are to ignore them, to dismiss them as insignificant in comparison with the preoccupations of our working lives; so accustomed as we are, in our adult way, to being severe with ourselves, to subjecting any need we have to interrogations and pitiless scrutiny and suspicious fault finding.

And then there is Jeff, who neither of us are keen to betray, who we're both fond of for similar reasons, with his habits of firmness and good humour, with his expectation of being respected, of his being accepted and listened to and agreed with. A man of an athlete's simplicity, who approaches problems in terms of best response, as a simple matter of quality and aptness of reaction. Someone less affected than most by doubts and self blame and regretted decisions and difficult memories, by memories of expressed anger and the unjust treatment of others and the taking of advantage of others and the abandonment of others and the past bitterness toward others. Jeff, with his negligible memories of being taken advantage of, of being fooled and duped and disbelieved and doubted and mistrusted. Jeff, with no source of emotional reek, no expanding or infiltrating influence that can, at any time, threaten to sour his front of house composure. Instead he is all conversation about cars and luxury destinations and sports, and is long accustomed to moving forward, to a momentum of accomplishment that seems, at times, to rotate the horizon towards him.

And also perhaps, with Suzie and I, there is the memory of all our other relationships, the memory of our dealings with all those we have loved and desired, or just loved, or just desired, and the memory of the well traveled paths of romance, with their signposts and stage markers, their familiar obstacles and avoided hazards. There is a biting of the lips and the exercise of self control for us both now, with our recollections, negative and positive, our memories of our refusals and of giving ourselves away, of trusting and then next time not trusting, of our misunderstanding another and of our being misunderstood by another, and the consequences thereof.

Perhaps it's the contemplation of this process that keeps us at opposite ends of the table, that makes us linger there, Suzie content to tuck the hair aside from her eyes and glance towards me, and me to sit as if fixed, apparently paralysed, able only to breathe more deeply than usual and have my inner voice debate and caution and advise.

Or even it could be our mistrust of language that keeps us prone, considering the slight hatred everybody has for any taint of hesitancy in their voices, revealed in particular when straying beyond our usual range of communication, of our voices when they are exposed as tentative and exploratory, when they try to vocalize thoughts we are unaccustomed to vocalizing, or express thoughts that we don't habitually express, or thoughts that we feel might come back and strike us hard, like uncaught boomerangs.

In fact it's likely that we are more willing to expose our bodies as naked than our voices, more comfortable with that kind of physical exposure than another; more likely to consider our most delicate parts to be revealed when we speak than when we are undressed. Perhaps what is being guarded is our erratic maturity, with its peaks and troughs; its spectacular developments and its unfenced areas; its persistent combination of childish outbursts and mature exercises of authority; its inner city like form, with coexistences of tempered and seasoned structures alongside ghettoes of urgent feelings and instincts. These are vulnerabilities that our veteran adult selves are more protective of, keener to shelter than when we were teenagers or students; when our whole existences necessitated acts of exposure and admitted to vulnerabilities, when our every move was tentative and unprotected; when the possibility of correction or admonishment lay perpetually in the background.

Or maybe my inaction is due to my aversion to commit, perhaps because I'm still in a condition of trauma, perhaps still sealed in a block of frozen emotion, after Hannah's death, just over two years ago.

'You've got absolutely stacks of DVD's, Josh.'

Suzie has stood up and taken her mug over to the counter. After speaking she stretches by arching her lower back and pushing her hands, palms inwards with intertwined fingers, up towards the ceiling.

'I don't think I've ever seen a flat with quite so many.'

She walks over to the zigzag shelving and pulls one out.

'How are they organized?'

I stand up and walk over and read the back of the DVD cover with her.

'That's the first film by the guy that directed *The End of the Ocean.*'

'I've never heard of it.'

'For some reason it was only released in Germany.'

She hands it to me and pulls out another.

'That one stars Morton Greaves. It was his breakthrough.'

'I recognise this. Isn't it on TV all the time?'

'He looks really young.'

'Josh?'

'Mmm?'

'It's sort of over for me and Jeff. I only came back for my stuff.'

She doesn't look at me; instead she is reading the back of the DVD.

'Oh, so, umm.'

'Yeah.'

And in a moment we're kissing, hard, her hands pushing up under my shirt, my left hand behind her shoulder blades. It's kissing where we both have to pause to breathe, kissing that I'm glad I'm doing rather than seeing, like two fish fighting and thrashing over a morsel of food. Suzie steps forward and pushes, forcing me to step back, and her long fingernails are twisting in my hair, which hurts. For a second I think she might raise a foot onto my belt, and pull on my scalp to climb, so her shins end up on my shoulders.

I have a brainwave, and start kissing her neck, then dropping down, small nibbling kisses, and then pull aside her T-shirt at the collar, so I can continue there. This makes her relax her hands, and her knees buckle, so for a moment it seems she might fall down.

'Let's go to the sofa,' she murmurs.

She seems drowsier, almost in a trance, as we kiss on the sofa, and presently I'm lying between her legs, kissing her bare and supple stomach, running my fingers along the firm muscles that run beside her spine. She has one of those tummy buttons that sticks out slightly, and I bite it, playfully, which makes her arch her back. Then I'm plucking at her bra strap, first one hand then two, a confident surgeon removing the first bandage from his potentially recovered patient. Her breasts, as I knead them with my thumbs, are a little disappointing, small, without any bold contours, offering only mild resistance to an upwards push, the peaks more Saharan dune than South American mountain.

It's a while later, after forty five minutes or so of panting and postures in the bedroom, of handholds and biting and tongues, when our clothes are all over the floor and we're prone on the bed among misshapen pillows; when we're both sweating and lying on our backs, exhausted, like sailors shipwrecked in an uncharted ocean, washed up on a sandy and unexplored shore, that I realize I haven't drawn the curtains.

Chapter Six

The training with Jakub began fairly steadily. We started by meeting at a private gym in central London, and he spent two hours a day, for three days a week over a fortnight, instructing me in the basic use of the equipment. There was the elevation on the running treadmills, a feature that I'd never experimented with, on which Jakub demonstrated how to steepen the gradient every seven minutes to exercise the widest range of muscles in the legs and buttocks. He taught me correct techniques for the dumb-bells: how to do bench presses with them, a more versatile and complete action than with the bar-bell, how to use the dumb-bells for shoulder presses and for bicep curls; how to lie face down on the bench and lift each weight up to chest level to exercise the deltoids. Jakub showed me stretches for the calves and the thighs, for the waist and neck and the shoulders. He taught me to do squat thrusts after finishing running, lifting fifty or sixty kilos on the shoulders to bulk up the thigh muscles, and then to stand on tiptoes, raising the same weight each time, to strengthen the calves and the collar of muscle and tendon around the ankles and the muscle on the front of the shin. He demonstrated a range of press ups: one type where the hands were placed by the waist, others where they were placed close to the shoulders or far apart, another that involved thrusting the upper body clear of the floor and clapping once or twice or even three times. There were different sit ups: where the knees are raised, ones where the raised upper body is rotated, where the straightened legs are a little elevated and the knees or the tips of the toes are touched. Then there were back stretches and breathing exercises and star jumps and shoulder dips.

All this was done in the same pattern, where he demonstrated the move or the action and then I did my best to copy or mimic it. If I failed in this, which was often, he simply demonstrated it again, and I repeated it, until I copied the action correctly. He didn't speak much during this process, instead wagging his finger at me or shaking his head and smiling before crouching down to repeat himself; we must have looked like mime artists practicing a routine.

All this took place, of course, in the fierce clarity of the gym, a space that was entirely brightly lit, amongst the concentration of the other users, the basic clothes that were worn, the grey unshaven faces of the men; the as-if-scripted conversation and banter of the employees; the smell of sweat and the mumbling rumble of the active machines; the thudding of the runner's toes and heels; the buoyant resurfacing motion of girls doing sit ups; the swish swish of the handles of the cross training machines, the rasp of men breathing, this sometimes drifting into tandem; and all of it sometimes threatening to converge into a hive-like rhythm of unconscious synchronisation.

At the beginning his practice of not talking much during our training sessions was charming or amusing.

'Oh I see,' I would say.

In the first couple of sessions it became a joke I humoured him by playing along with.

'Oh right that's it,' I would say, as he bent in demonstration, his eyes glittering in my direction.

But finally it began to bother me. At the end of the second week we finished the session with some sparring; he and I were alone on the padded floor of an exercise studio.

'Try for my chest. Here or here,' he instructed.

Each lunge or grab of mine met empty air, as he stepped or swivelled aside. Then Jakub began to cuff me around the head when I missed, laughing to himself, and smiling at me when we paused for breath and I frowned and half smiled and rubbed the bruised crown of my head. He had gnarly hands, protuberant knuckles and bony finger joints, and these rapped across my skull more painfully than I would have thought possible. During the first rest I glanced over his fingers to check for rings.

'You're hot in the head now,' he said and laughed.

Eventually after fifteen minutes of this, confused and annoyed, I sat down on the bench.

'Yeah look that's enough.'

'Is it? More next week eh?'

When we stopped, and I sat there and watched him: light on his feet, sinewy necked, his skin a little dark but also tanned, his teeth bright under his moustache, my perception of his red and white tracksuit blurred by the sweat in my eyes, its colours appearing as more like flag colours, like Napoleonic era European infantry, like the red and white of nineteenth century British infantry in paintings. Then it occurred to me how colonial he looked, how much like a young version of some long forgotten Victorian ancestor of mine, a swashbuckling lieutenant brimming with memories of duelling and plucky daredevilry and fortitude and good luck.

In those two weeks Hannah's working life also shifted up a gear. I arrived home early one day to discover her there, packing clothes and rinsing out some plastic bottles and beakers and thermometers in the bath. She was wearing a baseball cap to hold her hair up, a sign, in my experience, that she was feeling stressed.

'Alright?' I said.

She glanced up from her crouching position by the bath.

'Josh be a love and go and get the kitchen paper.'

'Haven't we run out?'

'No there's some by the toaster.'

'What's going on?'

'Just hurry can you?'

I fetched the roll of paper and then stood watching whilst she dried off a piece of kit that resembled the bowl and blades of a food blender.

'The toilet paper's too thin,' she said.

'Can I help?'

She didn't look up.

'You could make me a piece of toast.'

'Only if you tell me what all this stuff is for.'

'There's an infection site near Oxford. Everyone from the lab is driving up tonight.'

I went downstairs to make the toast.

'What's this thing then?' I asked when she was seated downstairs, gulping down the toast and swigging from the cup of tea I'd made her.

'Don't worry about it. How's that film coming along? Is it going to be made?'

'Oh. Yeah,'

'Are you quite sure?'

'I think so.'

She looked at me and took her cap off, and shook her hair out, then put the cap back on. Finally she smiled, quickly.

'That's a relief.'

'So are you staying up there?'

'I think for tonight and tomorrow. It depends what we find. We'll probably have to quarantine the stables.'

'Is your mobile charged?'

'Yes. Is yours?'

'Err. I'll have to check.'

'Josh I've got to go. The van left from the lab an hour ago.

'Yeah. Shall I take this out to the car?'

Hannah went for her jacket and gloves while I carried each of the two plastic crates of equipment and then her luggage out.

'Look after yourself,' I said.

'And you.'

She hugged me and I kissed her and then she was at the wheel and driving away. This wasn't the first time Hannah had stayed away from home to assist in a livestock or equine crisis. In the past, during the various agricultural crises of recent years, each one extensively televised and reported on, she'd left home to be involved and I'd watched for her on the news. Then I'd tried to identify her in the background during an interview or longer feature, tried to decide which of the figures she was, which of the attendants enclosed in white plastic suits and black masks, unwinding black and yellow striped tape around a farmyard or standing guard at the sealed-off turning to a country lane.

There was always an unreal quality to these suited personnel, as they stalked across the farmyards and the barn courtyards and the paddocks and the meadows; their movements hindered by their plastic suits, often raising their arms at the same time as they lifted their legs, swiveling their heads more carefully than normal, moving like astronauts in zero gravity or deep sea divers underwater.

These news reports, with their images of stacks of smouldering cows or pigs or sheep, or footage of bulldozers shovelling the corpses of livestock into freshly dug trenches or pits, always seemed otherworldly or scarcely credible; as if the reports showed the results of an extra-terrestrial invasion, the aftermath of a massacre of thousands of cattle. Or, it was as if the news teams were reporting on the onset of a plague; the early hours of the kind of national crisis that has long been predicted and imagined and discussed; and the figures in white suits were not vets but soldiers and doctors, in the process of quarantining a regional city like Nottingham or Leicester or Coventry. And these ghostly figures seemed to have wandered clear of people's minds, now loose and straying across the television screen; as if at any moment they might appear outside, wandering close to the window, stepping dozily like sleep-walkers and inhaling their audible breaths.

After Hannah had left I slung my gym clothes in the washing machine and then I went upstairs and ran a bath.

'Ooh god,' I said, as I lowered myself into the hot water.

Lying in the bath was a wider immersion in the familiar and reassuring things of home: of Hannah's female clutter in the bathroom, her bottles of shampoo and moisturizer and conditioner and balms, of the towels that we didn't wash often enough or dry out thoroughly enough, of the toilet seat that I tried to remember to leave down, of the zip-up travel bag she'd insisted I keep my toothbrush and shaving gear and deodorant in, rather than the random plastic bags I was inclined to use.

Now, the bath I have here in the flat is an altogether different affair. It is black and gleaming, entirely ample and voluminous. It is the bathroom ornament of an LA pimp or an Italian footballer, and every time I see it, I feel partially ashamed and uneasy. At times I even grimace when adjusting its Jacuzzi fittings. A television has been installed in the bathroom, a screen that descends from a slot in the ceiling, and there is an alcove that holds a silver bucket of iced champagne.

It is a bath to hold forbidden parties in, where an escort girl in lace and high heels might recline and peel off her soaking underwear, or the underwear of her decorative and expensive companion, where a grinning man or men might swig from glasses of champagne or iced tumblers of whisky, where the brown curve of buttocks might be pondered as they submerge and wallow amongst the steaming water and foamy bubbles.

Needless to say it distracts and concerns my visitors.

'Hey has your mother seen that bath?' Jeff asked.

'Yes she has.'

'Did she like it?'

'What do you think?'

The first time Jeff used my bathroom he backed out into the bedroom when he saw it.

'Dude what is that?'

'It's just the bath. I prefer the shower though.'

'In America folks campaign to outlaw those.'

'I thought every flat here had one.'

'Uh uh.'

'Well it takes twenty minutes to fill.'

'Is that marble?'

'I'm not sure.'

'Moving here was a mistake for you. You know?'

Even Suzie couldn't keep a straight face. She had a moment of gloating after she first used the bathroom.

'I thought you were a nice boy,' she said.

'What?'

'That bath is too much.'

'God. Please don't talk about it.'

'Was it here when you moved in?'

'You know it's a reason not to let journalists come here.'

'If you hate it then why don't you chuck it?'

'I don't know. I suppose it's good for a soak now and again.'

'Oh I bet.'

'What?'

One of these days Suzie and I will end up in that bath, and then who knows what we'll do, or how much mess we'll make. But the bath is soothing, with its pummelling water jets and multi-directional geysers, its wide bathing space, broad enough to accommodate all manner of sprawling and turning over and twisting around, so that any part of the body can be manoeuvred alongside at least one of the submerged nozzles.

In fact I would rather be soaking in it right now. At the moment it's mid morning, and I'm sitting in the Piccadilly office of a Caribbean airline, waiting to book a holiday, and the service so far has been disappointing. I have a ticket with number forty four on it, and the digital read out above the counters is thirty seven. I've been waiting for twenty minutes, and there are only two employees at their desks, both of whom are dealing with long and drawn out complaints, involving the presentation of numerous forms to the employees, who seem to respond to each form by making telephone calls, which then require further telephone calls.

The two customers making the complaint, both women, one Indian and one African, have their backs to me. These backs, and the women's postures generally, have an air of patient stolidity, like veteran players in a night long poker game. The employees facing them are becoming by degrees more frantic and flustered, clearly more and more desperate to dismiss these immoveable women. But the women continue to sit, as patient and as resigned to patience as fishermen, shaking their heads from time to time, explaining their points quietly, possibly even, God forbid, naming names of other employees consulted in recent former sessions of complaint. Perhaps even, horror of horrors, being reasonable, being utterly and unquestionably justified in their demands for compensation or repayment, making arguments using the small print; the same small print that the employees are, even now, being told over the phone by their managers to quote to undermine and use against the obdurate complainants.

In these last twenty minutes I have witnessed the gradual fragmentation of the professionalism of the employees, both in their mid twenties, both superbly groomed, the man with hair that is waxed and jutting, the woman with impeccable eye make-up and lipstick. Regrettably they have already given cause for offence, the young man already having raised his arms in the air once and shifted his chair back from the situation and slapped his hands onto the desk, the girl having narrowed her eyes too much and repeating her queries too loudly and shook her hair and is now frowning and is perhaps wondering if this isn't a training activity of some kind; and if this woman in front of her isn't a representative from head office who is about to produce ID and a checklist clipped on a clipboard and start behaving normally.

I sit, contented not to be recognised for once, or at least not to be confronted and required to acknowledge who I am. Perhaps my anonymity is due to my anti-paparazzi outfit, which consists of a blue baseball cap and sunglasses and a striped Paul Smith scarf wrapped as high as possible around my lower jaw; so high that it seems that I am attempting to conceal surgery or prevent infection or anonymously plan an atrocity. So high that I usually remove it before entering a bank or jewellers, so as not to frighten the employees or alarm their security guards.

Besides I am in no hurry, and have in fact largely invented this errand as an excuse to leave the flat. The task, of ordering the holiday tickets, is something I could have done online or even over the phone, but I wanted some new shoes, and had intended to visit this end of town anyway. The holiday I am buying tickets for is one of those January tropical holidays, the ultra expensive kind where Premier League footballers acquire their mid season tans, where young royalty are photographed on jet skis, where upwardly mobile professionals are occasionally robbed or raped or beaten by aggrieved locals. The island is the kind of paradise destination that celebrities mention in interviews, frequented by Sean Connery and Roger Moore and Pierce Brosnan; a place where resident billionaires moor all their latest yachts and luxury cruisers. As a holiday option it is unaffordable and barely considered by most people.

My fortnight there will be very different to the holidays Hannah and I once had. Principally our rambling holidays, when in red and yellow waterproof jackets, we walked the length of one or another long established route. There was the East Anglian coastal walk, when we spent a week treading by the margins of enormous tide flattened beaches and in single file along the dry embankment paths. Then there were our hiking trips to the Lake District, where we struggled up the sides of ridges and spars towards the highest peaks, enduring the deafening and dumbing and freezing effects of the hillside weather.

'I love this fresh air,' Hannah used to shout, standing atop some slate-cored and sparsely vegetated outcrop, relishing the view; while I nodded in agreement, my hands on my knees, too breathless to speak.

For meals we usually scheduled stops at country pubs, and here we'd chew our ham sandwiches or cottage pies and watch the other ramblers enter and order and sit down; see them removing their woolly hats and their mittens or gloves and their bright plastic jackets, like ours not only waterproof but porous too to the internal evaporation of sweat. Jackets that are always ornately labelled inside, much diagrammed, dependent on these science educational drawings to outline the overwhelming practicality of their features to any potential customer, that are eager to convince their buyers of the sheer scientific improbability of their wearers ever becoming even remotely damp.

And the hikers and ramblers sit down, a little radiant, slightly pleased with themselves, partially satisfied with their morning's accomplishments, their happiness no doubt in part derived from their belief in having worked off some calories, that they have managed this morning to incrementally reduce the likelihood of illness, that they certainly have, out on those rainy hills and muddy paths, diminished their chances of a static and immobile old age.

And perhaps they believe they have learnt to endure a fraction more, to withstand a fraction more, and that their morning's resistance to the outdoor elements will somehow crossover generally, and that they will find their innate stamina increased. This, so that all the trials and torments of their lives can be better persisted through and more fully braced against: those irritating supermarket queues, those lengthy waiting times to talk to advisors at call-centres, the crowded Saturday mornings in high street banks, those days when the car or the washing machine or the shower or the dishwasher or the central heating malfunctions, forcing them to interrupt their finely honed schedule to attend to its fixing.

Like us, they order non alcoholic drinks, usually ones they believe to contain a less than average quantity of sugar, and then they order their food, careful, like us, to order food which they don't imagine will affect their digestion during the afternoon's walk; no steak and chips, nor the beef and ale pie or the fish and chips. Neither, however, do they order food which, in their opinion, has an insufficient quota of vitamins and proteins and salts and minerals, considering the almighty task that they are in the midst of submitting their body to. The radish salad is left well alone.

And so Hannah and I sit there, among the other hikers, convinced of the value of our best practice in its contribution to our safety and security. Sure that we have, in some sense, fulfilled our side of a bargain, and that we can now reasonably hope for the best. As a result none of us, really, have much expectation of being the victim of the unforeseen or bother to put our energies into preparing for any likely dangerous events. It is possible that none of these ramblers carry bandages to bind up a sprained ankle, or spare boot laces, or have a mobile phone that they know receives a signal in the lowest contours of these hills; I wonder if any of them ever vaguely doubt the weather forecast.

That isn't to say the hikers aren't unequipped. On our holidays, staying in beds and breakfasts and small hotels, there have been a few occasions when, in the course of an enthusiastic demonstration, some specialist piece of equipment has been shaken at me. These hotels usually have common rooms, and while sitting in them, sore but relaxing after a day's walking, I've humoured men who have been keen to show me their toys: hand-held flares, luminous compasses, pistol launched flares, reflective Arctic survival blankets, miners' torches on headbands, unbreakable ropes, breakable ropes, self heating gloves, rubber heeled socks, nutritional oatcake bars from the NASA recipe, solar-powered radios, reviving isotonic drinks, wind-up radios, waterproof matches, fireproof maps, wind-up torches, waterproof gloves, windproof lighters, radioactive watches and solo-assembling all-weather tents.

All these things, of course, still clean and unused, included in case of life threatening emergencies which have never materialised. These are objects that seem more suited to the wilderness catastrophes which occur in other countries and in other hemispheres: to avalanches in Canadian national parks, plane crashes in the Andes, to canoeing incidents on Peruvian rivers, vehicle break downs in Egypt's Empty Quarter desert or to mountaineering accidents in the Alps. Better suited to the kind of situations reported on the news, situations that are typical subjects of real life documentaries on satellite TV channels. Perhaps some ramblers even have vaccinations before venturing out to roam upon the hills.

Now, in London, back in the travel agent, one of the women is finishing her complaint. She has been handed another form, which she stares at a little dully, listening as the representative explains its contents. There is mention of the airport authority and I realise that the complaint is about lost luggage. It is now clear that the employee has been telephoning foreign airports on the woman's behalf, and that this latest form is a direct, faxable request to the airport that has the lost bags. A signature and written description of the bags and their contents is required, and the customer bends down to complete these details. Then she passes the form back to the employee, who, with a sweeping flourish of her shampooed and conditioned hair, disappears into the back area. The woman then leaves, walking slowly by me, clutching her paperwork to her chest, and the static expression on her face belongs to someone who is unsure whether they have won or lost.

Later, when ordering my tickets, the transaction contains an instant of pride as I hand over my platinum credit card, which verges on the awesome, and I'm consequently treated to the impressed tiny smile of the employee, and her reappraisal of me.

'Don't I recognise you from somewhere?'

'Umm, I don't know.'

'Aren't you in that phone advert?'

'No.'

'Oh.'

A conversation which deflates the growing sense of interest between us, that closes the tiny chinks of receptivity that have opened in her persona, scattering the privacy that has begun to filter into our exchange. The formality of the moment reasserts itself, she takes refuge in concentrating on her computer screen, and we continue as before.

'Is there only the one resort you'll consider sir?'

'Yes.'

When we've finished, and I have the receipt for the tickets and the hotel booking, I wander into the street outside. It is typically busy, the suddenness of the traffic noise loud enough to be startling, in the way that a cold shower can be or someone unexpectedly yelling your name. It takes me a moment to orientate myself, to plan the best route to the turning I want, and then I'm off, settling in behind a trio of adolescent French tourists, following the path they create through the oncoming pedestrians.

In those first few weeks of the equine crisis, Hannah was barely at home. She'd arrive one afternoon and leave the next morning, and I'd return from training to find the washing machine revolving and her asleep in our bed. When awake she'd prop herself at the kitchen table in a dressing gown, sipping chicken soup from a mug, rubbing her eyes and apologising to me.

'Don't worry,' I'd say.

'At the moment it's our worst case load ever.'

'Can't you take a few days off?'

'I'm heading up this new unit now, Josh.'

Without Hannah in the house I began to drink more during the empty evenings; my habitual glass of red wine or can of lager being increased to two or three. My housekeeping, usually acceptable, deteriorated and the crusted plates and cutlery and cooking implements were left in a stack each night. Letters and free papers and fliers began to litter the sideboard and kitchen table and the living room table, and the floors and the kitchen and the bathroom seemed, even when cleaned, never quite reset to their proper state of pristine and cosmetic sparkle. In the solitary evenings the television's noise and glare echoed around and floodlit an apparently vacant ground floor.

More and more I was affected by introspection. A usually submerged clamour of thoughts and feelings began to creep into and skulk about my mind; long buried grievances groped their way to the surface, and banished self doubts reappeared, blinking in the open and healthy spaces of consciousness. At times I had to exert an effort of will to drag myself away from holding my own gaze in the bathroom mirror, as if my optic nerves could be peered down and the problem diagnosed.

Unfortunately Hannah was away when the police made their second visit. As it was I had to deal with the situation alone. The detective arrived on a weekday evening, soon after I'd returned from my day's training with Jakub; this time only one officer came to visit.

'There's not that much more to say sir,' the bulky detective said, once he was seated at the kitchen table with a cup of tea.

'OK.'

'We do believe your house was targeted, as there's been no reports of arson activity at any of the other houses on this estate, or on the other lot off the roundabout.'

'That's bad then.'

'It's not ideal no Mr Haddon.'

'Perhaps I should glue up the letterbox.'

'You might consider that. Best all round though is to keep your new address quiet. Don't mention it to anyone if you can. Be careful what forms you fill in.'

'Right.'

'There was one other issue. My colleague had a word with the landowner who has the wood behind your old place; now he did have a gate pushed down, properly driven over, that week of the fire. But he's not sure which night. Now even if there is a connection there's only this to say, and that's whoever it was wasn't local.'

'Not hoodies then?'

'No.'

An exchange which did little to ease my state of mind that evening, as I watched the news on TV and ate my spaghetti bolognese. Before bed I filled the washing up bowl with water, and pressed it against the front door under the letterbox. Hannah kept a rape alarm in a drawer in the bedroom, and I faced the front door for a time, thinking over whether to sellotape or superglue the alarm onto it so that any opening of the letter box flap would trigger the device. Eventually I went to bed, determined to buy some home security kit; the DIY place on the retail estate sold infra red and touch sensitive alarms; these were what I thought I needed.

Once in bed I lay awake, dwelling on being broken into. We owned none of the domestic weapons that couples normally have in case of a break in: no half metre US police style torches, no baseball bat under the bed or behind the bedroom door, no hammer or commando knife near to hand. Lying there, gazing around the bedroom, I realised that if forced into self defence, my best bet was one of Hannah's perfume bottles.

Now, in London, I am a mile from the airline offices and I have two new shopping bags. In one of these there is a pair of leather shoes, from a Spanish brand, with distinctive coloured laces and tinted leather. In the other bag is a new pair of gym trainers, very expensive, of the latest design incorporating a virtuoso range of rubber and plastic and stitching technologies. With these in my possession I feel somehow fresher, more alive to and in tune with the possibilities of the day, as if my transactions have reconfirmed my right to walk these streets.

Before I became famous I used to dislike shopping on my own. Then it was largely a passive exercise, as I wandered from shop to shop, identifying more and more of what I would like to buy, but was unable to afford. On these trips I wistfully fondled materials: the pliant cotton of expensive shirts, the resilient soles of gleaming leather boots and the Merino wool of designer jumpers. I used to expect to be mistaken for a shop lifter, due to my constant lingering amid the menswear and incessant trips to the fitting rooms. In those days I was someone who practiced self-restraint until the sales, who coveted certain shirts and trousers and shoes until the day of their discounting, at which point I would arrive and gently claim them.

Since the onset of my fame and celebrity I have shopped more courageously. These days I am bold with my credit card and masterful with the sales assistants. Prices rarely restrain me now, and I stroll through and feel at ease in all but the most exclusive Mayfair stores. It is a carefree feeling which was only present, in my past life with Hannah, on certain supermarket shopping expeditions. It occurred during those trips when we had to buy food for barbecues or birthday parties: tins of canned tomatoes, or packs of sausages, or cans of kidney beans, or boxes of frozen white fish, or racks of barbecued ribs. Then I would plunge my arms deep into the shelved banks of product or the frozen stacks of it and haul out the bulk size quantities, glad at the brief freedom from the necessities for and burdens of calculation.

Even if Hannah had worked normal hours over those weeks I'd have hardly seen her. The training with Jakub was intensifying, and I was arriving home later and later each day, and going to bed earlier and earlier. Those days became a blurry eyed and sweat soaked haze, full of my panting and nodding in dumb agreement to whatever Jakub proposed or had to say. By halfway through each morning session I had generally lost all composure, and was transformed into a sweating and grunting golem, staring as if punch drunk at a fixed point ahead, exerting all my efforts and will into meeting the forty minute objective set on the running machine.

These were sessions where my knees knocked together, where the fatigue during circuits on the indoor running track would make me clash my feet and stumble, where I brought three t-shirts for each day because they soaked through so rapidly. I re-experienced feelings and sensations unknown since playing sports at school: the raw ache of a stitch, the nausea that suddenly arises during any rest or lull in activity, the sense of the inadequacy of one's limbs to the angle of the slope; the awareness of the futility of the body's warming mechanisms versus the refrigerating British weather.

The house became nothing more than a recovery space, a place to pause in to allow my energies to reaccumulate and my body to rebalance itself; somewhere to eat and drink and lie around and moan softly. I've never stooped for so long under such piping hot showers as I did over those few weeks, or gone to bed so early or quite so gratefully, or eaten so much rare steak and mashed potato.

When Hannah did call or when I phoned her I patiently listened to and sympathized with her over a harsh decision she'd had to make or a period of ceaseless work she'd undertaken. The ordeals she described were more like those of a doctor in a war zone than a vet in Oxfordshire.

'Maybe you should put in for a residency after this,' I said one time; during a conversation in which she'd cried and asked me to drive up there to collect her and bring her home

'We're having to take the foals away.'

'Don't the mothers get them back?'

'Not always, and the mares get distressed and kick the stalls and damage their hoofs.'

'Teaching might be easier than this.'

'I know.'

For both of us the weekends were the worst. Hannah was working on a shift system, but this itself was constantly over-ridden by fresh outbreaks of the infection, by the necessity of making the three hour round trip to fetch equipment from the research complex near Reading, by an injury to one or another of her colleagues from the agitated horses. Equally it seemed that her superiors had been absorbed into a Whitehall bureaucracy that was expanding to supervise the crisis. There were committee meetings to be attended at different government departments, House of Commons briefings, Customs and Excise question and answer sessions, mornings with policy units and afternoons in think tanks; there were presentations to be given to this and that scientific organisation or agricultural union or farmer's support group. Our conversations left an impression of reserved men in tweed jackets waiting for early morning trains, men that perhaps resembled the Duke of Edinburgh, tall and reluctant in conversation, apprehensive of divulging; of their being ushered later through classical doorways in stately buildings near the Thames; of their consultations and meetings with officials in ornate rooms. Rooms high and spacious enough to rebound all sounds as clipped echoes and startling reports: of rhythmic shoe heels on marble floors, of dropped fountain pens, of the brass studs on the base of leather briefcases, of the wooden or metalled or hardened tip of full length umbrellas. And then an impression of the result, an institutional scrutiny swivelling to face the benign greenery of Oxfordshire, a shift in vigilance of accomplished minds, an emerging set of problems being sought for and then clarified and meditated upon; like architects imagining their sketches of future buildings. So Hannah and her colleagues who were close to middle management had to shoulder more responsibility, and the usually staid politics of her workplace were disrupted.

As a struggling actor in those years I often used to envy Hannah her office politics. The adrenaline immediacy of dealing with it stimulated her, that sharpening necessity of having to react to situations. Whereas my work problems felt less graspable, seemed less responsive to whatever course of action I chose. The instincts and hunches of directors and casting producers, the clash of schedules, my suitability or unsuitability for the role, the ignorance over which actors I was competing against, the prior decision that might reduce an audition to a formality for the chosen actor, a legal necessity for the director and to wasted time for the other candidates; all these were issues over which my control was non-existent or negligible.

'God, Roger's a wanker,' Hannah would say, standing in the kitchen, speaking while taking her coat off and looking at me on the sofa.

'Oh really?'

'He's put me and Martha down for two weekends in a row.'

'Right.'

'He's just trying to push us into a confrontation.'

'That's terrible.'

She walked over and ruffled my hair.

'He knows that I won't complain because of Martha, and Martha won't complain because of me.'

'Ah ha.'

'Maybe I should call her.'

'I think the washing machine might be broken.'

'He's a fucking prick.'

A conversation that was, of course, followed by her settling in to watch soap operas, themselves punctuated by similar conversations and tensions and exclamations, as Hannah sipped her cup of tea, avidly paying attention, rarely blinking.

As I exit the next designer shop I'm hailed by a wolf whistle from across the street. A black soft topped jeep, its khaki hood down, is turning left into a side road. In the rear seat are two girls, more or less student age, standing or kneeling high on their seats and facing back towards me. Judging from the deftness of their make-up and the even tone of their tans and the bouncy gleam of their studio hair they are dance school students, aspirant pop stars maybe; perhaps being driven through central London on their way to a music industry meeting.

This is the kind of recognition I always welcome, the kind that one easily tolerates. The jeep accelerates up the side road, hauling the two girls out of sight, but not before I have managed to raise my arm, heavy with a shopping bag, to acknowledge them both. For a few seconds eye contact between us is maintained, and their radiated excitement is palpably glossy and cartoon squirrel like, as they accelerate from view.

This little moment cheers me up, and when I flag down a taxi a couple of minutes later I smile pleasantly to the driver.

'Have you ever had anyone famous in your cab?' I ask him when we are underway.

'Only that Prescott.'

'You sure?'

The driver glances at me in the mirror, and the narrow band of his eyes and upper nose and lower forehead is reflected there; a familiar moment in any conversation with taxi drivers, but one that is never less than unsettling. It is the view that prisoners in dungeons must have of their guards or captors, when the slot in the iron door is slid across, and the distressed captive is peered at. It was perhaps once also the final view of dying knights on battlefields, when having fallen to his knees, the mortally injured man looked up at his armoured opponent, to see this same strip of eyes and nose and forehead, exposed by a raised visor.

The taxi driver squints and frowns.

'Oh fuck off,' he says.

'Yeah.'

'Which film are you in? Christ I know.'

'With Morton Greaves.'

'I know I know my son's got the DVD of it.'

'Almost two years ago.'

'Shit. You've got me there. Sorry.'

'*The End of the Ocean.*'

'That's it.'

'The film of the year.'

'Been shopping have you?'

'Yeah.'

After the cab driver drops me off at the building, I take the lift upstairs and then linger in my living room, wondering how to spend the rest of the afternoon. The script reading work is almost finished, and I want to make what remains of it stretch over a couple of days. I shouldn't go to the gym, as my regime instructs that I leave a recovery day between exercise sessions.

Instead I take a nap. Sleeping during the afternoon, this is a luxury departure from an ordinary working life. That working life with its headaches and backaches and elasticating effect on a person's powers of tolerance, its tendency to make relentless demands on one's time and energy, its indifference to health and levels of stress or sanity. And the luxury of an afternoon nap is the solitude of it, which is part of a wider solitude of money, distancing a person from immersion in ordinary things; and from all the negative feelings familiar to the workplace: from the inevitable tensions of mutual irritations and grievances, from the suspicions over motives and decisions, from the repetitive performance of repetitive tasks, from the jealousies and envies and anxieties that shape any working week.

And then there is the expectancy of the pleasure of waking, a pleasure rare in the working life; when the act of waking is always disfigured by the tones of alarm clocks, by the early wakefulness that is an inevitable part of thinking about who said what to who and who is more responsible for this or that problem, by the neighbour's car, by the demands of children or partners, by the whirr of the milk float or by footfalls in the street outside. Even on Saturdays or Sundays, when a lie-in can be hoped for and expected, there is always some interruption to the natural process of waking: the turning on of a bedside light or the drawing of a curtain, a cough or the opening of a door; unwelcome events that can propel a person remorselessly through the barriers of REM sleep.

Equally there is the pleasure, experienced just before dropping off, of contemplating the relaxed stages of early evening: when the television can finally be turned on to watch the news, when the contents of the fridge can be mused over, and vegetables chopped and potatoes boiled and alcohol drunk, all in relative comfort and in peace of mind.

Unlike the evenings after the days at the office, when one hastily returns home, and an insubstantial meal has to be assembled from odds and ends. When the chicken fillets have to be cooked straight from frozen, and the vegetables are a nuisance: celery or courgettes or carrots; and the store of cheap rice in their plastic bags in their cardboard box has been used, because the basmati rice, that golden grain of India, the foundation of nations and nourisher of dynasties, that confetti of numberless unions, has all but run out. And the milk has gone off, and the only bread is crusts, and there is no more dark or even milk chocolate, and there is ironing to be done before tomorrow, and despite all that needs to be done the latter evening is spent in front of the television, sometimes even ending in the eating of hot chocolate powder from the jar with a spoon.

And forming a background to all this is a familiar sense of feeling vaguely afflicted and harassed and uncomfortable; due to the white collar tasks of the office having only incompletely engaged the senses and the mind and the body; and so only a state of partial stimulation has been reached; and each evening has to be passed enduring its dissipation.

There is a blue covered duvet on my bed, and I stroll to it. There I caress out the faint creases and dimples with the palm of my hand. Then it is time to lie down, chest first, and spread out my arms. Outside in the street the traffic grates, but my sense of sleepy ease gradually overcomes all its bother and noise.

Not that I habitually sleep during the day. Until quite recently, for example, the noise of the decorators passing to and from the financier's flat was enough to keep me awake. The men were installing a new kitchen, and the music from their radio, their constant singing and their calls to each other, and the unsupervised and boisterous nature of their presence made afternoon naps all but impossible.

When I lived with Hannah afternoon naps were a sore point.

'Don't sleep during the afternoon,' she'd say over breakfast.

'I hardly ever do.'

'I know you're a 'resting' actor but…'

'Oh, c'mon.'

But in truth I rarely took naps when we lived on the estate. The tepid and airless quality of the place seemed to spoil them; it felt there that if I lay down, I might never get up again. A residual immobility had saturated the streets and houses there, and during our period of residence, I often imagined its background presence altering me. It was easy to believe, in the midst of a quiet afternoon on the estate, that all the inhabitants in the houses nearby were having a nap. The idea of this occurring in unison, of each of them lying down at the same time, and then later awaking together, each one using the same excuses to justify the nap to themselves, each person equally oblivious of their sleeping neighbours, unsettled me.

Chapter Seven

It's quite late, around nine thirty, when the doorbell rings, and Suzie is standing outside. She's holding Jeff's laptop, and she doesn't look as happy as I'd expected her to. In fact I'd spent most of the early evening imagining our first post sex meeting: the tactile hugs and kisses, the sense of trust granted, her eyes lingering and expressive, the fresh ease and sense of companionship between two people who've been intimate with one another. But Suzie's holding the laptop in a casual and slightly careless way, one handed, hanging beside her thigh, with the screen open and angled up; the way that people sometimes carry newspapers or magazines.

'Well you've got to see this,' she says, pushing past me.

She's still wearing her work clothes, a short brown jacket and tight brown trousers, which gives the situation an extra frisson of tension, as if we're professionals responding to an outrage.

'What is it?'

Angry women always make me feel dithery and fat-tongued and awkward, as if I'm an inflatable inflated with vague and benevolent emotions that are utterly inappropriate to and wholly useless for the situation. I tend to bob around and make indeterminate noises, staring with open-wide eyes, like a domesticated emu.

'Oh fucking hell, you won't believe this!' she says.

She smacks the laptop down on the living room table. It's still turned on, and after a moment of frenzied tapping, she brings up a website.

'Oh my God!'

The website she's bought up is a celebrity monitor blog, where fans or paparazzi can post their photos; it's one of the sites that generate tabloid exclusives and unfounded rumours. On the title page is a photo of Suzie and I last night, standing by the wall-window that overlooks the square. We are close, facing each other, and her left leg is wrapped around her right, and she is gazing up at me, and I'm smiling. The photo was taken from the square below, and although it's fuzzy and badly lit, it's clear who, and how intimate, we are.

'Fuckers!' I say.

'I can't believe it. Are you under surveillance here or something?'

'Has Jeff seen it?'

'How should I know?'

'He didn't email you or anything?'

'No.'

'How do you know about this then?'

'The press people at work.'

'Oh right.'

'Can't you get a lawyer to take it down?'

'Err, aren't you a lawyer?'

'Josh.'

'Sorry.'

She closes the laptop and goes and flops down on the sofa.

'Can I have a drink?'

'Gin and tonic?'

'Please.'

In a moment I'm in the kitchen, rummaging in the booze cupboard, feeling lightheaded with all the emotion, glad of a moment's breathing space.

'Besides, it'll be too late now to stop the photo getting out. I wonder what else he took.'

She's staring at the drawn curtains, almost distracted by them, replying as an afterthought.

'Really?'

'Yeah, usually The Family only use those sites to whet peoples' appetites. The photographer might offer other pictures to magazine editors today.'

'The Family?'

'You know. It's what Jeff and I call the paparazzi.'

'Oh god of course.'

I walk over and hand her a tumbler.

'Thanks. Sorry I didn't mean to be quite that dramatic. Have you had a nice day?'

She sips her drink.

'Yeah, it's been fine.'

I lean down and we both kiss for a long, delicious, moment.

'You don't think it might be a member of the public?'

I shake my head.

'No. You need a long lens for a picture like that.'

'Do you think Jeff will find out?'

'Yes, in fact I know he checks that site. He's been thinking of suing them.'

'Oh.'

'I know.'

I walk over to the curtains and draw them, opening a view onto the square outside. There are a few people hanging around, smoking cigarettes or talking into phones, and the usual moving clusters of friends and colleagues, no doubt going to and from restaurants or pubs at this time of night, but no one holding a camera, or looking anything other than a passer-by.

'Josh, last night, in the bedroom, didn't we kind of, move off the bed at one point?'

'More than once I think. Why?'

'Well, I think I might have, I'm fairly sure I put one of my hands on the window, to steady myself, kind of thing.'

'Oh no.'

'It's probably nothing, and it would have been much later than the other photo.'

'Paparazzi work shifts on the same spots, like beggars.'

I'm moving into the bedroom, and turning the light off, so I'm not lit from behind, I sidle over and stare at an angle onto the glass. Sure enough, there is the faint trace of the upper part of a palm, patches of the lengths of the fingers, and a definite thumb print.

'Oh fuck!'

'What?'

'You did. The glass is marked. I can see your handprint.'

Suzie is silent for a moment.

'What shall we do?'

'Nothing, yet.'

I walk back into the living room.

'I might just go outside and try to work out where they were standing. The angle up to the bedroom is a bit different.'

'OK.'

'Make yourself another drink.'

'I might run a bath, if that's OK.'

'Whatever. I'll be back in a minute.'

Picking up one of the anti-paparazzi hooded tops from a coat hook; I go out of the door and take the stairs, bounding down the steps. The stairs exit into the lobby at a point not visible from the outside, round a short curve at the back of the atrium, and I dawdle there, until a group of people exit the building together. Then I jog out behind them, head down and hood up, as if I'm setting off for a run, and quickly turn into the side-road. I make my way down a handful of streets, until I approach the photographer's likely position from the rear.

There's nobody stationary or watching, but one of the street lights isn't working, creating a patch of darkness where the alley joins onto the square in front of my building. At this point I stop, and look up at the building. Sure enough the length of my flat is clearly visible from here, and it would be no problem for someone, with the right equipment, to take photos of both the living room and bedroom window. Luckily the angle is quite steep, so interior shots would be impossible. Next I examine the ground. There are quite a few cigarette ends here, curled and orange and larvae like; and as I'm staring at them, pondering their significance, a vehicle turns into the street behind me, and trundles forward.

A glance tells me it's a black SUV, and then I'm walking, ducking round onto the square and quickly slipping into the nearby doorway of a sandwich shop. After a moment the bonnet of the SUV appears where I've just been standing, and the lights switch off. It remains stationary, and no-one climbs out. This front end of the car is sinister, somehow vigilant and predatory; it reminds me of the snout of a wolf in a cartoon, sniffing the air in the entrance to some burrow or den.

By looking through the sandwich shop, window to window, I have a clear view of it. It is very similar, if not identical, to the SUV that Jakub used to drive. Its proportions are larger than is usual, or than is strictly necessary. Both the rear and the front of the car are elongated, apparently containing extra compartments, and its entire structure seems barely to fit in the narrow alley. The windows, though not blacked out, are a shade darker than usual. The overall impression is of a vehicle designed for militaristic official duties: to form the lead and rear vehicles of presidential convoys, to transport bodyguards and their armaments, to follow and provide support in cases of rendition when the silver van with the sliding side door has already set off with the suspect. It is a car I would half expect to see diplomatic plates on, or even the outline of an agent in the driver's seat, wearing dark glasses and a suit and muttering into his wrist.

It reminds me of the training, because as the weeks had worn on, we'd begun to make greater use of this SUV. Jakub regarded the gym training as having limitations, so after the first month we'd done more outdoors. The first few sessions were in Hyde Park, but the traffic fumes and crowds of visitors were a hindrance, so we switched to canal paths and river paths, old Roman roads and green lanes on the outskirts of London. During these sessions he made me carry a ten kilo weight, then fifteen and then twenty kilos, wrapped tightly in white towels and wedged together in a body hugging rucksack with stomach and chest straps.

Sometimes we trained together during these afternoons or mornings, but on the other days he tracked me in the SUV. Running along I'd glance up to see the bonnet poking through the bushes, and then hear the engine's ignition once I'd passed by. Next it'd be just ahead, on a road bridge above the path, black and monolithic. At these times I felt as if I was a Roman legionnaire, happening across the cult stones of some pagan caste.

The first time we drove to Wales to train it was in the SUV. On that occasion Jakub had given little explanation.

'There's an idea I have for you,' he'd said.

He'd mentioned this idea of a training trip to Wales on the Wednesday, and as Hannah was busy, I'd agreed. On the drive there on the Friday afternoon I slept most of the way. On the occasions I awoke it was in a garage forecourt or in a lay-by, as Jakub refuelled the tank or stood outside making calls on his mobile. The week's training had left me sore and pulverised, a shaken looking man in the passenger seat: a passer-by might have taken me for Jakub's hostage.

Over the next month we took many long journeys together in that SUV. Jakub was fierce when he drove, all acceleration and deep sighs and palpable frustration. And I sat, seeing his etched face, his mountain soldier's face, in profile. This face, which was by turns haggard and noble; a particularly expressive face whose skin slackened and became spongy when Jakub was tired, and which tautened and darkened when he was bullish and fierce. One whose alternate expressions were either full concentration or contemplative melancholy, either rapt upon the landscape like a hunter, all senses deployed; or distracted, close to both smiling and regretting, as if touched by memories of conversation with intimates now dead.

'There is all this traffic here.'

For my part I had to contain an urge to make confessions. The throbbing pain in my left ankle, the background exhaustion that seemed to well up and make me nod off whenever I sat down, the clicks from my ribs and occasional flashes of soreness deep in my hips; these were what I resisted describing to him. There are some men who respond well to such confessions and admittances, men who tend to respond in kind with their own list of secret torments and difficulties and hidden habits of tolerated discomfort. There are men that I could have spent those journeys pleasantly with, sharing thoughts and finding areas of agreement.

But with Jakub I found it hard to predict what his response might be to my confessions. Perhaps he would nod and move his tongue around his mouth, and then reel off a list of possible injuries and their symptoms and the fastest ways to heal them. Perhaps he would laugh and then tell me I was a European and an Englishman and that I was ignorant about pain. Or maybe he would merely frown and grunt and nod and then keep staring at the road and his own muscular forearm; exposed by rolled-up shirt sleeves, as they lay angled to the upper rim of the steering wheel. Possibly he would pat my leg and look at me as he might look at a child and shake his head and smile, enjoying having his own convictions confirmed. At the worst, he would lean his head back and laugh too forcefully and too loudly, which was an unappealing mannerism of his.

Either way the moment of attempted contact would be typical of other failed moments of attempted contact in my life. All those times, particularly when younger, when I said this or that misjudged thing to a person, and they failed to understand what I wanted them to do, or understood but felt inclined not to cooperate, or frowned and stiffened and were embarrassed. All those times in part time jobs when I'd talked about acting or plays or some other cultural matter, or when even younger asked girls about their jewellery, or tried to make small talk and ruined a silence which others were enjoying and relishing and allowing to grow; because those others knew how rare any shared and observed silence between people is; and could judge expertly what conversational aside to cast into it, in order to most fully expand the character of the moment.

Back here in London, now, after waiting for a few moments, pretending to be texting a message into my mobile phone, I walk away, keeping close to the side of the square, not looking over my shoulder.

Presently I'm back in the flat.

'Hello?' I say.

'I'm in the bath,' Suzie replies.

'How is it?'

'I'm watching TV.'

'Good. Yes it's fun isn't it?'

'I'm only sleeping with you because of this bath.'

'You know I thought you were a bit like that.'

'Oi.'

'Someone probably did take photos from down there. There were cig butts, and a weird car came along and parked there.'

'I'll just be a minute.'

I can hear the sound of the shower, and I wonder if she's drying her hair. So I sit down and switch on the news. It is one of the TV programmes that I watch regularly, that I notice if I miss. There is news on different channels, and at different times, and there are one or two broadcasts I prefer over others. But in general they share enjoyable common features. There is the opening melodramatic and urgent music, usually combined with aerial footage of central London or a chiming Big Ben, a combination which evokes a sense of national order and spirit that is otherwise always obscure, that is rarely glimpsed or given shape to in the everyday course of things. But whose rare manifestation is somehow thrilling and exciting and dangerous and forbidden, in the way that a magical spell is in fantastical stories or computer games; when an alignment of elements, elements that are separately passive and benign, are being invoked to unite to create mythical energies. Or like one of those spells of summoning, spells where a stone golem or species of devil is called upon to materialise in a pentagram, into a blood and candlewax design dripped onto a stone paved floor; and a monster duly appears, over which the conjurer has uncertain or only partial control.

Then there is the statement of the headline or headlines, described in grave and sombre terms, where even a relatively trivial event, an event that is only worthy of becoming the headline on a slow news day, can be cast in the most serious and significant and momentous tones. An instance, again rare in life, when one glimpses the mechanisms of democracy and power, when one is at the receiving end of facts cast as truths that flare briefly in the mind; bright moments illuminating the vast spaces of personal gullibility and desire to believe and desire to have faith and desire to trust; those feelings on which politicians rely.

Then the main story unfolds, and then the day's other topics are presented by the articulate presenters, with their expensive suits and their flamboyant ties and socks. And one is drawn in, one is kept in the audience, at least in part by a sense of being made privy to things, by an impression of being reported to and consulted with; as if one were a cabinet minister or similar personage, an individual with decision making power, and these gorgeously socked and well-tailored gentlemen are personal advisers making a regular briefing.

And perhaps if someone watches regularly, then that someone might notice the same striking socks and ties on the diplomats and the dignitaries and the representatives being interviewed, and then that person might also notice more strongly the illusion of involvement the news provides; the illusion of participation in the inner functioning of democracy; an illusion that is perhaps only broken when one looks down and regards one's own socks, which are almost invariably black and in a disgraceful state.

During the training with Jakub, there was a television in the cottage in Wales, and watching the news was one of the few luxuries Jakub permitted. He never watched television, and instead liked to sit on a comfy chair, listening to music through headphones. We took it in turns to cook, but generally I got to see the headlines at least. Later we'd be early to bed, exhausted after our days hiking or jogging in the hills.

'For the thighs,' Jakub liked to explain.

Over the period of time of training in Wales I began to develop the excessive strength of bouncers or inmates or soldiers, a kind of reactive strength that is difficult to regulate, but which can regenerate a man and make for a more robust disposition. My chest thickened and broadened, and my physique became the sort that intimidates pensioners and alarms small children. I started to feel affinity with the shaven headed of the world, all those marines and conscripts and wrestlers and athletes; I took pleasure in becoming encased in their rigid physicality, pleasure in the same aerobic resilience and capacity for sustained exertion.

Our runs up the hills and along the ridges had an isolating intensity: the hoarseness of my breathing suppressed any distant sound, and concentrating on the muddy and rocky paths and tracks prevented me noticing the views or any of the scenery. Early on I bought some Welsh rugby shirts, and at the end of each morning my face was as blood red as the dragon insignia on my back and breast. We carried packs here too, loaded with water and half sacks of coal, and each stamp of a foot felt weighted and heavy; a hammer blow to force the mountain further down towards the earth's core. Up and over the ridges and spars and contours we ran, spurred on by the drumming of the blood in our arteries.

The paths themselves were damaged by overuse, trampled into gullies and trenches by others like ourselves, runners in training or competitors in a race. Marathon entrants and triathletes, heads bent and nodding as they concentrated and endured, formed a steady weekend traffic over the hills; giving the trails some of the scoured appearance of overused city streets or major train stations or public football pitches or exhausted farmland; places with scarce opportunity for any recovery or replenishment, without any sprouting grass despite the milder weather of the changing season. These were paths suffering from an excess of purpose, paths with the taint of confinement, paths suffering from a lack of variety and fundamentally in need of a holiday.

Aside from the training there were a few incidents. There was my snoring, which troubled Jakub.

'Stop you bastard.'

I'd wake to find him shining a torch into my eyes.

'What?'

'You're like a pig. Your noises.'

'Sleep in the other room.'

'No you.'

One afternoon a wild cat climbed in through a window, a creature I discovered after an afternoon's training session. Jakub was absent, having driven to the supermarket, and when drying myself after showering I had that peculiar sensation of not being alone. There was a noise in the sitting room, and thinking a bird had accidentally flown in, I pushed the sofa aside with a broom. The wildcat sprang out and careened around the furniture and walls, leaving gouge marks on a few cushions and knocking over a pile of books. After that it holed up under my bed, hissing and spitting, and tore a mop ragged when I tried to push it out. Fearing injuries to my face or genitals, or the foul spray of its pressurized and fear induced shitting, or its effort to wriggle up and then horribly suffocate in the chimney, I opened the bedroom and then the front door, and shut myself in the kitchen. Eventually the cat escaped after a scrabbling dash through the hall, and I watched its feral, coarsely hairy tail and arsehole bound away into the bushes.

The cold I caught was also a problem.

'I need to sleep for a couple of days.'

'This is all too much. Stand up. At least leave the sofa for me and go to your bed.'

Jakub had none of the British familiarity with colds, none of our resigned expectation of catching them; he quickly became impatient.

'Look I'm always like this with these things.'

'You have just stopped.'

'I have to.'

'Do you like me caring for you? Are you a baby?'

'What?'

On my ill days Jakub sulked around the cottage, fiddling with the jigsaws from the cupboard or browsing in some of the thrillers from the shelf. Or he wandered up and down in the garden outside, seeking a hint of reception for his mobile phone. One afternoon he even, out of boredom, visited a museum, only to return resenting me and denouncing all elderly Welsh villagers and all tourists.

'They never understand what I said.'

'They're like with that everyone. It's worse if you're English.'

'What is their problem?'

'They're locals. Don't worry about it.'

But on these visits to Wales, in general we just kept on, resigned to the intermittent drizzle and gusting wind, panting our way up the stony paths, circling above the valley on the hillside trails. We passed or were passed by a number of others, men and women in lycra leggings and acrylic jackets; all of them far from their usual communities, no doubt seeking respite from the confusing and contradictory demands of work and family, as if each pump and push of the lungs cleared their minds for an instance, forcing their preoccupations to the fringes, affording them a momentary uncluttered view. And afterwards it was easy to imagine them returning home, allowing themselves a gaze at their physiques in the mirror, convinced that this wasn't out of vanity, but for health reasons instead, to check on the fat swelling around their midriff or their muscle tone. And then perhaps later feeling a little empty, or a little sad, as the adrenaline wears off or subsides, finding less solace and renewal in their aerobic routines than they once did, feeling inadequately restored and reorientated by it; staring out at the view from the bedroom window which is just the same, perhaps troubled for a moment by a sense of incompleteness, by the fleeting apprehension of other vaguer and less recognisable needs, which rear and almost coalesce in an amoebic way just on the edges of consciousness.

Men and women who, no doubt, in their neat houses on neat estates, or whilst sitting behind computer terminals in offices immaculate enough to still resemble the interior designer's sketches, like to remember the rawness of the mountains; and to think of their encounters with the external elements there. People who consider the wind in their throats and the rain in their faces to be reviving; who in some way rely on the feeling of entire animation they find in the mountains; who take strength from their memories of these sensations, when sitting in the car on the drive to and from work; in the measured channels of traffic and the familiar progress of their weekdays.

Sometimes, in the cottage, I'd catch Jakub watching me, in the exasperated way couples look at each other when they're angry, the sullen gaze that is usually directed at a person when the object of it is not looking, when they're unaware, busy reading or tidying up in the kitchen. It is a gaze full of frustration carrying with it not only the accusation that the person being viewed is a burden or an encumbrance, but equally that they are the responsibility of the viewer, and so fuels the viewer's own self loathing that they have managed, yet again, to create an unwanted situation for themselves. So I'd have to bear this heavy and loaded gaze from this face that was the site of so many simultaneous conflicts: between youth and encroaching age, between frustration and compassion, between patience and impatience; one that was fleshed out or shrunken by the variables in his temperament.

Next door, in the bedroom, I can hear Suzie moving about, opening and closing cupboards.

'There are more towels under the mirror.'

'Oh thanks. I'll be through in a minute.'

While I wait I go and stand by the window, and draw back the curtain. The SUV has gone, and the square is almost deserted. On evenings like this I don't always watch the television; sometimes I turn one of the armchairs to face the window, and then sit viewing the city. I've considered buying a radio, a CB style device capable of receiving the well used frequencies. Then I could listen to the radio chatter as well, and make connections with the content of the view and what is being said. There are the police cars and fire engines and ambulances active in the streets, usually singly but sometimes all together, as if they were pursuing one another, or were all converging on a place nearby. On other nights there is the blinking light of a helicopter, an air ambulance or airborne police unit, hovering above the rooftops and drifting in front of the financial towers. The later I stay the more the proportion of taxis increases; black or maroon cabs with the deep gleam of polished boots or shoes, which jostle in the side streets and mount the pavement corners. On the limit of my vision is the river, and here tourist boats ease along, lit like chandeliers, until they are concealed by the hull of a larger vessel, a barge or container vessel perhaps, an industrial cargo buoyant on the swell of water.

There are nights when I've fallen asleep in the chair, slumped before this view of the city, only to be woken by the reflected streak of a headlight across my face or a surge of noise from a duo of car horns. In these sleepy moments after waking, when too drowsy to move, the window facing me resembles a public TV screen, similar to those mounted at cricket grounds or outside the entrance to the courts at Wimbledon. And in this position I'm unsure if I'm a viewer, sitting before a screen, or an actor, installed behind it. Either way, the illusion is maintained by the proliferation of glass and steel buildings extending to the limits of the visible terrain, all appearing televisual at this hour of night; as if monumental televisions were clustered all the way to the horizon, dormant and in storage, without anyone to watch them; each containing their share of actors, all slumped and bored and inactive and essentially confined.

This impression, of the cluttering and uncontrolled and replicating production of automata, is familiar from motorways, when the thickening traffic can seem to be forming a metal layer over the tarmac, as if all the cars intend to interlock together and become an aluminum surface, a crunchy and slightly collapsible road for the future robotic marvels that will grind and roll along it. This is a sense that applies to plastic bags in the ocean, in rivers and in landfill sites and in shanty towns and on

Pacific beaches and on roadside verges; as if the plastic bags are artificial organisms that divide and subdivide, which replicate throughout and populate all the latitudes of the Earth.

It's on these occasions and at this time when I have most regretted being single. A girlfriend would never let me doze off in the chair, would never let me drift into the advanced state of absorbed abstraction necessary to fall asleep there. When I started living with Hannah there were certain bachelor habits that were hard to maintain. One of these was a casual love of late night television, a Friday or Saturday tendency to wander, in the hours close to midnight, among the down market channels; to browse indulgently and perhaps choose a Jean Claude Van Damme or Steven Seagal movie, or arrive and settle in half way through some other late starting film.

And there is a freedom at this time of night, when a person is too tired to read anything serious or work related, when the eyes have had enough of computer screens, when the daytime's opportunity of devoting oneself to any useful or wholesome or life advancing task has passed. These are hours when the channels are scanned, in the vague desire for pornography; hours when the break down in each channel's usual content seems to mirror the fragmentation of one's own personality, in response to tiredness, to the after effects of the demands of the week. The late hours, before a final submission to sleep, when one's points of resolve and resolution, when one's long established understanding of oneself, can seem to loosen and come under threat. Times when this or that project or plan begins to seem futile and ill conceived, naïve and under financed; times when grievances towards friends or family seek to reinstate themselves as preoccupations; times when all half forgotten and pressing but undone tasks are remembered in full clarity: the clearing out of the garage, the trimming in the garden, the replacement of a piece of gutter, the email response to an acquaintance or the invitation of a particular couple to dinner.

These are the hours when alcohol is most easily drunk, when one or two glasses can become three or four, or two beers can become five, or one bottle can become two. The hours when most promises are broken, when regretted decisions are made, when ideas which would be dismissed instantly by day are entertained and considered and taken seriously; hours when a person is most receptive to daring proposals and unusual liaisons.

It is the time of night when celebrities lurch round to each other's flats and raise the subject of strip bars. The hours when Jeff, in his occasional days of drinking following a defeat, comes and knocks on my door and attempts to take me out.

'Listen man the girls wrestle on the stage.'

'I was about to go to bed, Jeff.'

'You're always about to go to bed.'

'You'll be recognized.'

'Screw it.'

'That's not what your agent'll say.'

He leans on the doorway and stares into the flat.

'What's that?'

'It's a windsurfing board.'

'Oh.'

'Where is this place?'

'South of the river.'

'It sounds horrible.'

'No man it's wild.'

It is also the time of night of the longest telephone calls, when rates are cheapest and distant time zones intersect; when the quiet murmur of a loved one's voice can seem to penetrate more deeply than at other times; when that voice can remind the listener why the other is loved, speaking as it does to more parts of the listener than any other voice; seeming to the listener to have more bells and rings and chimes and notes in it than any other voice; seeming to the listener to rouse what is best in them, restoring to them their sense of the person they most are. The voice that has more sympathy and understanding in it than any other, that contains the necessary ratios of generosity and tolerance and the necessary impatience and intolerance considering the listener's personality; the voice which encourages and chides and warns and praises, only at the right time and in the right tone, so that the listener feels advised but never tyrannised, reassured but never patronized, loved but never possessed.

It is the time of night when a person is forced to acknowledge their own interior monologue, forced finally to face up to or face down that drearily insistent voice that is perhaps only distantly heard during the week; which is perhaps only dimly audible in a few moments of silence, when walking down corridors or along pavements or sitting in the back of taxis, that is pushed into the far off background when one is coping with the immediate communications of the day; when one is speaking and listening to colleagues, or typing or concentrating or planning or eating lunch and laughing about something with someone. The voice that is more than anything like having a stranger in the house, a person you scarcely know occupying a locked room, a stranger who talks all the while and who can barely be heard in the kitchen and the living room and all the parts of the house that are busy with life, but who is nonetheless there, and who eventually must be attended to.

A voice that has its own peculiar demands and pleadings, that are almost always a little strange and obscure, that are difficult to meet given the current conditions of one's outer life, that in fact seem to seek to undermine this life. A voice that is routinely dismissive of normal comforts, with requests and wishes whose fulfillments seem peculiarly designed to destabilise your life, the one you keep telling yourself is the best for you, perhaps the only possible life for you, given the circumstances. The existence that you have so carefully built up, with its concessions and its trophies, its sacrifices and its pleasures, the life you are so convinced that you are happy and content with; this is the life that the inner voice, the hidden voice, is so frustrated with and concerned about.

Chapter Eight

'Morning Mr Haddon,' the hairdresser's receptionist says.

'Hello.'

'Well, are we?'

'Fine thanks.'

'With Jason, is it?'

'That's right.'

'Here, put your coat on that.'

'Thank you so much.'

I have my hair cut every three weeks or so, and always at this salon, with one of two different hairdressers. My appointments are made well in advance, and I try to arrive ten minutes early by taxi. One of the casualties of my celebrity has been a free and easy approach to haircuts. In the old days of obscurity I wasn't fussy, tending to wander into any salon that wasn't too downmarket, nor too upmarket. Of course I knew enough to avoid the old men's places, those barbers' shops that one half mistakes for morgues or funeral parlours or crematoria; the barbers' shops that are near chemists and post offices and launderettes; the kind with brown floors and walls where on passing, one might see a solitary pensioner tipped up in a bulky and rather industrial chair, perhaps even lathered around the jaw and chin. And there, alongside him, is the hairdresser, often unkempt, perhaps guilty of cutting his own hair from time to time, who prods at his customer's hair as if he were Dr

Frankenstein putting the finishing and final preparatory touches to his creation; as if he were, after months of obsessive work, soon to cry aloud and yank the lever.

Equally I used to avoid the more expensive salons, the places where women go to have their hair highlighted and coloured and waxed and lengthened and trimmed and touched up and sometimes even cut. The kind of salon where the staff are very young and noticeably beautiful; where even to enter, as a person over the age of twenty five, is to feel that one is interrupting a teenage party or music video. Where the floors and the ceilings and the walls are done in white tiles, almost as if it were a fashion photographer's studio, and the staff are skinny and in black, and the silver aluminum hairdryers are coordinated to match with the combs and the mirror backs and the slightly unnecessary rail that often divides the basin section from the hair cutting section.

Instead I used to visit the salons which aimed themselves at fashion conscious men, those with brown or black leather sofas and copies of GQ and Arena and Maxim magazine. Salons where the staff are tattooed and amiable and talk about bands and nightclubbing and holidays in Thailand and occasionally, joy of joys, their sexuality. Salons where there is banter, where the hairdressers argue with each other and discuss their acquaintances in wide and expansive detail, where they forget what you do for a living no matter how many times you go in there.

These carefree days are now over. More than anything else, the arrival of celebrity has obliterated my hairdressing arrangements. Gone are the days when I could venture into a salon and slump down on the sofa, glad of the break in my routine, grateful for the opportunity to read magazines I could never persuade myself to buy. There is a privacy in anonymity in public places, a sense of loose tolerance and freedom from interference, which I used to appreciate while undergoing a haircut.

After the film was released, at first I tried to continue my haircuts as normal. But this proved to be impossible. A gleeful and expectant atmosphere would pervade the salon in the minutes after I entered, a hopeful and anticipatory hush that seemed to pass between the staff and the customers, as if they were all nudging each other and silently pointing me out. The overall volume of conversation would diminish, and every time I looked up, I'd sense a redirecting of eye contact from everywhere in the room.

When my turn came, the hairdresser available would regard me with an expression of conquest; as if I were a pouting and nubile young lover, poised naked upon a plush and silken bed. He or she would shake out the gown with a flourish, and then invite me to sit. Clearly these people, these impresarios of small talk, saw me as a serious challenge, a threat even. Here I was, among them and their peers, a first rate source of desirable anecdotes and provider of high class gossip. The others would expect their colleague to force me to talk, to make me do more than merely talk, to compel me to gorge their ears with a colourful portrayal of undisclosed celebrity life; to hold the entire salon spellbound with details of quarrels and seductions and extravagant behaviour.

So, in the early days of being famous, having my haircut became an imitation of torture. There were the early inconsequential questions, the ones intended to create a rapport between myself and the hairdresser, to establish a bond of trust. Then, once the haircut proper was underway, when I was fully captive and committed, the true objectives of my stylist would emerge.

'Haven't I seen you before somewhere?'

'Yeah. I act.'

'That's it!'

'I was in *The End of the Ocean*; the one with Morton Greaves in it.'

'Got you. I know.'

Then a silence would ensue, like the moment, in an inquisitor's dungeon, after the first application of pain and resulting sharp intake of breath; a moment in which all possibilities seem to lie before two people, and only the direction of travel is for sure.

'Mate. I loved it.'

'Oh. Great.'

'Just keep your head still for us.'

'Sorry.'

'Take long to film did it?'

'No not too long.'

Then, once into the foothills of the conversation, our chatter would retain this tone for a time, while all the weight and thickness was cut out of my hair, while the sides were graded to the correct length. Then at the moment of maximum impossible departure, at the moment when half the hair on my head was significantly shorter than the hair on the other half, when any attempt at an outraged exit would undoubtedly attract the attention of and provoke hilarity in any passers-by, the serious questioning would begin.

'That Greaves bloke was the lead wasn't he?'

'Yes he was.'

'Was he ok? Was he as bad as the papers say?'

'No, he was fine. A nice man actually.'

'Really?'

'Yup. Very much the professional.'

'He wasn't still banging that singer then?'

'No. That was all rumours.'

'Oh was it?'

In the early haircuts I would keep this tone throughout, a kind of detached ambivalence, a sort of resigned patience that offered very little, and confined itself to discreet responses to any questions asked. But I began to realise that this was a mistake, that it made the hairdressers vengeful and frustrated, and that this unhappiness caused their forearms to tense up and their fingers to tighten. They felt I was withholding on them, being patronizing perhaps, and as a result I had some very patchy haircuts indeed. So I learnt to relent, to play the game more, and to impart salacious tit-bits to keep the atmosphere charged.

'I mean he did throw his weight around a couple of times.'

'No.'

'You see that scar on my ear?'

'Yeah.'

'Well Morton and I were doing this one scene and...'

It was statements with beginnings like this that ensured my speedy release, which allowed me safe passage to the streets outside without serious damage, which enabled me to look in the mirror when I got home and breathe a sigh of huge relief. These regular masquerades ended when I contacted an expensive and famous salon, to ask for a private appointment. Since then I've been coming to see Jason or Tanya, and things have been much easier all round.

'Mr Haddon?'

'Yes.'

'Jason's ready for you now.'

'Lovely.'

Jakub and I were training in Wales when Hannah's accident happened. It was a Saturday morning, and we'd been running for a couple of hours. At the rest and rehydration break, near the crest of a hill, I checked my phone in my rucksack. This had been on silent all morning, so as not to interrupt the run, and I was surprised to see four missed calls from Hannah's mobile. Thinking she must have gone home and forgotten where I was, I rang her back.

A man's voice answered.

'Hello.'

'Hi yeah I'm trying to get Hannah. Is she around?'

'Is that Josh?

'Yes.'

The speaker paused and swallowed.

'Her husband right?'

'Yes.'

'I've got some bad news I'm afraid. There's been an accident here. An incident with one of the horses and now she's in intensive care. We've been trying to call for the last couple of hours.'

The man spoke respectfully, like a doctor or a funeral director, as if practiced in delivering unwelcome news, as if he understood how to negotiate with the distressed and the bereaved.

'Really? How bad is she?'

'Well she was knocked out.'

'Oh my god. Fuck.'

'Yes. Are you close by?'

His tone was polite, but equally, urgent.

'No. I'm running up a mountain in Wales.'

'Oh.'

'Can I call you back?'

'Of course. I'm one of Hannah's colleagues in Oxford. I'll text you a couple of numbers for us here.'

I ended the call and looked over at Jakub. He was stretching, extending his arms over his head and bending his torso from side to side. With him this movement was more than just the dip and flex that one sees practiced in the gym, or done in lines before amateur club or school team sports. When Jakub did this stretch his outer hand could touch the ground, and the practiced wrench of his lower spine was almost audible; his nearside ribs would touch to the left and right of his knees.

'It alright?' he asked.

'No. That was a colleague of Hannah's. She's been hurt. She's in the hospital.'

'Motherfuckers. OK. Come on. Now we go down.'

We picked up our rucksacks and started down the trail.

'I'll drive you.'

'Thanks.'

'Not too quick. Not too quick.'

As we ran down the path Jakub kept shouting. And running down there with him felt like the midst of an incident in a warzone, as if we were retreating combatants, fleeing the slopes in fear of a bombardment or a helicopter raid, as if our sparse and meagre position, our native and revolutionary position, was finally about to receive the brutal attention of the allied forces, of their technological capacity and awesome firepower, of their withering and exacting scrutiny.

Thankfully it was a sunny day, and the mud was firm rather than slippery. By the time we reached the cottage I could feel sunburn on my face, for the first time that year. Inside we crashed about, having two minute showers and packing clean and ironed clothes to wear. It was the kind of hurry where I almost didn't bother with socks, where I put my underpants on back to front and where the towels were left where they fell, uncollected and uncared for, sprawled and disorderly upon the carpet; among the forgotten and more ignored clothes: the plastic green waterproof trousers, the oversized fisherman's jumper that seems to materialise in every Englishman's wardrobe when anywhere near the outdoors, the checked shirt in country colours that I had bought in anticipation of polite drinks in hotel bars and unexpected but welcome invitations to dinner in grand estates and country houses; the hastily bought tracksuits and shapeless exercise clothes that were, in hindsight, far too hideous to wear, and made me appear to have escaped from somewhere; as if I were an outlaw or desperado on the run, sure to be pursued by helicopters and sniffer dog teams, through the lush and otherwise peaceful valleys.

'Eat something,' Jakub said.

In the end we got in the SUV holding blocks of orange cheese and bread rolls and tubs of hummus.

'I'm sure she's fine,' Jakub said.

'We just need to get up there.'

'OK.'

'Fuck, hang on, my toothbrush.'

I ran inside and swept all our personal hygiene equipment from the bathroom sink into a plastic bag and then rushed back out to the SUV.

'Let's go let's go.'

'No, the phone chargers.'

'Shit the phone chargers.'

I ran inside again, found them, and rushed back out to the SUV.

'Go.'

And so we set off, on one of those hasty journeys through the British countryside, the kind that often occur at weddings, when the aim is to reach a tiny village church somewhere in Dorset or Berkshire or Norfolk, and the motorways are overcrowded, and against all better judgment a short cut is proposed and agreed upon; and so the A roads are diverted to, and the car is then trapped behind a succession of tractors and timber lorries and slow coaches and beeping flashing highway patrol vehicles of obscure purpose and unnecessary width; the kind that seem to infest the roads whenever one feels any urgency or is in a hurry. A type of weekend journey that is always quickly arranged and agreed to, usually involving a passenger rendezvous or a short detour of collection; a journey that one has felt increasing anxiety over during the preceding week, realizing more and more how unfamiliar the roads are, how precisely imprecise the directions and hand drawn map are, how effective or otherwise the satellite navigation device might be.

A journey usually made in spring or early summer, when the landscape is wearing its party clothes, in green and yellow and vivid red; and one feels relief at not having to stare out at the drab winter vegetation, at the stick thin and underdressed trees; as if they were all ragged and undernourished refugees, fleeing through and into England to escape the destruction of summer in some far off place.

One of those journeys where the number of wind turbines is noticed and remarked upon, where the changing character of the landscape registers with the passengers, where the driver comes close to being dangerously distracted, and says so, forcefully. A journey where mental notes are made of picturesque hotels and homely villages, and vague inner vows of return are made, and castles are seen for the first time, shockingly so; because people always think they know where every castle is, that they are acquainted with all the castles, and so to see a new one is amazing.

A journey where names and places known from the television and newspapers are passed by and remarked on: horse racing tracks and nuclear or coal power stations, prisons and villages where an infamous crime was committed, army and RAF bases and airports, famous factories and wildlife reserves and one of the nation's largest rivers. Journeys that go close to places where childhood holidays were taken and cousins or aunties or godparents lived, places where you often return to in your memories, times before all the difficulties and troubles, times whose happy tone you wish you could restore; but can't because too much has been said and too much has been unsaid. Because too many of the early expectations, the early expectations of the parties involved, have gone unrealized; those initial hopes and budding desires and hints of promises, those feelings that crowd the first stages of any favourable human encounter, have gone unmet and unanswered. And so the parties involved venture on, continue their search, drifting away.

During the journey Hannah's colleague called me again.

'Josh, it's the hospital out on the ring road. You'll see the signs.'

'Are you with here now?'

'No we're on the way there too.'

From the cautious slowness of his voice, this laboured quality to his voice, it sounded as if he was injured, as if he was speaking in spite of or over the pain of a wound.

'Any news?'

'Nothing concrete sorry.'

It was during the journey that I made the call to Hannah's parents.

'Hi Stephanie, its Josh.'

'Oh hello.'

'Stephanie, I've got some bad news I'm sorry.'

'What is it?'

'Hannah's been hurt. No now I'm not sure how badly, but she's in the hospital up at Oxford.'

'Oh God. Was it in the car?'

'No, I think a horse knocked her over.'

'That bloody epidemic. Josh this line's not very good.'

'Do you want me to call Ronald?'

'Don't worry I'll do that.'

These were conversations that were continued later, amid hugs and tearful expressions of sympathy, in the lobby and then the café of the hospital, as we waited for Hannah's doctor, while Jakub stood nearby, or sat discreetly in the corridor, stirring a coffee and saying almost nothing.

'Ronald's in bloody Ireland.'

'When can he get here?'

'He wasn't sure.'

We managed to rendezvous with Hannah's colleague, a tall and matter of fact man called Steve, who explained to us that Hannah had been kicked by a horse and the impact had bashed her head against a stable wall.

'Poor girl,' Stephanie said.

These days, I see Stephanie now and again. She and I have remained friends, and when she visits London we go out for a meal or have a drink in the West End. There had been talk of her coming down to see me today, maybe to go shopping in the sales, or wander through an art gallery or an exhibition or two. But her plans changed last week, and now she can't make it until next month. This is a shame as I look forward to her visits, as they're an opportunity for me to be a tourist with her, and do things in town that I would never otherwise find time to do; like visit the theatre or the latest retrospectives, or attend the performances of foreign orchestras or watch a ballet. Also these are situations where people tend to be gracious about my celebrity, where discreet requests are made to autograph programs; where women raise their hands to cover their mouths and then whisper to their companion; where men are informed of who I am by their children or their girlfriends or their wives, and then nod and watch until I leave their field of vision. All this provides me, and Stephanie when she is at my side, instead of at the far end of the room gazing at another painting or sculpture, with a feeling of being a rake or a debutante at a society ball. A similar feeling is felt, perhaps, by the people remarking on us, as if for a moment our wide and disparate society is incarnated and made immediate, and we are, for an instance, each granted roles.

So without Stephanie I am doomed to return home far too soon, to do nothing more than mooch about after my haircut, prolonging my time outdoors, looking at watches in jewellery shops and finding a deli in which to order an interesting sandwich; one of those with egg mayonnaise and pastrami ham that I like, or even one involving chili jam, the condiment whose novelty is now sadly fading. A smoothie may also become necessary, one with strawberries and blueberries and yoghurt and honey; a treat to take the edge off my sweet tooth for the rest of the afternoon.

But eventually I will drift home, probably by taxi, definitely not by tube, perhaps by bus. Not the tube as the nature of celebrity recognitions there are difficult. On the tube no one has ever approached me with any dignity, not in the trains nor on the platforms nor in the bustling ticket halls. The tube is where men with greasy and stringy hair inform me about astrology; where Asian tourists or South American families make complicated and time consuming photograph requests, involving sign language and extreme smiling; where people ask me to kiss their friends or colleagues or legal representatives; where drunks shout Haddon from the opposite platform; where teenagers film me on their mobile phones and stick out their tongues however I react; where anyone of crude inclination, feeling faintly bored or unsettled, can harangue me and try to incite some sort of mob response among the other passengers.

'How much money do you reckon he's got on him?'

or

'Give much to charity do you?'

Passengers who rarely do more than mutter and rustle their newspapers or attend to their electronic organisers, who glance sidelong at the offending man or boy, or who, without a newspaper or an electronic organiser, stare at the ceiling and try to ignore the situation. The situation is, of course, starkly different on the bus, when I am almost never recognised, when the pensioners and the part time workers and schoolchildren stare out of the windows and at each other blankly, or with mild interest. On the bus where even the merest hint of recognition causes the viewer only to reflect that I resemble a famous actor, and how strange that must be for me. The bus, where the presence of a celebrity is assumed, by a proportion of the passengers, to be that day's first hallucination, another symptom of the mental illness they are currently suffering from; the mental illness whose anti-depressant or anti-psychotic prescription prevents them driving, and therefore obliges them to take the bus, where they sit, bloated and rather pale, wondering why their heads feel so fuzzy.

After the haircut I decide to take a taxi home, having bought a chicken and avocado sandwich to takeaway. Once home, and sitting on the counter, eating my sandwich over the wrapper, with a glass of blackcurrant and apple squash to hand, I contemplate my long and most probably uneventful afternoon. There is the usual script work, and also there is a novel I should start to read, a task I had forgotten until this morning, when I saw the book on the shelf, and remembered that I'd agreed to read it.

Unfortunately Suzie went back next door after her bath last night, as she had such an early start. So the sofa and the table and the chairs are as I left them, in a state of mild disarray and lumpen untidiness. The sofa's cushions are moulded to the shape of my back and buttocks, in a boldly private and starkly unappealing way; and the table has its breakfast scattering of opened envelopes and plastic wrappers and bottle tops; as if a refuse lorry had shakily passed by, scattering its looser and more mobile contents upon it. There is a morbid quality to these signs of light occupation, as if they are a proof of the depth of my bachelorhood, indicating that nobody ever attends to the flat except myself. The state of the table is as much an imprint of me as the shape of the sofa cushions, and to be confronted with its mess each time I enter is dispiriting.

Nevertheless I tidy up, sweeping the odds and the ends from the table into a supermarket bag, and puffing up and reshaping the cushions by swatting at them with the palm of my hand. And in this way the afternoon begins, passing onward like the predictable spectacle of an annual military parade: starting with the settling into a viewing position and the sipping of tea, then the march of the fingers among the papers and the pencils, then the slow trundle of the hands along the pages, followed by the rolling of the eyes and the rising of the eyebrows, interrupted occasionally by the cannon boom and trumpet of a cough or a sneeze.

An afternoon like countless afternoons before it, where any justified opportunity for movement is to be taken, where any interruption to the time consuming and concentration demanding work is lingered over and enjoyed. Afternoons where even trips to the toilet become pleasantly anticipated; where an almost sensual pleasure is derived from the function of the necessary muscles; where the relieving of lower body pressures is welcomed as a refreshing break to the monotonous hours.

The fetching and drinking of glasses of water, the making of cups of tea, the adjusting of the window blinds: these are all tasks that I'm glad for during my script reading time. These can be spaced at intervals in the hours, excuses to stand up and walk around that I can reward myself with. When starting my work I usually remain stationary for an hour or so. This is when I try to muster the necessary quantities of concentration; when the mind is allowed to descend into its deeper, thoughtful regions; when it begins to activate in its fullest and broadest part; when it, so to speak, shakes and puffs and fans out its plumage; when it engages its deep space engines and primes its hyper drive.

So, after a while, a time arrives when I'm reading smoothly. A time when the pages begin to flick over rhythmically; when the speaking characters in the script are talking clearly in my head; when I can easily visualise them, moving around their location, adequately lit and appropriately dressed and appealingly made up. This is the time when camera angles occur to me, as well as additions to the dialogue, both of which I note on the page. Also the actions and the positions of the characters: what they're holding, where they're standing or sitting, what their eyes and hands and feet are doing, are most readily visualised and duly noted. Once this evenness of concentration is established; once it is teased into existence and set onto its course; once it is hauled into an upright and elevated position and fixed in with pegs and guy ropes, this is when I can relax.

The making of toast with chocolate marmalade, the fondling and gentle unwrapping of Kit Kats, the rinsing of a few mugs or plates: all these are tasks that will now fail to constitute an interruption. Sometimes I even stand and say the dialogue aloud, even position myself in the room to best reconstruct where the character is as described in the script. There is, though, a limit to this three dimensional manner of reading. To be in the kitchen facing the lounge, reading a line aloud to an imaginary intruder, is acceptable. To be naked in bed, murmuring sweet dialogue to the pillow beside you, is not.

But most of my time, in these working afternoons, is spent very still. The occasional snap of a page turning is like the crack and sputter from the embers of a fire late at night, when the flames have burnt down, and the glowing logs are furnace orange and molten. And the noises outside, through the insulating glass, have the smoothed edges of sounds heard under conditions of departure. Like those heard, for instance, when one is falling asleep in a crowded house, perhaps a relative's house in the summer, when taking an afternoon nap in an unfrequented upstairs bedroom, half listening to the faint conversation of friends and family, and the falling back of curtains raised by the breeze; sounds which have lost their direct clarity, which have slackened into softness in the moderate spaces there. Or the sounds heard when one is walking away from clusters of people in conversation, perhaps at a summer party, wandering away through an ornamental garden with hedges and walls and orchards; and gradually each voice loses its pristine and distinctive quality, until eventually all the voices churn and mutter together, an indecipherable blend.

My feelings about the reading are shaped by the weather. On the sunny days, when the yellow sun and the blue sky heightens the green in the tree leaves and the colours in the hanging baskets in the street below, then I am more likely to feel content with reading for those few hours; more likely to convince myself that it is a productive and worthwhile activity. However when the weather is overcast and dull, and grey clouds advance to obscure the sky, billowing like a substance tipped into water, or as if to surround and blockade and seal off the city; then the hours spent reading become harder to justify. At these times reading is a task I chafe against, and I wish I was acting instead, even in a matinee performance or in a radio play; something real and evidently career enhancing, as opposed to these silent hours alone.

I suppose the benefit of the reading is found in the character of the scripts. Most are long enough to take a day or two to read, and I prefer to read each one through two or three times. Their reading has become a practice, a ritual which helps me to guide myself through each day, and I've come to see the scripts as more than just distractions, as more than mere devices of entertainment.

The slow descent into the reading, the gradual immersion into an imaginary world, this is something which recalls my mind to its rational state, which helps to reorder my thoughts and chasten their excesses. Afterwards I am refreshed and rebalanced, as if the daily convoy of my thoughts is now passing at its proper distance and in its proper state. In these moments I feel like a cowboy in the saddle, content and smoking a cigar, watching the steers and cattle, in their compact herd, streaming together and making progress among the cacti and red boulders of New Mexico. It as if the company of another mind has made me more comfortable in the company of my own.

I did plenty of reading in the Oxford hospital over those first few days. The reading of newspapers in the café; the reading of thrillers and blockbusters by Hannah's bed in the hours when guests were allowed, the reading of information leaflets and medical pamphlets and website pages related to Hannah's injury. Stephanie and I took turns to be present in the hospital during visiting hours, in case of a worsening in Hannah's condition.

On that first day, after an hour or so of waiting, the doctor arrived to escort us to Hannah's room and give us the speech, the serious illness speech, which he had no doubt performed in many different variants before. The speech, perhaps most often used with cancer patients, involving words like 'gravity' and 'appreciate', and percentages and statistics are given, and the doctor manages to be both businesslike and apologetic, wholly serious and yet often quite sexy, in a high culture way, at the same time; as if he has a red sports car outside and two tickets to a concerto or an operetta in his jacket pocket.

The kind of speech where the institution of the hospital first begins to impress itself upon you, this gigantic and ceramic white mechanism; and it occurs to you that these days there is an institution for everything; that every human eventuality has its uniformed staff and polished corridors and helpful receptionists. And here, amid the intense illumination of the overhead lights, and the tucked-in sheets and the disposable gloves and the damp mops and wheeled trolleys, it seems to you that the old death of churches and priests and bedsides is very far away, that old quiet and peaceful death or old agonised and noisy death. The deaths where hands were held and brows were mopped and water was dabbed onto lips and trickled, ever so carefully, into dry mouths and into swallowing throats. It is perhaps here in the hospital that you really notice and are jarred by the convenience, by the slick and ultra fast and keep-them-moving convenience that exists everywhere. Convenience that is in the tone of the nurse's voice as she asks you if you'd like a coffee, that is in the apologetic smile of the cleaner as he or she enters to sweep and wipe, that is in the charges in the expensive car park outside, that is in the regularity of the bus services to the hospital and the size of the drop-off area in the hospital forecourt; a convenience that possesses everything and everyone except you, as you sit there near your loved one and experience the ebb and flow of your feelings as your wife or brother or mother or father decays or dies or weakens.

Once in Hannah's room the doctor showed us X-rays of her skull, and described the injuries using the usual medical jargon, the terminology that is always half recogniseable from television.

'There is a slight ocular fracture and the rear lobe is distended.'

And Stephanie and I peered at the faint lines on the image, and at the cloudy outline of Hannah's skull, and tried to concentrate and breathe deeply, and glanced now and again at Hannah, who was enmeshed in cables and transparent tubes, with a masked face and bandages over her forehead and eyes, and also on her left arm, limp and comatose. Then, after the doctor had gone, Stephanie and I sat, each side of the bed, alongside Hannah's oddly deflated and pressed-down-on body, her diminished figure which seemed to have lost its bulk and substance and filling.

'I need a cigarette,' Stephanie said.

I touched Hannah's arm.

'Poor baby,' I said.

Stephanie put a finger in her mouth, and a tear trickled down her cheek.

'Oh. Sorry,' she said.

'Do you want a tissue?'

She sniffed, and wiped two fingers through each eye, drawing them together, in the way that people do when tired.

'No. Don't worry.'

'Where is Ronald?' she said.

'I'll try him.'

'He's on his yacht.'

'On the yacht' had been among the cited reasons for their divorce, along with infidelity and incompatibility; the yacht that had been in the boatyard for years, the yacht where Ronald would usually be whenever Hannah and I visited him for the weekend, rubbing the tar or paint or caulking or varnish from his hands while smiling at us in greeting; smiling in his bemused and cautious and guardedly cheerful way. Ronald, emerging from that yacht as if it were a shelter; some dug-out in which he was accustomed to seeking refuge from Stephanie's rampant and forceful expressions of dissatisfaction and frustration, her remorseless listings of all that had and hadn't happened.

'Where were you when I called?'

'At the garden centre. In the office.'

I was silent for a moment and maintained eye contact, both forms of subtle emphasis lost on Stephanie as she leaned over Hannah to pluck free a few strands of hair trapped under her bandages.

'Mummy's poor girl.'

A peculiar irony of Stephanie's and Roland's divorce was that they had both forged new careers in the activities that they had used to avoid each other. For Roland, this had been yachting, and for Stephanie, it had been her landscape gardening business. Each of them, unable to bear the other's presence at the weekend, had plunged their Saturday energies into these occupations, and had consequently made rapid advances. Stephanie became known as a landscape gardener who worked all hours, and so her business expanded and flourished. In fact she became so wealthy and knowledgeable that she bought and made profitable a local garden centre.

Whereas Ronald, who for years had been a family solicitor in Bristol, passed all his yachting exams and diplomas, then set up an Anglo-Irish sailing festival; an event for which he applied for and received all manner of tourism development grants, and after three years was headhunted to consult for a marina company, which now paid him an ample salary with generous benefits.

'Have you seen Ronald much recently?'

'No. Not since Christmas. He almost lives over there now.'

'Is it still the same number?'

'As far as I know.'

At this point we both noticed the sign forbidding the use of mobiles, and so I had to go to the car park to begin the process of calling Ronald, which turned into one of those epic telephone adventures. The kind of multi-faceted and multi-layered phone call which is very rare, which can only naturally occur when making a complaint, and when a caller is diverted and put across and switched over through the hierarchies of a company, where in the worst examples you are actually transferred between continents. Phone calls where the caller is constantly reassured by insincere but extremely confident employees, who represent themselves as taking career endangering risks on your behalf; who put the caller on hold to shout queries across open plan sales floors; who without hesitation procure for you the mobile phone numbers of their immediate and later their distant superiors; employees who actually speculate with you the caller over the benefits or otherwise of transferring your call to private phones installed in limousines and small jets and, God forbid, personal helicopters.

The phone call to Ronald became, after his original number was unreachable, a tactical exercise like this, one which navigated the inhospitable terrain of the emergency services and the coastguard authorities; then the various mobile phone numbers of the organizers of the race; then the radios of the other boats in the race, and found victory in a direct link to the radio on Ronald's boat.

'Ronald, it's Josh.'

'Who?'

'Your son in law.'

'Josh? Hello. Why are you on my radio? Are you OK?'

'No not really, there's bad news.'

'What?'

'Hannah's in hospital.'

'Oh. Is she?'

His voice flattened.

'Yes. She's unconscious. Her skull is fractured. She's in the hospital in Oxford.'

'Christ alive. Christ. What happened?'

'She got kicked by a horse.'

There was an intake of breath.

'Is Stephanie there?'

Suddenly the rasp of his breathing was audible.

'Yes. But not this second.'

'Right. I'll try to get to you for tomorrow then. Are you on the mobile?'

'Yeah.'

'I'll text you when I'm at the airport. And Josh, look after Stephanie won't you?'

'Of course.'

When I returned to Hannah's room Jakub was standing in the corridor outside. He had taken off his jacket and was holding it against his groin and thighs, tucked over his joined hands. He looked pale and put upon and dejected standing there, as if he were a bereaved relative, as if he were preparing himself to grieve.

'Listen man I'm sorry she's in there.'

'I know look…'

'Do you want me here?'

'Don't worry. I'm sure she'll be over it in a day or two.'

'It's wrong for me to go now.'

'Her mother's here and her dad's coming tomorrow.'

Jakub nodded and was solemn, looking tired and heavy lidded, as if he hadn't slept the night before, as if he had found Hannah's body, and accompanied her to the hospital, and sat up by her bedside. He put his hand on my shoulder and stared into my face.

'Years ago I had a kid that died. In a hospital like this.'

'Really?'

'Yes. A bad situation.'

He bent his head forward and frowned. I wondered, for a moment, if he was coming down with a cold or flu.

'OK. I'm going to Wales. To that stupid small house.'

'I'll call you tomorrow.'

'Mm.'

And oddly enough it was easy to imagine him at a funeral, among the crowd of relatives on each side of the pit and the coffin. Jakub standing in a windy autumn or in the light rains of spring, hugging and consoling a sobbing and haggard woman or younger sleek woman; perhaps attended by military colleagues, with a few uniformed men present. Jakub in a suit no doubt, ready to have the conversations one always has at funerals: the conversations about health and the passing of time, about one's more recent contacts and dealings with the deceased, about other mutual friends and acquaintances, about what one has just finished doing and about what one is soon to do.

Funerals where the aerial view is like a mutilated clock face, with the pit and the coffin the damaged centre, the mourners the numerals, and one of the rotating hands has been stolen. Funerals where there is always a tree, a tree that is near to the pit and to the coffin, behind or alongside the mourners; a tree that manages to appear in any photographs taken, and that is always offensively, abundantly and defiantly alive; that always seems to be bustling with sap and vigour, that seems a threat and an insult to the privacy and dignity of the ceremony.

Funerals where one is mesmerised by the coffin, by the polished wood of it, by the gleaming brass or imitation handles, by the rigid and angled and uneven way it lies in the soil at the bottom of the pit; in the same way that a boat rests on the sand or gravel of a beach; or a spade or fork that is forgotten and left among the turned clods and clumps of soil in a garden.

Funerals where the smell of earth and the green trees reminds you of woods and gardens, places where you yourself played, where perhaps you played with the deceased, or where the deceased played a few years before or after you. The woods whose closeness of branches, whose hideaways of bushes and thickets, whose enclosing nest of nature is recalled by you as you stand here amongst this scent of bare earth, and the sound of these branches shaking in the wind, and the intonations and chants of ceremony. A ceremony of the kind that childhood is, in your memory, thick with or punctuated by those weddings and christenings and funerals and baptisms and Easters and Christmas's and Thanksgivings and Anniversaries and Remembrances.

Occasions whose essential components seem unchanged to you now, as if the priest here is the same priest that you remember, as if the mourners here are the same as the church-goers you remember; and where only you are different, where you as your adult self are alone in violation. Occasions whose resemblance to memories induces in you a kind of emotional nausea, a sense of being overcome by a surge of feelings from past times and past places, the emotions of childhood with all their dependencies and anxieties and confusions. So much so that you take a deep breath and grip your hands in your pockets and frown and

142

stare at the ground and try to focus on who you are and where you are and what you have to do.

In the hospital room with Hannah I faced the same questions that I face now. It is odd to think how quickly I accepted the possibility of her death, strange to think how quickly I slipped into preparing for it, how quickly an inner dictation began to create a psychological readiness; it was as if my mind immediately recognised a survival situation. And those questions were over whether I had made her feel loved enough, whether if together we had known the limits of happiness, whether I had been an adequate or extraordinary or less than adequate lover and friend and husband.

I asked myself then, and still do, on these nights alone here, whether my thoughts about happiness were correct. Ours had always seemed to me to be a recognizable type: the kind based on contentment and ease of proximity, one where a deepness of compatibility expressed itself in the gradual saturation of ourselves with our feelings for each other. Since then I've considered the limitations of this view, and wondered how much it imposed on her. Perhaps she had wanted more; perhaps she had concealed all the secret, violent, charges of her heart.

What I try to forget are the times we argued, the times we disappointed each other, the times we doubted each other or felt doubted by the other. What I feel guilty about are the times I let my feelings wane, when I wasn't strong enough or persistent enough or steady enough in the encouragement of my best feelings. The times when I let myself believe the worst of my thoughts about us: that we were ordinary, that we were clearly ill-suited, that our marriage was no more than a formalisation of our desire to depend on and take advantage of the strengths of the other.

These were thoughts that at times I failed to fight off, that I allowed to sour my responses during some of our more difficult exchanges. These usually took place when one of us was ill or tired or overworked for a week or more, times when the responsibility of running the house had fallen on the shoulders of one person for too long. In these times the usual measures of patience and generosity would be thinned down and worn away.

These arguments always seemed to happen in mid morning, in the kitchen; in its featureless spaces, when the housework and unmade phone calls and other unattended tasks rose up sheer around us.

'Why do you get so sick at this time of year?' she'd say.

'I don't know. It's the end of winter. I'm depleted.'

'Other people don't get ill for as long as you.'

'Well. I don't know. Just deal with it.'

'Looks like I'll have to.'

These arguments replayed themselves in my mind as I sat by her hospital bed, watching Hannah and talking, in a low voice, to Stephanie. Occasionally Hannah would make moaning noises, or breathe in sharply and shift about in the bed.

'Don't worry angel,' Stephanie would say.

The room acquired an atmosphere: an air of patience, of stilled feelings, of the quiet assembly of tragic thoughts. Its qualities of silence: the reflective stillness of churches or of churchyards, the waiting silence of second homes near the coast in winter, the secluded silence of hilltops and forest trails, seemed misplaced in the bright and efficient hospital. But the digital screens of the room, and its harsh white floors and walls and lights, these failed to dispel what was a congress of silence.

All this has had a lasting effect. Often now, when alone, the atmosphere of the hospital room returns to me. It seems to drift in, quietly and invisibly, from under the furniture and from behind the bookshelves and pictures. Presently I am submerged, and my everyday concerns and preoccupations recede, and the memories of the hospital room become foremost. Perhaps I'm always pressed to remember it, and when alone just more so.

Now, back in the flat in London, it's late afternoon, and the reading is done. The novel is still on the table, and I haven't opened it. It's currently the subject of a high profile adaptation, and the screenwriter is, apparently, in the final stages of the script. My agent has passed the novel onto me for preparatory reading, as she expects the production company to send in the script very soon. It will have to wait until tomorrow.

In a fit of curiosity I rush over to my laptop, which is in an alcove by the bedroom door, and type in my name, and then click search on Google image. Sure enough, there are two or three reproductions of the photo of Suzie and I. There is the same one that we saw, on the blog, but alarmingly the picture is now on the website of a celebrity gossip magazine. When I click on it, and follow the link, I see the photo is part of a gallery, which includes a daylight shot of Suzie leaving the front entrance.

My mobile is among the scripts, and in a moment I'm looking at the latest text message Suzie has sent, then calling her. She answers almost immediately.

'Hi, did you get the last text?'

'Have you seen what's happened?'

'I know. It's going viral. Have you checked your email?'

'No.'

'Do. Jeff has sent us both one.'

'Is he pissed off?'

'Err. Yeah. Of course he's pissed off.'

'Oh fuck!'

'Look Josh I'm about to give a presentation. I'll call you later. I want to stay over by the way, you lucky boy.'

I hurry back over to my laptop and open up my email account. Sure enough there is an email from Jeff, principally to Suzie, but copied to me. The photo from the website is attached to it, and the subject box reads "???**WTF**???". There's no message in the main body of the email.

Unsure as how to respond to this latest development, I retreat to the kitchen, and fill the kettle.

Reflecting on Suzie's comment it occurs to me, as it has done before, that virtually everybody in the building, apart from me, uses their flats almost wholly for sexual purposes. In fact it often seems that many of the owners have bought their flats for hot cock reasons. Here, it is like living in a pornographic outpost, it is like being in a colony established by sexual explorers, in the hinterlands of a more chaste region. It is the place where the residents come to come, the place where they can forget the inhibiting sexual mores of the surrounding territory.

As a result of living here I have begun to see London as being full of sexual migrants, full of people in search of a wilder sex life. Sometimes I think the professional side of London is secondary to this, that getting laid with greater frequency and ferocity and imaginative use of furniture and even use of oven warmed kitchen implements is the chief attraction of the capital.

Perhaps London is largely populated by those who have exhausted the frottage opportunities of their home towns; who have made passes at and seduced all available partners; who have progressed beyond that to their partner's parents and siblings; who have even slept with distant relatives. People that have got bored of doing the rounds of the local pubs and bars, that have learnt to recognise and avoid the other one night stand specialists that masquerade as drinkers there. The time arrives when they know that only in London will they make progress.

That I live in a residential block in the centre means that I experience all this the more intensely. Right now, if I knocked on all the doors in the building, no doubt many would be answered by middle aged men in dressing gowns, girls with tousled hair in leggings and lacy bras, tall muscle bound Italians naked from the waist up wearing riding breeches, timid boys with earrings and reddening lash marks across their chests. I can only hope that the architects catered for this in the original design, for the possibility of a synchronicity of pelvic thrusting; and that the combined energy of all these simultaneous penetrations won't one day cause the entire tower to rock and sway, and bring the whole edifice toppling over.

And then I go back to my flat to patiently endure the end of the afternoon and the start of early evening, the time of day when one's progress through the list of tasks, the list of tasks that we all have and keep close to hand, begins to slow; when it starts to be pursued with less stern resolution, with less clock watching and frowning and nervous irritation. The time of day when a drink can be considered, when tomorrow can finally be thought about, when the waning of one's energies are welcomed after the vigour and determinations of the day. The time when natural limitations are accepted: the loss of daylight in winter, the decline in powers of concentration, the early stirrings of hunger, the need to break the routine or monotony of what you have been doing for all these hours. The time when heads are raised from reading, when arms and backs are stretched, when computer screens are finally ignored and backed away from and turned off, when the journey home is contemplated. The time when friends and family are thought about, hopefully with a sense of relief, when their likely daily activities and pursuits are considered and imagined, and their complaints and needs and requests are anticipated.

The time when you stand on a train platform, like all the others standing on train platforms, and perhaps take comfort in this succession of regularities, this succession of trains and taxis and commuters that seems to mimic the succession of your feelings: your relief at the end of the day after the usual tiresome and unrelieved slog of the afternoon, your energetic and decisive morning, your pleasure on thinking about the pleasant comforts of home: those gentle arguments that unravel over weeks, those touching insights and denials that your wife or girlfriend or boyfriend or children like to banter with you over, the cuddles beside the counter and the fridge or on the sofa that are one of the rewards of a settled life.

It is the time of day when the patrol of reality's more treacherous and enemy infested shores is over, and they can be steered away from; or when reality's front lines and forward trenches can be withdrawn from. The time of day when the realm of duty is departed and the necessity for uniforms has past, for the time being at least. The hour when all life's threatening and difficult encounters can be momentarily forgotten about, and the newspaper opened, and the kettle put on.

Recently it is the time when I've begun to browse the internet: to read the news on news websites; to jealously observe the career moves and lucky breaks and starring roles of other actors; to watch interviews and trailers on YouTube; to try for sure, for sure this time, to avoid the pits and traps of pornography; to even glance through the interviews and features and photographs of myself, looking stylish and lightly amused whilst being informative and engaging about my work and background. This is the time when I read and respond to my emails and check my social and networking profile.

The networking profile that is remarkably useless, that seems barely more than an excuse for truncated written conversations, for hasty chats with distant memories of people, as if one had encountered them in a dream. The profile where all the photographs are of the people as you remember them, or as they themselves would like to be remembered: on holiday in the sun or standing on beaches or being extrovert in bars or gardens or laughing at parties. The photographs that make a person's page profile like a holiday brochure of a life, containing all the best angled shots in the high season, that present all the rooms and the buildings and the staff to their best advantage, that make it seem an attractive place to be. The photographs that always make you think that your friends are doing OK, that you don't need to see them after all; that your concern or interest in their welfare is essentially misplaced.

It was also the time of day when Stephanie and I had to leave the hospital, as the visiting hours matched regular working hours. After leaving, on that first night, we stood for a while in the forecourt at the front of the hospital, feeling shaken and drained. We felt as if we were doctors or nurses at the end of a long and particularly difficult shift, as if we had, for hours, been urgently and ceaselessly tending to the injured and dangerously ill and dying. Stephanie drove me to a hotel, a sprawling country pub affair, where she'd reserved two rooms. Rooms which I was expecting to be dark and wooden, featuring the kind of paneling that may or may not conceal a secret door; rooms that I was expecting to have toilets with old fashioned cisterns, the ones that make loud gargling noises as they fill, often accompanied by a grinding whining noise; a sound of an almost mechanical nature. Instead my room had a table made from driftwood, and an exotic, tribal theme; the main lampshade verged on sculpture, and the lamp in the corner was positively totemic.

I showered before meeting her downstairs.

There we, exhausted, ate a long and largely silent meal, during which I felt we were accomplices in some horrific crime; a situation where our feelings of guilt, and fear over the certainty of our capture, suffocated all other emotions. Afterwards, sitting in front of the log fire, each of us holding a double whisky, conversation came more easily.

'What have you been up to recently?' she asked.

'Well, not much acting. Hannah told you about this film?'

'Oh yes. She mentioned it I think.'

Stephanie sipped her drink, relieved, it seemed, to hear something other than her own thoughts.

'As part of it, for the preparation, I have to become fitter and everything. You know how film actors do that these days?'

'Like the new James Bond?'

'Yeah that sort of thing. Well the director, you know Audrey, I've talked about him before.'

'The one who likes you?'

'Mmm, he's decided I need to become more an action orientated kind of actor. So I've been doing a course with this personal trainer.'

Stephanie took a moment or two to absorb this, and tipped her drink a little, watching the ice cubes slide together and then come to rest against the side of the glass.

'My friend's got one of those.'

'It's quite intense though. He's this Russian guy, does a lot of work in Hollywood,'

I burped and swallowed and coughed, making an alarming hemorrhaging noise.

She frowned.

'Are you alright?'

'Yeah. Jesus. Anyway we've been going to Wales on these trips, running up mountains and whatnot.'

Stephanie shifted her chair round, to face the fire more. Then she threw the remains of the drink onto the burning logs, which fizzed and hissed. Bubbles flared up on the blackened logs, a hyperactive frenzy of steaming; as she spoke she watched the agitated, evaporating liquid.

'You two have had a difficult time recently.'

'I suppose we have.'

'When does the film start?'

'Quite soon. In fact I think the production team's moving into location at the end of the month.

'Where's that?'

'Scotland. Somewhere up near John O'Groats.'

'Oh.'

'In fact I think I'm meant to be doing some reading rehearsals next week. Maybe it's the week after.'

A conversation that continued like this until after ten or so, when both of us began to quieten and stare at the fire a little more, began to feel a little graver. When each of us started, no doubt, to think of the arrangements and the commitments we had made for the next week, and how best to reorganise them in light of the current circumstances. When each of us, privately to ourselves, thought about the strangeness of our reactions, wondered why we hadn't become more emotional and hysterical, wondered how we were coping and still functioning as if nothing out of the ordinary was happening.

When both of us sat there, awaiting the arrival of the main force of our emotions, convinced that everything we had felt so far was nothing more than preliminaries, nothing more than the forward scouts for the mighty army of our emotions. Neither of us, really, at that stage, with much experience or knowledge of trauma: with much understanding about how it can affect a person, with much insight into the different ways that the body can respond to it. Both of us expecting an emotional meltdown, a sobbing collapse in the manner of war zone mothers and wives and fathers on the international news; involving a falling to the knees and a beating of the hands upon the ground, some purging disintegration and utter abandoning of usual and everyday conduct.

Neither of us anticipating the actual process, the actual experience of trauma; that seems more than anything to wrench apart a person's mechanisms for dealing with grief. The effect of trauma, that often leaves a person trapped in the initial emergency stage, the coping stage, of their response to grief. The effect of trauma, where the secondary stage of managing grief, the emotional explosion stage; the wipe the slate clean and reset the clock stage, becomes detached from the first. And so the first stage, the lets stay calm stage endures, the nodding accepting stage, the just get on with things stage, this persists. And people are left trapped forever, raised high up and bound up, held as if dangling; above and out of reach of any surface where they might gain traction; where they might be able to step back onto a road towards the fullness of themselves.

Later on, in the room that night, I lit a candle, one I'd taken from the dining room downstairs. This is a practice that has stayed with me, and now and then, when thinking about Hannah, and our years together, I light a candle. They are always similar, nothing ostentatious; often the penny candles, the wax in those small aluminum circles, that are bought in clear bags of ten or twenty; or the marble white candles that are lit above dining room tables at Christmas; those longer ones with the stiff wicks, that are used in churches in batches at Easter or for Midnight Mass. That night, in the hotel room, I lit a candle, and tonight, I'll light a candle also.

Then it was to hope for Hannah, a beacon for her, as well as to remember our best times together, which were often candlelit. The holidays we'd taken in the tropics, for our honeymoon and on other occasions, and eaten in beachside restaurants with candles on the table. The time we'd rented a ramshackle but cosy cottage in Ireland, and lit candles in the evening, and undressed and talked in their soft and yielding light. When we'd wanted their guttering light, their inconstant fiery light that was all the dead generations had to know their nights by, when we'd wanted our candlelit night to be one in a procession of such nights, stretching away into the past. And even her birthday parties, when there'd always been a cake and candles.

Now, when I light the candles, it is to remember her, but also something more. The flickering candle now reminds me of other times and places when candles are lit: in churches and chapels and cathedrals, for funerals or on religious days. Now I see these occasions differently: as the sole fixed or permanent points in a surrounding and unstable landscape, in the way that the gleam of a lighthouse is to sailors, when near to shore. The candles are now a reminder of the flow and turbulence of seconds and hours and minutes, of the permanence of impermanence. In these moments, it seems that the churches and the chapels and the cathedrals are all that remain and endure; are all that aren't washed away or submerged by the tides and floods of days and weeks and months and years.

Now, in the flat in London, as I continue to browse the internet, looking at news sites, resisting the urge to check the sports pages and see how far Jeff has progressed in his tournament, there is a knock on the door. Going over and peering through the peephole, something I always do, despite the fact that it is totally unnecessary and that I've never not opened the door as a result, I see a policewoman standing outside. She is glancing up and down the corridor, her hair up beneath her hat; after a moment I recognize Suzie.

I open the door a crack, on the chain.

'Yes?'

'Josh, let me in, I feel like a total idiot.'

She marches in, takes off the dapper hat with the black and white checked band, puts it on the table, and shakes out her hair.

'There are photographers outside.'

'Where did you get that outfit?'

'It's Jeff's, don't ask.'

She comes over and we kiss, a long lip tugging smooch, in which we resist each other's attempts to pull away; eventually we break off, and Suzie sits down at the table.

'I quite like wearing it actually. People get out of your way.'

'So you've worn it before?'

'Half the time it's the only way to get to his changing room. He gives tickets to the chief constable, or something.'

I stare at her for a moment.

'Right, fuck it, I'm going down there.'

I walk over and pick my coat off the back of the chair.

'Oh Josh don't.'

'No, I'm going.'

By now I'm by the door, slipping on my trainers.

'You'll only make it worse.'

'I don't care.'

As I left the flat I thought that if Jeff saw me denying the affair with Suzie, or read an interview or an article in which I denied the affair with Suzie, then the situation would become more manageable. In a moment I'm in the lobby, waving to Joe and manically smiling as I ignore his pointing outside and mouthing of "family". As he moves out of my line of sight his hands go up to his face, a gesture of despair. As I progress across the lobby I'm working to build up a momentum of charisma: rolling my shoulders to loosen them, fluffing up my hair at the front, priming my smile and warming up my right eyebrow muscle.

And then I'm outside, and the oxygen is the oxygen of publicity, and the nearby group of paparazzi, loitering men holding cameras; drab and functionally dressed, bald or inexpensively barbered, inclined towards being overweight, men whose clothes are the indeterminate and functional blues, dark greens and greys, of spectators at lower division football matches, of fishermen by murky canals, of bookie regulars. These men suddenly perk up and face me and drop their cigarettes and activate their cameras.

'Oh we're on,' one of them says.

They rush over, their cameras clicking and flashing away. I swing my head from side to side, giving them both profiles, and smile lasciviously, in a way that I imagine is devilish and handsome.

'Where is she, Haddon?' one of the paparazzi asks.

'For the record, gents, we are in no way romantically involved.'

'Is that a quote?'

'No, my darlings, it's the truth.'

This statement renews the urgency of the cameras' clicking and flashing. The camp tone of my last remark, carefully calculated to entice, to lengthen this encounter, to invite more questions, seems to work.

'Isn't she Jeff Brazer's girl?' asks a gruff voice.

'She is absolutely still involved with Jeff Brazer.'

'You sure?'

'I think that's called misconstruing the evidence.'

And with this I decide to leave, whirling around in a manner that I imagine is commanding and magisterial, reentering the lobby, ignoring the shouts and swearing. As I stride towards the lift, confident that none of them will follow, I wonder how soon the first video, or sequence of photos, will be posted on a blog.

That evening Suzie stays the night, and at first, with the curtains closed, everything goes fine. We laugh and chat over a pre-dinner bottle of Malbec; we compose Jeff an e-mail that explains the misunderstanding; a jokey, making light of it, kind of e-mail. We talk about films and acting and I describe the history of some of the paintings on my walls, one of which was once owned by Alec Guinness. During the meal, after most of another bottle, Suzie does her gerbil impression, which Jeff has told me about; then she spends too long talking about her sister.

It is as we are finishing our beef stroganoff that events go awry.

'You see Josh, the thing is,' Suzie says.

'Oh yeah, what's that?'

I look at her, raising the last forkful of rice to my lips.

'Well you see you know I'd said I'd broken up with Jeff.'

She takes a mouthful of the wine.

'Yes.'

She swallows and then breathes out deeply.

'Well that's not strictly true.'

'Strictly?'

'In fact that's not quite what happened.'

I'm chewing, and my jaw speed seems to slow, as if the rice has become gluey.

'It's difficult,' she says.

'So have you actually broken up with him?'

She leans forward, and tucks her fringe back, but doesn't make eye contact.

'Well what we said was that we'd break up when he got back.'

'So you haven't?'

She stands up.

'I'm going to the roof to smoke a cigarette.'

When she comes back down I'm clearing the dishes and loading the dishwasher. She stands in the middle of the lounge, finishing off her wine, watching and waiting for me to say something.

'No wonder he's pissed off.'

'Josh, there's nothing else to say about it. We're as good as separated anyway.'

'This is all just about you sending him a message then?'

'No it isn't. It's because you're nice and he's not.'

I turn to face her, holding a damp wooden spoon.

'I don't know.'

'Can we have some coffee?'

'Fucking no.'

Later, after we've made up, and come to an understanding, and watched TV together, with her head on my shoulder, it occurs to me that Jeff probably made the conversation difficult. It's likely that he claimed to be in a hurry, that he did his very best to postpone any serious talking as indefinitely as possible, and that he perhaps used the tournament in

153

Australia as an excuse, saying he needed to 'maintain his emotional equilibrium', saying this or some other over-worked phrase.

Around midnight, when Suzie and I have sex, it is a typical second sex session; the kind of slower, more exploratory, sex session that often occurs after the first, wild, slightly harried and desperate one. A bout of lovemaking that is more thoughtfully lit, that makes less extreme demands on the pillows and bed linen; pubic gymnastics in which the pliancy and firmness of parts of the body are, more carefully this time, measured and tested; sex in which first impressions, first impressions that have, in the intervening days, been doubted and disbelieved, are reconfirmed. These are hours when technique and rhythm and pace can be worked on, when like partners at a naturist school sports day, a clumsy synchronization is found.

Chapter Nine

In the morning, after Suzie's pre-dawn departure, I have one of my ordinary mornings. One where I am conscious of others leaving and going to work, conscious of movement in the corridors of the building, of doors opening and closing, of the grind of the lift hauling up and down. A morning whose earliest and clearest sounds: of a car or a taxi, of brief snatches of music, become lost in the general groundswell; a mass departure and migration that reaches a crescendo and peaks at around eight thirty. Usually it is the combined volume of all these mundane noises that prompts me from my bed: the clatter of toasters, the hard torrents of showers, the opening of drawers, the coughs and sighs, the turning on of washing machines and the draining of sinks.

It as if I am affected by all the human action around me, as if my neighbours and I are in loose tandem, like a flock of birds or shoal of fish; where the steerage of the mass affects the direction and momentum of each. When the other residents stand and rise and go to shower, I am rolled over in my bed. When they towel themselves, briskly and vigorously, I rub my face and head. The resolute leaving of their bedrooms and striding to their kitchens yanks me into an upright and standing position. It is energy from their multiple front door departures that powers my lurching and unsteady progress towards the kettle.

Sometimes Jeff used to pop round, for breakfast, after his morning run. He'd stand in the kitchen, repeatedly filling a glass of water, and drinking it in one long swallow.

'Man.'

'Umm.'

'Are you a drug addict?'

'What?'

'Your face is all mushy looking.'

At times, in these exchanges, Jeff would open my fridge, find and egg, and crack it into his mouth.

'I'm not too good in the mornings.'

'Oh OK. What does that mean?'

'What?'

'Some people are at their desks by now.'

There were occasions when he'd lift a leg onto the kitchen counter, and lean forward to touch his toes.

'Are they?'

'Yeah. Big time.'

'Just pass me the sugar.'

Certainly the horizon to horizon scale of the movements in the city helps to rouse me into action. As does my dislike of the passing by of unused daylight; that scraping and grating sensation as the waited out hours shift by, the regret and guilt over the stern facing down of promising and useful time. After rising I stand by the window in the lounge, sipping from a mug of tea or coffee and watching the people and the traffic hurrying along in the street below. Sometimes, if I'm lucky, there is an accident or an arrest or an argument or a fight, and the unfolding drama can be watched safely from my vantage-point; usually though nothing happens, and eventually I eat toast and shower and proceed with the day ahead. However there are mornings when I linger, remaining in my dressing gown until well after nine. Today is one of those invalid days, when like a convalescing patient I am content to merely exist; and so I go to make another cup of tea and to switch on the radio.

It's also the time of day when the management of the building, every few months or so, chooses to test the fire alarm; a practice that Jeff and I discovered the hard way. The first time we met in the corridor, recently awakened and disorientated by the ear splitting and overpowering siren.

'What the fuck is going on man?'

'I don't know.'

Jeff put his hands over his ears, and tried to run down the corridor. He stumbled, and bumped against the wall. Then he turned and spoke from a half crouching position.

'I should get my stuff.'

'No just get to the stairs.'

'This is noise, dude.'

'You need to put some more clothes on.'

'I've been home two hours.'

'Jeff, you can't go down there in those.'

'Fuck that.'

'They're fluorescent.'

Eventually, after my second cup of coffee, I decide to venture out. The weather is fresh outside, and I want to clear my head. It is windy but the clouds are very high; a day whose air seems worth tasting, whose weather seems particularly rare and bracing. The kind of weather one hopes for in London; that blows all the pollution from the streets; that can bring with it the earthen and rain drenched scent of the farmland to the south and west. However, in the lobby downstairs, Joe, the Nigerian receptionist, beckons me over.

'Mr Haddon.'

'Alright Joe.'

'The Family is still outside.'

Joe had a faintly pleading expression on his face, a look that was begging me to be predictable, to not repeat the behavior of the night before. It occurred to me, in a distant, nagging way, that my encouragement of the paparazzi would make his job a great deal harder.

'I expected this.'

'There is a man with a long lens.'

'Where is he?'

'Over the road now. He was by the post box before.'

'They don't let up, do they?'

'You mustn't hit him.'

'No I know.'

'Not even a little slap.'

'Yeah.'

'Mr Haddon.'

'What Joe?'

'There is something here.'

I turned round.

'Sorry.'

'It is this.'

Joe knelt down and then stood, one of the boxes underneath the desk clutched to his chest. He placed it onto the desk.

'These are Mr Brazer's. He stores them here.'

Joe lifted the top off the box.

'Perhaps he would want you to use them.'

Inside the box was a pair of rollerblades and a compact rucksack. The fibreglass of the boots was black and gleaming, and the laces were broad and white. They were appropriate to an internationally famous circus act, suited to the feet of a teenage Russian twin, glittering in the light as she launches off a ramp to grasp the outstretched hands off her trapeze borne sister; a costumed and athletic girl swooping by in a low arc overhead.

'No.'

'They are for these situations with the photographers.'

'What size are they?'

'Size 11.'

'Here let me try.'

'I think it will be ok.'

'Yes.'

As I'm putting the boots, sitting on floor behind the circular desk, leaning up against it and wriggling my right foot into the first boot, I glance up and see Joe's face above me. From this angle his head is upside down, but a benevolent, paternal and vaguely relieved expression is still perceptible there. It is the timeless expression of butlers and personal servants, those men who've mastered the art of the subtle suggestion, the emphatic cough, the demure proposal; it is a parental face that knows the value of framing a choice.

'You're his friend.'

'Of course.'

'The rucksack is for the shoes.'

'Oh OK.'

'How do they feel?'

'Fine. Great actually.'

'Good luck Mr Haddon.'

'Thanks Joe.'

'You're welcome.'

And then I was off, gently out through the automatic doors, round the corner of the building in three easy glides of my legs, ignoring the sudden shout and flurry of movement from the lurking paparazzi; a situation that was quickly put behind me. In a moment I was on the walkway by the water, gathering speed, legs slicing more deeply to the side and rear. One of the truly successful escapes of my life, a cartoon style departure; which surely must have left behind a fat man cursing and stamping on his bowler hat; the photographer tracking me with his lens and swearing as I made the corner an instant before he focused, a tramp or an elderly lady cheering and waving a fist in the air as I made my getaway, perhaps even pairs of nuns or policewomen hugging each other.

An escape that was quickly consolidated by my arrival at a large and crowded café, the early spring season having brought out the office employees and tourists, and within moments I was installed at a corner table inside, with a clear view of the doorway and the various approaches. Feeling like a victorious musketeer after a duel, I slipped off the rollerblades and ordered a mango juice. In fact I spent the rest of that morning in a giddy state, repressing urges to pat small children on the head, to straighten the ties of passing businessman, to tickle baby's chins and to begin cheery and impromptu conversations with strangers.

The kind of conversations that I'd always imagined as being commonplace for celebrities; conversations where I am respectfully questioned and my advice is sought, and autographs are signed; conversations that manage to be rewarding for all the parties concerned; conversations that contain implicit understandings of the rights and responsibilities of everyone involved. Those conversations where my hand is touched in emphasis, or even shaken as a mark of respect, in which people nod in agreement or sympathy or deliberation. Conversations that perhaps take place on holiday, in summer and Mediterranean destinations: alongside hotel swimming pools or on beaches or amongst the first class seating of planes or between restaurant tables or between the decks of yachts when moored in marinas. Conversations whose tone reflects the standards of communication that celebrity life is habituated to, all talks and chats and phone calls and emails occurring in a spirit of consultation; the possibility of the other's deferral and submission and tacit compliance hovering and undeniably there.

Imaginary conversations that didn't, for example, consider the possibility of inebriation. Acts of the imagination that utterly failed to conceive of the levels of drunkenness involved in many approaches to celebrities. Flights of fancy that never, for a moment, considered the presence of drunken groups of sizeable women in restaurants; that never imagined their tottering progress towards your table or their repetitive and insistent stage whisper questions and then later, their passionate invitations. Imaginary scenarios that would never have entertained the possibility of two or three or even four of these women ambushing you in the toilets, of the efforts of two or three of them to remove your trousers whilst the other, unbelievably, held the door closed and smoked a fag.

Imaginary speculations that never dwelt much on the drunken behaviour of guests in hotels, that never covered the celebrity conversations which occur through locked and chained hotel room doors.

'Please fuck off.'

'My friend fancies you.'

'Right.'

'Think she's a slapper, do you?'

'It's four o'clock in the morning.'

'Lemme in or I'll say.'

Idle musings that never ventured into the problems of long distance plane journeys, which never much imagined the attentions of gangs of children and enthusiastic grandmothers, of bored businesspeople and cynical jet set folk.

'Actually you're not that famous are you?'

'No probably not.'

'I mean compared to Brad Pitt or someone.'

'True.'

'Do you like being famous?'

'I suppose so.'

'God I'd love it.'

That also never mulled over the hotel room conversations one has with oneself when famous, those conversations that occur in front of televisions, the conversations where the stress and tension and pressure cause one to deliberate out loud; causing a person to mutter to him or herself over what course of action to take when the paparazzi are patrolling the corridors and occupying the lobby; when every hotel staff member is a potential paid insider; when any eye contact with anyone in the building fizzes with possible meaning and intent.

Stephanie and I stayed in the hotel near Oxford for five nights. By the end of this time Hannah's condition was stable and, although she was still critical, the doctors considered it unlikely that she would suffer a sudden or catastrophic slump. She'd passed into a full coma, of the kind that, in reality, are rare outside medical reference books; comas that almost never end with the abrupt awakening of the patient, and their rapid escape and locating of a weapon; nor with the successful assassination of the patient by an assassin who failed the first time, and has returned, most likely disguised as a surgeon or policeman.

On the second afternoon Roland arrived, weather-beaten and a touch dishevelled, wearing shorts and sockless, flapping along the hospital corridors in his canvas yachting shoes. When he first saw Hannah he gripped the rail at the end of her bed and pushed down on it to relieve his tension. The bed shifted and so he let go, balling his hands into fists instead.

'Mind out,' Stephanie said.

'I can't believe it,' he said.

Stephanie and I were seated to one side of the bed, in two white folding chairs, and we leaned forward together, staring at Roland as if he was a stranger, as if he was capable of anything.

'She's barely moved since we got here yesterday.'

'But she knew her horses so well.'

'The poor girl.'

Roland and Stephanie shared a look, one that was dense with frustration and shame and regret and confusion.

'I'm going to get a coffee,' I said.

'Okay Josh.'

So I left Stephanie and Roland together. Roland, with all the accoutrements of a single but wealthy and professional middle aged man: his artificially topped up tan, his springy and boyish hair, his sturdy legs in his faded red designer shorts; his faint air of golf courses and open top sports cars and illicit and regretted motel sex. Roland, with his cigarettes never too far away, with his designer sunglasses, with a Spanish villa no doubt; with his watch that you glance at again, and think you recognise from magazine adverts; a model that you have admired in the duty free lounge of an airport, one that you have even considered stealing.

163

In fact more than just stealing, a model that has inspired complex fantasies of theft, as you've sat drinking coffee in a café opposite or within sight of a jewellers; a model that has caused you to remember everything that is generally known about Rolexes. The fact that they must be declared at Customs with their ownership documents, and also each genuine Rolex has an identification number that links it to the buyer and the retailer and the original factory.

Information you consider as you fantasize about cutting through the ceiling of the jewellers during a thunder-storm, so as to provide a plausible explanation for the sounding alarms, and to ensure uncrowded streets for the escape; or even consider electronically tracking the man who delivers the Rolexes, to discover if there is a national depot. Fantasies in which car tyres squeal and only expensive suits are worn and where ties are confidently adjusted and cuff links are nervously rubbed between thumb and forefinger. Fantasies that are no doubt sun-lit and feature cocktails and pool loungers; which involve buyers and their briefcases full of bound wads of dollar bills, and feet in patent leather shoes hastening across plush carpets in hotel lobbies and corridors.

When I returned to the room Roland was alone, sitting low in a chair with his legs thrust out in front of him, frowning deeply.

'Alright?' I said.

'Stephanie had to get some air.'

'Oh. I didn't see her.'

'She felt a need.'

I walked forward and sat on the side of Hannah's bed.

'You can hardly hear any breathing,' he said.

'I know.'

Roland, who wasn't going to discuss with me, or probably with anyone, what Stephanie had just said. I would guess she had pointed out his talent for late arrivals, for being unpunctual when attending family occasions. She would have raised the issue of priorities, and probably been dismissive of his yachting. A different man to Roland might have told her that this was neither the time nor the place to continue their feud, might have accused her of insensitivity in using this situation to revive it, and told her to shut up and then asked her to tell him what the doctors had said.

But I doubt Roland had done any of these things. More likely he'd provided the detail on a series of excuses, that he'd looked harassed and unsettled, and that he'd clumsily changed the subject to Stephanie's past few days. A set of responses likely to have infuriated Stephanie, and which had provoked her into leaving the room; recognising in them as she did an English and middle class way of sidestepping others' emotions, a tactic that marriage to Roland had taught her to resent.

'Are you tired?' I asked.

'Knackered. Absolutely. I had to drive to Belfast for the early flight.'

'Ow.'

'There wasn't anything from Cork.'

Roland talking in the way he often did, reluctant to make eye contact, in his speaking style that is almost staccato, that delivers information as briefly as possible at first. A way of communication that asks permission of the listener, that treads carefully around the listener, one which seems to expect a rebuttal or sharp retort.

'Oh no.'

'The yacht almost capsized two nights ago. I haven't really slept since.'

'I think Stephanie had to take something last night.'

'Look at Hannah.'

'I know.'

'She's like a sleeping little girl.'

'She's been like that all the time.'

'Oh dear.'

Roland leaned forward and put his head in his hands and ran them through his hair.

'I'll need to be around for a while.'

In the corridor outside a nurse pushing a trolley stopped, just outside the door to the room, and we both glanced at her. She, in her tidy uniform, knelt down to sort amongst the boxes on the trolley's lower shelf, and for a moment we both thought she was preparing to enter. Instead, when she stood up holding a tub of cream, she pushed the trolley on.

'I'm here for the foreseeable.'

'Were you at home?'

'No. Wales. On an acting thing.'

'Oh.'

'This is the medical report. Have a read.'

As a man, Roland seemed unsuited to dealing with tragedies. The last time I'd seen him had been at a Twickenham rugby match. Then we'd all sat together in a corporate sponsor's box, and drank glasses of champagne, and spent the game constantly half rising from our seats to shout or clap. Roland had played the host: talking about the recent form of the different players, discussing the pros and cons of the team's strategies and the latest changes to the rules, describing previous games he'd been to and telling anecdotes from his days of semi professional rugby union. Then he'd been convivial and generous in his attentions, he'd bantered and flirted with the other business people, he'd made introductions and known people's nicknames and been hearty and prominent and boisterous. At Twickenham he seemed long freed from the concessions of home life, and the awkward negotiations of his fractured domesticity.

Watching Roland in the hospital room I had an urge to send him away to the nearest pub or restaurant, a place where he could be called and informed of the latest developments, where he could be insulated from the worst of this horrific situation. He seemed unprepared for this instance of life's hard treatment, broadly unadapted and vulnerable to such painful eventualities and inevitabilities. Sitting, reading the report, he emitted an air of dismay and hurt confusion, as if he had just unexpectedly failed an important exam or been dropped from a sports team.

'It's bad isn't it?' I said.

'Yes.'

He looked up and met my gaze.

'Yes it is. Severe.'

'Mmm.'

'I suppose the best we can do is make her comfortable.'

Roland then stood, and went over to the side of the bed, and put his hands on his hips.

'Yeah I think.'

'How's Steph been?'

'Not great. But better today.'

He stepped closer to the bed and picked up Hannah's limp right hand. We both stared down at her pale face; the face that was so different from her sleeping one, that gave no suggestion of the soft frown that creased her brow when she napped in the afternoon; the same frown that formed when she slept on the beach in summer holidays, which was always accompanied by a slightly pouting mouth and apparently swollen cheeks, creating an expression that was childish and puffy. Nor did it

166

resemble any of her usual poses in deep sleep: the faintly smiling face she made when lying on her back, the one where her eyelids seemed to be very lightly closed; or where her mouth was very slightly open, as if she was swimming on her back in the sea, and closing her eyes as a protection against the glare of a summer, unclouded sun.

No, her face in the hospital bed was very different from these. It was whiter and more angular, as if all her curves and roundness had been struck into harder angles by the shod blow of the impact. The shading and colouring had altered too; her skin was traced pink above her cheekbones and over the sockets of the eyes, as if she had been exposed to the coldest weather. It was like seeing a face that was underwater or beneath the two sliding glass panels of a shop front freezer.

'I remember buying her first horse.'

'It's so unfair. She loved horses. She loved treating them.'

'True.'

'I might go and find Stephanie.'

'No. I'll get her. You stay here Josh.'

And later, in the hotel, Stephanie told me that he had almost walked past her in the corridor, such was his exhaustion and confusion and inner disarray, and that she'd had to say his name to stop him, and it was her voice that had caused Roland to stop and face her and recognise who she was and remember what he had to say. A situation that was caused in part no doubt by the hypnotic and reflective brightness of the corridor itself, and the fact of both of them having aged, and that he had never anticipated a conversation like this. Perhaps as he'd walked along he was thinking of Hannah's birth; that other time he had stood by a woman in a hospital bed, and had consoled her, and was tender.

Or perhaps he was thinking about divorce and consequences. Perhaps he was thinking so much about Stephanie, the younger Stephanie, the imagined Stephanie; that he failed to recognise the older, real Stephanie, as she walked towards him along the corridor. Perhaps he was thinking that nothing could end well, after their divorce, and that everything begun in that time was bound eventually to collapse and fail, even Hannah.

Perhaps he was thinking, as he had thought before, and tried not to think before, and tried to deny to himself before; that divorce is like a curse, that it can seem the origin of misfortunes which linger over the lives of those involved. Perhaps he was thinking this, or was even comparing divorce to viruses, never quite dormant viruses that sometimes revive and upset a person's health. Perhaps he was thinking of all those times that he's tried to convince himself, and let others try to convince him, those friends and therapists and strangers and family relations, that his marriage, that all marriages, are only temporary arrangements, extensions of the casual affairs we all have before we marry. Perhaps it was their arguments that were repeating and repeating in his head, when he failed to recognise his ex-wife in the hospital corridor.

Or perhaps the origin of his distraction was due to his own counter arguments, by a line of thinking that saw divorce as the final and ultimate betrayal, a line of thinking that accepted how different men's wives are from their girlfriends, a line of thinking that inquired what it was, besides sex, that had compelled him to uproot himself.

Now, in London, in the large and crowded café, I sit for a while, sipping the mango juice and people watching. A man leaves the toilet flying low, spectacularly so, to the point where the blue cotton of his underwear is directly visible. He has on a pair of slacks, in a light tan colour and baggy style more common in the States than here, and the open fly gapes wide, the zip unsupported by the thin fabric. The occupants of several different tables immediately notice, and heads turn round, and a woman's hand goes to her mouth, and a couple of men look down at their plates and smirk. The unzipped man compounds the problem by standing at the bar to make a complaint, or to make some complicated request or booking, and leans across the stools, thereby stretching his midriff and angling his crotch towards one half of the room. His underwear then projects substantially, almost as if it were a napkin he had tucked into his waistband, to the extent that the material might flap and flutter in a breeze. Eventually he finishes talking, and, blithe and confident, strolls from the café and off along the street, all the while unaware of the small blue prow that extends before him.

A situation which for a celebrity. might tip and upset their career, and would certainly provoke some imaginative tabloid headlines. It is moments like this that Jeff and I tremble about, when we discuss the hazards of our being famous.

'Wheelchairs man.'

'What?'

'Never get photographed pushing a wheelchair.'

'Sorry?'

'It's like the thing that signals the end.'

168

I stared at him.

'Also watch out for pets.'

'Seriously?'

'Yeah people don't want to see that shit. They don't want you to be caught up in the same stuff as them.'

'What about a dog and a wheelchair?'

'In seriousness man. In seriousness I think dogs are better than cats. Cats are like an international emblem of craziness.'

'Aren't labradors okay though?'

'Dude the blind people.'

Jeff, who was a veteran of daring paparazzi escapes: a habitué of laundry and grocery vans and hotel service doors and kitchen exits from restaurants, a frequent occupant of car trunks and who would no doubt consider being rolled up in a carpet or being pulled down an alley hidden within a freshly cleaned wheelie bin. Jeff, who I know has activated fire alarms in hotels, just to be able to flee the paparazzi under the cover of the general evacuation. It is interesting that Jeff has never mentioned the rollerblades to me, and this makes me wonder what other methods of escape he has in the building. Perhaps there is a motorbike in the basement, or even a speed boat somewhere, perched atop a ramp that leads to a concealed exterior door, one that opens onto a waterway nearby.

I leave the café after finishing the mango juice, still wearing the rollerblades, and skate on a little further, towards the square in front of Canary Wharf tube station. There I decide to practice skating, to attempt jumps up at and slides down some of the concrete features, to practise turns and changes of direction and braking and sudden accelerations. Fortunately I have my sunglasses, and wearing these usually reduces the chance of my being recognised. Also the passersby are mostly hurrying to work, but still I keep an eye out for photographers.

In fact I became so engrossed in the skating that I almost forgot to check my electronic organizer, and almost missed my massage appointment. As it was I arrived at the parlour sweaty and red in the face, and was asked to shower before the treatment started. The parlour is a place where people glide instead of walk; where many of the employees are young or look young; where the maximum quality and quantity of possible beauty treatments have been expended on the employees, and as a result the older ones look radiant and glossy, but also slightly damp and with a similar gleam to polished and frequently handled wood; the wood of church pews, or doors or window frames in castles and stately homes; or the wood in yachts that lines the deck and is used as trimming in the cockpit.

There is always music in the massage parlour, gentle and unidentifiable music that is vaguely ethnic, involving pipes and wooden flutes and drums and the occasional harsh twang of a guitar or similar stringed instrument. This music seems to exist at the edge of hearing, so much so that one only becomes conscious of it when activity quietens in the reception and waiting area. There one encounters the waiting customers: their designer clothes and jewellery, their expensive handbags and shoes, their tapering legs or well done hair or facial surgery or personal trainer bodies. Occasionally there is another male customer waiting, invariably an athlete or obviously wealthy Russian or Middle Easterner, dapper in leather jackets and ripped jeans and trimmed stubble. All of these are people who emit an air of regular pampering and long standing adaption to comfort; they sit patiently and relaxed, strangers who acknowledge each other whenever their gaze should accidentally meet.

When I'm waiting there I tend to look through the leaflet detailing the services on offer. There is a bewildering variety of pluckings and waxings and laser treatments and enemas, an extensive range of tanning methods and bleachings, of acupuncture and electrolysis and cleansing top to toe applications. One day, I usually think, I will spend a whole day here, and emerge more fully metrosexual. For the time being though I'm content to sit, the rollerblades in their bag at my feet, slightly scruffy, aware that I resemble nothing more than a delivery courier awaiting a freebie.

In the hospital, during those first few days with Roland and Stephanie, Hannah had a daily massage. They were a regular part of her treatment, to aid her circulation and help prevent muscle shrinkage. The same nurse came in with a trolley each day, a surprisingly slight blonde woman, who, while making appropriate and concerned talk with us, kneaded and pressed at Hannah's body, and hauled and tugged and turned her around in the bed.

Often her arrival was a welcome interruption to the tension in the room. Stephanie had become preoccupied and more silent, overcome by an irritable watchfulness; her reflex response to Roland's presence. For his part, he paced up and down the corridor outside, smiled at and chatted to the nurses and doctors, disappeared to smoke cigarettes, and tried to limit his restlessness when sitting with us.

170

In the hotel, on the third night, Stephanie vented some of her feelings. She first turned and spoke seriously to me while we were waiting for drinks at the bar, in that drifting moment of time when most people are content to remain silent; when most like to quietly anticipate the evening ahead; when they perhaps look over the bottles behind the bar, and read the specials menu on the blackboard; when they glance over the other clientele, and generally begin to relax and find their bearings.

'Of course all the animals we kept was a way of keeping us together.'

'What?'

'Yes you know the goats. And that bloody pig.'

Our shoulders were almost touching, so her face was very close.

'Hannah said about the pig.'

'Roland did love him. He helped keep us cheerful.'

'Oh right.'

'But really Roland and I knew that we got them to delay things.'

Stephanie and I sat in the lounge bar until late that night, both of us drinking, me watching as her face seemed to become more compressed and more clenched the longer she spoke; as if the skin at her scalp was being twisted, and was gradually tightening around her forehead and chin and cheekbones. Stephanie, of course, with her numerous grievances, with her precisely recalled instances of disappointment and betrayal and loss of trust. Able, of course, to talk with clarity and earnestness about what had gone wrong and might have gone further wrong, about what might have been prevented and about what had been risked.

Stephanie talking as a woman that had been softened by the small affections of marriage, as a woman that had, in the reassuring embrace of marriage or under its benign reign, laid to rest her hard learnt skills of offence and defence. A woman who had gently let drop her ability to argue and insult and accuse and counter accuse, to shout and to shout back, or to argue insistently, or to ask questions persistently, or to deny and then accuse persistently. A woman who had lost the capacity not to be intimidated by another's anger, to withstand another's anger, and then respond forcefully, or respond in a more measured and deliberate way.

Stephanie talking as a woman who had been forced, by Roland's affair, by the divorce, to revive all these bitter talents; a woman who had suddenly found herself, under-prepared and ill-equipped, far from the mild pastures of marriage. It was near midnight when our conversation entered its final phase.

'I wonder what he's doing now.'

'I don't know. He's probably asleep.'

'I bet he's not.'

'He's still exhausted after getting here.'

'I bet he's talking to someone.'

'Like who?'

'Like Angie, you know who he sails with.'

By this time my role in the conversation, or the part that I was playing in it, had been reduced to something advisory, cautionary; it had become almost parental. This is a conversational position that I dislike, and I was beginning to resent Stephanie, aware that soon she would begin to resent me for setting boundaries on her spite, for reining her in. As she continued I watched a girl from the bar staff wipe down tables, on the other side of the room.

'That's been over for ages.'

'Try calling him, to see if his phone's engaged.'

'We should both go to bed.'

'If you won't call him, I will.'

'Don't Stephanie. Leave him be.'

'Why? He's kept me up lots of nights.'

'He won't answer if you call.'

'Well pass me your phone.'

'That's not fair though.'

Had Hannah been with us, a row would have developed here; a row that would have been the repetition of other rows, a repeat of the other spats and arguments and disagreements that had soured relations between mother and daughter. Rows that usually flared up at Christmas or on family visits and weekends together, rows that started with Hannah saying, in a quiet voice:

'Maybe you should ask him yourself.'

Hannah saying this, perhaps as she is sitting opposite her mother, in a restaurant, passing a plate of food to me that has been wrongly given to her by a waiter. Passing me the steak or sausages that the waiter should know a young woman would never order, but there you go; Hannah looking at Stephanie in a determined way, with a hardness which is a compression of emotions, a forming of anger under conditions of pressure. It as if all her usual and sociable feelings are mustering together, as if they are congregating into a threatening form.

And Stephanie responds by looking round a little, by glancing at the other diners nearby as if seeking eye contact, as if she wants to show to Hannah that she has their sympathy.

'I always do, my dear.'

Rows that never seemed to be resolved, that only ever seemed to subside and hibernate in periods of dormancy. Rows that were always nurtured in privacy and silence by both of them, rows that each were preoccupied by, that they dwelt on and mulled and deliberated over, that simmered and resurged in each of them, that occurred throughout the year with an almost seasonal reliability.

They often started like this

'Do you remember last Easter when you said...?'

Rows that usually ended with Hannah saying or shouting:

'Look, I'm not going to be your fucking messenger.'

'Try not to overreact, darling.'

Rows that ended with us driving home, return journeys in which I again listened to and commiserated with Hannah's long established list of complaints. Journeys where she told me she hated being the contact point between Roland and Stephanie; where she explained how much she resented being only a functionary; where she tried once more to identify the point in her adolescence when she'd become their hub or go between. During these journeys and conversations I always imagined the teenage Hannah: her tending to the animals, hair longer and tied up in a ponytail, of her feeding the pig and brushing the pony, looking pale and muted, in solitude; while her dissatisfied and fractious parents brooded in and soured the atmosphere inside the house.

'I'm sorry, Josh,' Stephanie said.

'Look it's OK.'

'It's just...'

She took a deep breath and let it out as a sob.

'It's just that he's turned up here, like he's some kind of boy scout or something, and his daughter's in there dying, and all he can do is wander around and sort of smile at people.'

'It's his way of dealing with it.'

She bent forward and rubbed at the tears.

'Oh I don't know. I wish he'd hug me or take you out for a chat or just do something real.'

'I don't think he knows what to do either.'

'He just looks so lost all the time.'

A phrase that was uttered in fits and starts, its tone and pitch disrupted by sobs and grief; a disordered phrase identical to one spoken under duress; the halting, intermittent, words of a speaker confessing during an interrogation.

'Calling him now won't help anything.'

'I know I'm sorry.'

She leant back and wiped at her eyes.

'Hannah would be so annoyed with me.'

'Do you want another drink?'

'No. Have you seen the time?'

'Look, napkins.'

'Thanks.'

Of course there have been other times a woman has cried in front of me, when Hannah or my mother or a colleague on a film set has started crying, and stood or sat there, shaking and a little helpless. Perhaps this is something that all men are more exposed to as they mature and age, these incidents of tears and sobs and shakings of the shoulders, these soddenings of tissues and shudders and deep near drowning kinds of breaths. And each time of course, it is clear what a primitive signal this clamour is, like the piercing scream of a girl or woman, a sound of alarm that carries so far. And the woman's tears always seem as much a feature of manhood as female nakedness, that the increasing frequency of both in a man's passing days is a sign of a shift in condition – the end of juvenile times. So much so that the first girl's tears are often a surprise; the first girl's tears that are generally in bed, that are usually connected to sexual activity, that are perhaps due to her pornographic humiliation; the first tears that wrench a response from the young man, that create an urge to console and to comfort, that can even animate these softer instincts.

Hannah had cried when our dog died, she cried the time I lost my house keys for the sixth time one summer, she cried when we went on holiday and our suitcases were lost by the airline. She cried over things that happened at work, when so-and-so shouted at her or so-and-so was dismissive of her. Hannah cried sometimes over her triathlons, after pulling a muscle or after another injury preventing her starting the race or forcing her to retire early. And of course she'd cried over the pain of animals, over trampled calves with broken legs, over under-nourished ponies with their protruding ribs and half blind eyes, over sheep and dogs maimed in collisions with cars. She'd cried after arguments with her mother, she'd cried when her father had failed to keep another promise, and she'd cried when our freezer packed up and all the meat defrosted and was spoiled.

And each man has these memories of women's tears and his responses, memories that are like the memories of his fights, that are like the memories of his public expressions of anger; memories that punctuate the years and the decades, that in hindsight are markers to the state of his character, that may cause him to frown when remembered, to pause a little and try to recapture what had happened that was so difficult and painful.

Chapter Ten

By mid afternoon I'm sitting in my agent's office, feeling limbered up and freshly massaged, settling into place in the comfortable leather chair across from her own. I've stopped off at home for lunch and to change, and am now my transatlantic and debonair self, ready to be the centre of attention, ready to be relaxed and witty, ready to charm and dazzle and impress the citizenry. My agent, Laura, is rustling me up a cup of tea, and I can hear her making cheery small talk with one of her assistants, in the kitchen down the corridor.

'How's Jeff?' she asks, when she comes back in.

'Fine, I think. I haven't seen him for a while.'

I'm thinking that she's seen the photos.

'Oh really?'

'He's competing in Australia. He's spending the month there.'

'God. Yes of course. It's that time of year isn't it?'

'Yeah.'

Laura's manner continues to be both breezy and matter of fact, and I realise that she hasn't seen them.

'Nice suit by the way.'

'Thanks. It's Brioni.'

'Oh. Very suave.'

She settles down behind her desk, a surprisingly old fashioned one, and as Laura shifts papers around to clear space it occurs to me how self-assured she is behind it; she looks like a pilot who's just climbed into a cockpit, flipping switches and checking his dashboard.

'How are things?'

'God. Busy.'

She laughs and runs her hand through her hair.

'It's all go here.'

I'd met Laura at the launch party of a small West End play, and for most of that first conversation I'd assumed she was the friend or girlfriend of one the cast. She'd seemed altogether too fresh and surprised and curious to be an industry professional, too interested somehow in the minutiae of the rehearsals and the back story of the development of the play. Later, when I knew her better, I came to recognise that her charm lay in this setting out on every new encounter so hopefully, that in its optimism there was a kind of deliberate forgetting, a recklessness and hope about where one person might lead another. She appeared not to practice any of the usual measured kinds of behaviour: no assessments and judgments and manoeuvrings, no sly cautiousness in crowded rooms; with her, there was rarely any sense of a mind sifting through its impressions.

Laura leant back in her chair and raised her feet, shod in leather boots, up to show me.

'You know what Rafael calls me?'

'What?'

'Posh in Boots.'

She smiled and I smiled.

'Does he? Is that nice?'

'Oh you know what he's like.'

'Yeah.'

I reached into my bag and pulled the scripts out one by one, stacking them on the table. Then the assistant came in with the tea.

'No sugar?'

'Yes, thanks.'

'Thanks Amy.'

'So Josh, have you read them all?'

'Every single one. Except one.'

Laura puts on her glasses, which are metallic and trim, and opens up a notebook. She has one for each of her clients, where she records each of their meetings in shorthand. Sitting there, pen poised above the fresh page, she resembles a student awaiting permission to commence an exam. At these moments, I always expect her to lick the blunt stub of her pencil.

'Oh. And?'

'I liked them all actually. Particularly the BBC drama.'

'The London Vampires?'

'Yes, that's it.'

She scribbles something in the notebook, a jabbing squiggle; a movement so impossibly quick that I think that she's only pretending to make notes in order to appear more professional.

'I liked it too. It's quite sort of naughty, isn't it?'

'Do you think I could get away with gothic?'

'Oh sure, you'll fit right in.'

Early on in our professional relationship, I'd wondered if Laura was gay. There wasn't much evidence to support this, but she had a fondness for boots and these petite, tweed, jackets. I imagined her smoking a cigarette in front of a fireplace, with spaniels curled up at her feet. It wasn't until I met Rafael, her theatrical producer husband, that I dismissed this thought. But even after this question was forgotten, I continued to suspect her of eccentric sexual conduct.

'A casting producer called me about you yesterday. He couldn't remember your name, and he kept saying you were the guy who looked like Frances Mason.'

'What did you say?'

'I let him suffer and go on like that for a while.'

'Do you think I look like him?'

'No. Not especially.'

Considering how famous I am now, it's peculiar how often this happens. Before my days of fame, I, like everyone else, was accustomed to being mistaken for others. On TV shoots, when acting in plays, I was only ever one amongst many, an unknown face in the assembled crew and cast. In fact people forgetting others' names afflicted all my acting jobs. Most of us were semi-anonymous, and only the lead actors had the privilege of being remembered. Then this seemed an advantage of success, one of its distinct benefits. During my years as a jobbing actor I came to accept this anonymity, to the point where I'd be surprised to be called by my name, instead of referred to as my character's name, or merely pointed at and beckoned, or was the subject of and participant in those circling conversations where the use of the other's name is avoided by both speakers, and each person calls the other "you", in a manner that always verges on the exaggerated and wary. And the casual nature of the profession itself, with everyone always moving on, constantly dispersing to other projects and other places, encouraged this. In the later period of my acting, when my face was becoming known from TV dramas, from those three part broadcasts and Sunday night one-offs, then I began to be known by the name of the characters I had recently played. Actors would call me after the name of the lawyer I was acting in one series, and other people on set would imitate them, often without knowing the TV series the actors were referring to, assuming that the name of the lawyer was my real one. Added to this, of course, is the tendency of people to describe others by comparing them to film and television actors. So when a new acquaintance or a new boyfriend or girlfriend is being described to family or to older, closer friends, part of the assembled description is a reference to an actor.

'He looks just like so-and-so.'

Or:

'She laughs just like so-and-so from so-and-so.'

Unfortunately, when you're the actor yourself, when you're the person who is the point of reference, this tactic becomes difficult. No actor, or nobody on a film set, can describe another person there whose name they've forgotten by comparison with another actor, or a character from the television screen. This only adds to the confusion. Equally as an actor, when you meet new people, a young couple say, and she remarks on how her partner resembles you in some film or some series, but is also quick to inform you that she notices how little you possess those qualities in real life, so to speak, an embarrassment and awkwardness sets in. She, and her partner, no doubt feel a little fooled, as if something they have believed in has been exposed as false. You want to console her, to remind her how commonplace her mistake is, but you sense that this might worsen the situation, so you smile and change the subject.

Eventually I began to see each new stage of my adult life as an assault on this anonymity. There was marriage, for example, with its guarantee of, at the very least, daily recognition. But since my celebrity, my anonymity has persisted, but in a different form. Now, instead of being anonymous, I am recognised, but rarely correctly identified. Instead I am mistaken for all sorts of people: for old school friends, for other actors, for cousins, for childhood playmates and for doctors. The expression, 'Don't I know you from somewhere?' is frequently directed at me in supermarkets, in the post office, or when queuing to buy tickets at train stations. And there's something incredibly strange about this, to be an audience to so many surges of camaraderie and feeling, to see so many strangers' faces animated and softening; to be a witness to all these small revivals of warmth and intimacies and better, almost forgotten times.

'I'm off of the telly,' is, I've discovered, the most satisfactory answer.

In the early days of my celebrity I used to say:

'Yeah. Hi. I'm Josh Haddon.'

This was said in what verged on an American accent, in a flat vowelled and drawling tone, often accompanied by a slight frown and a direct, brazen stare; as if I were a surgeon or a spaceship captain or a police detective or forensic scientist. And then I would extend my hand and smile; all of which usually led to a mystified and slightly distant response, and the beginnings of mistrust and aversion.

In the office, Laura is finishing making her notes. She is taking her time, and I'm waiting, listening to one of her colleagues talking on the phone in the main office behind me. It occurs to me that these visits to my agent are not unlike visiting a doctor.

'You know Morton's in town at the moment?'

She looks up after she speaks, and lays her pencil to one side.

'No I didn't.'

'It's for the premiere of that science fiction film.'

'Oh I know. I've seen the adverts. I don't know why he bothers with that crap.'

She is staring at me in a steady way, in a particular way of her's that makes me uneasy.

'You should have dinner with him.'

'We haven't spoken for a while.'

I'd first met Morton in those early weeks when Hannah was in hospital. After returning home I began to attend the early stages of the film shoot, mainly script readings in studios and empty theatres, and the first gatherings of the cast and crew. These involved spending mornings, feeling slightly ill at ease, in cavernous and under-heated rooms, being introduced and tentatively shaking hands; rooms gradually filling with men and women trying both to project confidence and to detect it in others, one of those situations where one always feels surprisingly naked and exposed, surprisingly compromised and vulnerable. One of those situations where everyone seems pale and either underweight or overweight, where the desire for friendships and alliances is almost palpable; where one smiles so much that smiling seems to lose its spontaneity, and become a forced and contrived gesture; where the onset of the proceedings of the day are awaited with relief so as to end the strain of the introductions.

Amongst the senior cast and crew these were more private. The director invited me to a dinner party at his home in Hampstead. The kind of house that was known to me then only in secondhand ways: from documentaries featuring interviews with venerable broadcasters and comedians and designers, where the book shelves and the cream sofas and the grand fireplaces are in the background; from news reports on this or that minor royal or misbehaving celebrity, when the press target hurries from the porch and along the path, and behind them there is the edifice of a stucco façade or a creeping mass of roses above a front door. The kind of house that, in these moments, stimulates the imagination, that is frequently more attractive to the imagination than the harassed celebrity. A house whose interior is less predictable than usual, which contains multiple possibilities, that is spacious and private enough to be mysterious.

And in many ways the director's house didn't disappoint, with its cream and faded lime colouring, with its heavy mirrors and its wide staircase and the solid timber of its banisters, and the stainless steel and glass tables, limited edition no doubt, and the ceiling tall cabinets full of books, and the paintings in styles by vaguely recognisable artists; canvases of varying sizes which held concentric circles or grid patterns or abstract shapes in primary colour, that were probably not reproductions, but where it would be poor taste for me to go and inspect them. And of course various statuettes and metal wrought figurines; as well as the director's souvenirs and mementos and heirlooms, such as a mounted cigarette holder and a picture frame containing three metallic tinted ties, props from his and from other, more famous Hollywood films.

A house whose lighting is as sympathetic and adjustable and discreet as any expensive hotel or restaurant, where anyone at any time appears to be favourably under lit, gently bathed in and talking from the warmth of their personal glow. A house with a theatrical or Shakespearean garden, the kind that is often attached to these imposing North London homes. A garden that is more often seen than entered into, that is glimpsed dozens of times each day through the windows on the landings of the stairs, by the wife or the children or the cleaning lady, or by whoever else happens to be at home. Seen so often from inside that it is more like looking at a painting than anything, with the window frame substituting for the frame of the painting; and also the image itself being a little fuzzy in the memory, imprecise and roughly depicted, due to the seasons' cycle of growth and withering in the garden, and the remembered succession of minutely different images overlaying each other.

A scent-laden place that is ruddily candlelit in summer, with its mature bushes and established shrubs and depth of shadows, which possesses the features and proportions of a stage designer's garden or a fairy story wild place: the hanging or drooping branches, the clusters of concealing undergrowth, the sheltered clearing and bench, the pathway from which the principals stray. The garden that is in complement to the house, as woods and glades are to castles and palaces in plays and in bedside stories.

So it was in this director's house that I met Morton and I saw Jakub again, for the first time in weeks. When I arrived the others were in the lounge, sipping at glasses of wine or at tumblers of gin and tonic and nibbling on finger food, and pausing to swallow and then continue to talk about the weather and their children and their demanding schedules and describing how they'd first met the director. These assembled guests featured an older blonde woman, in a black dress that sparkled, holding her glass of wine in both hands, her face in profile. All night she was complimented on this or that element of her appearance, and by the time the coffee came round she seemed about to levitate. There was a young Hispanic woman with her arms crossed; she was in black trousers and a lacy sleeveless top, her full bodied hair and pliant youthful skin making her look as if she'd spent her childhood swimming in pools below waterfalls, and then shaking her hair to dry it. Also there was a slight framed man of about my own age, with a black collarless jacket, balding elegantly, no doubt with the artful help of a discerning hairdresser, and wearing tight jeans. Later I found out he composed film scores, although his posture was so hunched that it became a distraction during our conversation.

Pretty soon, I introduced myself to Morton, who was as burly as he usually is on screen; he was unshaven and holding a bottle of beer to his chest; also he was more fatherly and stout, more smartly dressed and orderly than I'd expected. My introduction had interrupted a conversation he was having with another tall American, a man in tortoiseshell glasses and a thin, designer, blue blazer. Both of them considered me indulgently.

'Glad to meet you at last, Josh.'

'Thanks. It's a privilege to be working with you.'

'And you my man. I've seen your BBC work. It's promising.'

There was a pause whilst he swigged his beer and I sipped from my glass. One of those hierarchical silences began to develop; the kind that, as the inferior, it was my responsibility to fill and otherwise manage.

'And in the film we're going to be cousins.'

'Yeah and in that case we'll have to avoid sleeping together.'

'Yes. God.'

Throughout the evening Morton was exerting a constant pressure of self control. He seemed very deliberate in everything, even in his smallest movements: in the way he listened to others, in the way that he passed the food along the table or poured a glass of wine. It was clear he was making sure that he was attentive and respectful, to be no more than a guest at his host's table, to rein in and confine the power of his fame and celebrity. When stood up to visit the bathroom, or to get some air outside, he stalked past us all, passing his hands from chair to chair, walking stiffly, quite unconsciously giving us that sidelong, slightly baffled smile that was one of his screen trademarks.

Until dessert, the meal passed pleasantly enough. There was more wealth on show than is usual in London: one of the women was wearing a necklace that was certainly gold; the unmistakable twinkle of diamonds flashed from different points and places up and down the table, the sparkle that always seems more than mere reflected light, that seems more like light restrained and held and furious to move again. Also there were Italian and French accents, and for a while the people beside me conversed in Italian. And I remember the catering staff, who for a surprised few moments, I assumed to be the director's servants; and the way everyone there carried on so calmly as the young men and women bustled around with laden plates and cutlery, and fresh napkins and iced bottles of wine; as if it were the most normal thing in the world to be served like this in a private home, as if in fact, none of the guests had ever known anything different.

During the main course the director had to leave the table to respond to a phone call, one that had persistently appeared on the screen of his mobile phone, a repeated call that he had frowned at and tried to ignore. From the hallway I heard his voice, and I noticed some stress in it, as if he were refusing something to someone, or as if he was being forced to return to an argument that he had long considered over. When he returned he seemed irritated, and presently he left the table again to answer the front door.

This ringing of the door bell occurred in between the main course and the dessert, and some of the guests had taken the opportunity to smoke cigarettes outside, and had opened a verandah door that led out into the courtyard and garden behind the house. Morton was on the sofa at the other end of the room, making some notes on a touch-screen device.

'Really this isn't the best time,' I heard the director say outside.

'I have a right Dad,' a woman's voice replied.

Then the door from the hallway opened and the director came in, followed by a blonde girl who was unusually tall and imposing, not fat or obese but impressively sturdy and physical. She had on plain black high heeled boots and black trousers, as if she had just left an office party or works drinks. She looked at me, the sole remaining guest at the table, with a mixture of confusion, irritation and contempt. The director sat down at the table, and began to refill his glass of wine.

'Megan, this is Josh, one of the actors on the new film. Josh, this is Megan, my daughter from my first marriage.'

'Hello,' I said.

'Oh hello.'

'Megan I can't talk to you now. Really this is an interruption.'

On the other side of the table the other guests, some of whom were now in the doorway leading to the garden, exchanged glances and edged back outside again.

'You said you were having a quiet dinner night.'

'You know what I meant.'

The director pushed his glasses onto the top of his head, and leant back in his chair, and the light fell on his face at a less flattering angle, one which made the lines around his mouth more graven, and made his skin appear greyer, and less tanned. In this position his lips looked pursed, and this man, usually so analytical and logical, so sweepingly decisive, seemed fussy and small hearted.

'Dad, the bank are starting to make trouble.'

'This is why we're meeting at the solicitor's next week, rather than now when my cast is having this necessary get-together.'

'But if you weren't on these film things all the time then I wouldn't need to come over here like this. I mean your house is always full of bloody people.'

I began to stand up.

'No, don't worry, Josh.'

He waved me back down.

'Your father's a marvellous director, you know.'

Morton's voice spread across the room, swelling to fill the space; a projected voice that was deeper and more inflected than his conversational one. It was familiar from his film characters, from the investigators and the tribal warrior and the astronaut he'd played on screen. A voice as intimately known to us as one of our family's; or even our everyday voices, or even our private and inner and guarded ones, speaking out loud.

'Oh sorry. Hello there.'

Morton stood up and came over. As he approached, with his rolling, distinctive, almost bandy-legged walk, Megan's neck and face and head went through a particular series of reflexes, a set of responses common in people meeting celebrities: the face jolts forward, and then the head jars back, the neck undulating beneath them both. The movement mimics whiplash, but at a slower, frame by frame, speed. In Megan's case her blonde hair swayed, marginally out of pace with her rocking head. Morton reached out his hand.

'Hi. I'm Morton Greaves.'

'Oh God. I know who you are.'

'Well now I know who you are. You're Michael's first daughter.'

'Yes I am.'

'Pleased to meet you.'

And of course Morton had a very accomplished handshake, one of those truly special grips, like the handshake that a political leader must have; the kind of handshake that, through sheer repetition, has surely acquired considerable power. Watching, as if in slow motion, Morton's hand, his surprisingly rough labourer's kind of hand, grasp Megan's, resembled a martial arts demonstration more than a casual greeting. There was a sense of inevitability about it, a sense of a conclusion becoming foregone, of an impending victory and surrender that would be utterly final and complete. Their hands met, he closed his other over their clasping ones, and shook more vigorously than is the custom in Britain. And then he, absent mindedly and out of habit I assume, turned to me and smiled, as if I were a photographer. Then he spoke to her:

'Tell me, have you eaten tonight?'

'Well just bits and pieces.'

'I'm sure we can fix that.'

Then I was aware of someone at the verandah doors, and I glanced round, and Jakub was there.

'A warm evening,' he said, to everyone.

Morton turned and half smiled, as he accompanied Megan out of the room, one of his arms around her shoulders, to the kitchen. Megan's elbows and forearms were in front of her and raised up, as if she was a blindfolded child, being led to a spectacular present.

'Have you tasted these cigars?' Jakub asked the director.

Jakub showed him a pocket sized box, holding it up clutched in his palm.

'No. No I haven't,' the director said.

He was staring at the empty doorway into the hall, and he stood up, and went hesitantly into the corridor. Jakub stared at his back, before turning to me and smiling.

'Josh.'

'Alright you alright?'

'Would you like a cigar?'

'I've been training as much as I can. But things have been very hectic.'

He took one out of the box, held it between thumb and forefinger, and shook it, in the way that nurses and mothers shake thermometers.

'You're not pissed off?'

'No no. Can we talk over something?'

'I like your waistcoat. Is it Russian?'

He began patting his jacket pockets, frowning.

'I bought it in St James.'

'Hannah's still really ill.'

'I'm sorry for that.'

He paused and lit the cigar, concentrating, taking a couple of rapid puffs, which obscured his torso in trails, sudden spirals and columns, of smoke.

'Can we talk in private?'

Jakub beckoned by inclining his head, and I followed him outside, onto the crescent of brick steps leading down to the garden. The other guests had congregated on the lawn, and the garden's air was full of their mellow chatter and laughter, it was tinkling with their expressions of interest and enthusiasm.

'There is something I should explain. Now your wife is in hospital, this has altered some things.'

'Oh right.'

A couple of the women stepped backwards towards us, precarious in their heels, to create space for a burly, bald man to eagerly demonstrate a forward somersault, to prove a point perhaps. They glanced back to see that they didn't trip on the lowest step. The silvery dress of the closest, wrapped tight across her hip, flashed in the light; it appeared flimsy, but also chameleonic.

'Maybe this isn't the best place to talk. Are you busy this week?'

'I think I'm at the theatre again tomorrow. All day, with the others.'

After pointing his finger in turn at each of the immediate onlookers, his flushed face comically severe, the burly acrobat jumped and spun round his chosen axis. The man's hands clutched his heels and his chin touched his knees, and his goatee beard revolved; the movement a contraction, then a spin, of limbs and fabric. On the thump of landing his leather coat and jacket flew up over the top of his head, hooding him.

I laughed and clapped, along with the others nearby. When I glanced at Jakub, for us to share the amusement, I was surprised by how grimly set his face was. It was rigid with self-recrimination, pale and touched by traces of regret.

Momentarily I wondered if he and Hannah had somehow been having an affair, and this is what he wanted to confess to me. It's rare for anyone to receive a direct apology, in any kind of intentional or heartfelt way. An apology where the stage is set and the ground prepared, and the apology itself occupies the centre. Most apologies aren't as formal as this, they're more roundabout, they're given less freely and openly, and they're hurriedly moved on from, to encourage the participants to forget. Also Jakub didn't seem a man who was accustomed to apologising, requiring as it does the vulnerable position of the speaker. Examining him, with his compact beard and moustache, and his tailored suit that was continental and loose fitting, he appeared as more a seducer than anything else, as if it wasn't me that he should be speaking to, so attentively and privately, but instead one of the unattached women: the blonde with the gold necklace perhaps, or the publicist with her straight black hair, so evenly and thoroughly coloured that it must have been dyed. Indeed Jakub was a person that a woman might find it easy to dream about, as he wasn't the kind of man to repeat the usual opinions that everyone repeats, or one that always revisits the same topics in conversation. Nor was he the unapproachable sort who always occupies the centre of a room, and speaks loudly, and notes the comings and goings of everyone there. Instead he was someone that a woman might meet accidentally in an upstairs corridor, or when seeking fresh air outside the front door, and slip into conversation with. And also he was the kind that a woman might expect to meet, but hardly ever does, a person that is familiar to her from films and television, a kind that she is led to imagine can only be found in cities like London and Paris and New York. He is one of these rare creatures that is strangely absent from everyday life, a man she might hope to have a chance meeting with in a bookshop, or even walking in a park or by the river, or possibly an art gallery. A man she imagines to have a life that is quieter and simpler than hers, more dedicated to some skill or talent, without any of the compromises that she, on occasion, regrets. It as if she glimpses him, in the foreground of his separate world, from the midst of her own entanglements and responsibilities, and is attracted, and is envious.

Chapter Eleven

In London, in the office, Laura was frowning, rolling her pencil backwards and forwards on the table.

'I thought that Morton would have called you,' she said.

'You know how life is for him. He doesn't really do social calls.'

'Well I think he does Josh.'

'Look I've got something to say.'

She turned her head to profile and narrowed her eyes.

'You want a new agent?'

'No. I've fucked Jeff's girlfriend.'

'You've what?'

'I've fucked Suzie.'

Laura stood up and walked around and pushed close her office door. Then she paused there, with her hand on the doorknob; she took a deep breath.

'Did she want you to?'

'I haven't raped her.'

'Are you sure?'

'Yes.'

'Thank God. That's a start.'

Laura left the door and came to lean against the shelving. She spoke while looking at the wall opposite, only making infrequent eye contact with me.

'Does he know?'

'Yes.'

She nodded, and suppressed a sigh.

'How angry is he?'

'Very.'

'Was she good?'

'Yeah. What?'

'I'm asking the questions. Does anyone else know?'

'Yes. There's been some exploratory papping.'

Laura began twisting one of her rings.

'Damn. Is she rich?'

'She's a lawyer.'

'At last, some positive news.'

'She's broken up with Jeff.'

'Oh is that what she told you? Right get out, wait outside with the girls, I've got some calls to make.'

'What? What calls?'

'Editors, media Olympians. I'll be out in ten. Then we're going to the cinema.'

'Umm. Not sure about that.'

I was half way out of my chair.

'There is something by one of these directors playing at the moment.'

She picked up one of the scripts on the desk.

'I know. But I do have that rule.'

'Josh, it's a stupid rule.'

'They always are though, aren't they?'

'Listen Haddon wait outside. You're fucked, unless I help. The wrong spin on this story, and it'll be panto and soap operas for you. Seaside towns in January, I mean it.'

I scurried out the door, and stood just outside. The assistants looked at me quizzically, and I smiled and gave a tiny wave.

I don't remember exactly when I started only going to premieres. Of course it was close to the time that *The End of the Ocean* was released, but I don't think it was immediately that the film started showing. At first I refused to go and see the film, partly because I felt I would attract too much attention. The idea of being noticed in the auditorium, being engaged in conversation, perhaps being shouted to or at, repelled me. The thought of this continuing during the film itself, with constant asides and queries from some over keen and socially insensitive film goer, was too much to bear.

But, on examination, my reasons for not going to the cinema were more complex than that. I suppose I felt that my presence there would be an intrusion, that it would break the spell of the film and would pierce the bubble of make believe that the audience had paid to enter into. I imagined a situation where I arrived late to a crowded cinema, and was forced to sit in one of the front rows closest to the screen. There I would be, visible to the majority of those present, edging along past the knees of the seated viewers, muttering apologies, perhaps spilling or trying not to spill popcorn onto their laps. In other words merely another compromised human being, another clumsy and hesitant person, a potential figure of fun and scorn. And it seemed too much to expect the viewers to reconcile the acting man with this one in front of them, the figure before the screen, so to speak. The obstructing man, distracting them from their prized reality, smaller and scruffier than they might expect, not quite as well dressed or so virile seeming; who, just for a moment, is larger than the actor on the screen, obscuring him.

At first I only avoided *The End of the Ocean*, but then, once this line of thought had developed, I found reason to avoid the cinema in general. I felt myself to be a resident of the cinema world, and that my presence in the auditorium would disrupt the experience for the audience. To my mind, I would have seemed like a man in a women's toilet, or an adult learning among the pupils in a classroom. In fact my very presence on the street often felt like a transgression, as if I had obviously wandered clear of my sanctioned places, and the shocked expressions of the passers-by who recognized me were an indication of this, of my flagrant and scandalous disregard for boundaries.

About ten minutes later Laura came out the office, zipping up her short coat.

'Let's walk and talk,' she said.

She then locked her office door, stared pointedly at her assistants, and hastened us on.

'Right, the consensus is they're sitting on it for now, but you're going to have to pay.'

'Pardon? I don't understand.'

'We're talking about a half naked broadsheet photo sheet; probably at the time of your next film. We're talking reality TV, we're talking nipples and, yes, maybe even some bum-crack.'

'I'm sorry?'

We were going down the stairs, Laura clinging grimly to the banister. Her knee length skirt restricted her legs, and so she was shuffling slightly, in a way that suggested bowel problems. The square heels of her shoes were squeaking on the plastic edging of each step.

'Don't. And you're coming to the cinema.'

'You know I hate the cinema.'

We stopped on a stairwell, and she stared at me.

'It's ridiculous, I mean imagine a stage actor never going to the theatre. This is your profession, your lifeblood. You need to be inside cinemas, to see the people there, to see how they react, what they like and what they don't like. Also how can you know who's good and who isn't, who's directing messily and who's acting well? What about the competition for crying out loud?'

'Have you booked a taxi?'

Laura didn't reply and started walking again so her face wasn't visible, but it was obvious she had that satisfied expression, the pleased and catlike one she always has when she gets her own way. It was an expression clearly originating from her childhood, in it you could see a little girl that had learnt the value of protest; a girl that could barely conceal her pride over her instants of household mastery and one that rejoiced over successful incursions into the adult world.

Our conversation continued later, at first in a taxi, a taxi that Laura had summoned effortlessly, so punctual that it might even have been in a garage behind the office, that it might have been the same taxi that she always climbed into, or the one that had just dropped her off, or the one about to whisk her away. The taxi that was merely one of the metropolitan accessories that seemed to whirl around her, alive to her bidding and keen to obey her will. The taxi that was no different from the courier bikes that brought the scripts to my flat, the ones that carried cheques and sometimes cash to her clients and creditors; or no different to those restaurant menus that gently alighted in her hands, often twice a day, as if they were part of a winged cloud that fluttered close by her. Or alike to the theatre tickets and premiere tickets and tickets for classical music and pop music, tickets for fashion shows, tickets to see the opera or sporting events like the English Grand Prix, all of which seemed to accumulate within her reach. And the same thing happened with bottles of wine and bunches of flowers, which could materialize in Laura's right hand with the swiftness of a conjuring trick, as if flicking out from beneath a sleeve.

And then there were the complimentary gifts she received at Christmas, marching across her office, quartered on her desk, like a regiment of mechanical toy soldiers, unending and ceaseless in their advance: all those bottles of perfume and make-up kits and fountain pens, the electronic gadgets and shampoos and soaps and bath salts, the watches and sports clothing, the stacks of baseball caps. All of which made her, for her friends and family, particularly her distant cousins, a kind of central London Santa Claus, as if Father Christmas had appointed her a cosmopolitan distributor.

So we went to an Italian restaurant, one of those that aspires to be a chain, where she was known and greeted with familiarity, and where for once I was ignored, and the waiter gave the impression of being glad to see Laura there with a man, as if she came in alone a lot, and the staff worried about her, and talked about her eccentricities. And we ate some salad and we chatted about some of the actors that we knew, and about Morton Greaves, and the places he was likely to go to and the people he might visit. And then later we went to the cinema, and I scurried into the toilet and sat on a cubicle while she bought the tickets, and then once the film had started and she had found us seats I dashed out, feigning a coughing fit, keeping a fistful of tissues pressed against my face as I strode down the corridor to screen three. And once there I knew how right I'd been to agree to this, as I marvelled at how much more sophisticated the computer graphics had become, at how original and unique the directing style seemed, and at how gritty and raw the exact shade of colour on the camera filter managed to be, despite the fact that every year there is a new shade that evokes this rawness and grittiness.

And the visit also reminded me of some of the things I'd always disliked about the cinema. The moment for example, when there is a particularly bright flash on the screen, perhaps during the opening adverts or the trailers; a flash that illuminates a row of faces of the seated audience and makes them seem disembodied, or too pale and not quite natural. In this moment the viewers seem charged with the animation of the screen, as if they are receiving from it some element which they lack, and their visit to the cinema is an act of replenishment. It is a moment which makes the audience appear deprived, as if modern lives seclude people from vivid drama or force on them an adaption to an unrelieved passivity. This flash of light makes them all less than human, as if they aren't quite the people they should be.

Then there are the moments of carelessness: the spilled popcorn, the discarded sweet or chocolate bar wrappers, the conversations disturbing the people seated nearby, the noisy beeping of a mobile phone. It as if the cinema is one of the original transient places, a place where anonymity is assured, and therefore the feelings of others can be, if not ignored, then at least considered only marginally. It is as if everywhere is now like the cinema, as if the cinema rules have spread out, so now everywhere can be littered, and as if everyone is someone who'll never be seen again.

Fortunately where we are is fairly empty, so the experience feels more private than it might have. There is a cluster of people sitting down at the front, on the right hand side, and they keep standing up and walking past us to leave, and then returning. They are moving around more so than is customary, and it doesn't seem as if they're exiting to buy snacks or to visit the toilet. I wonder if they're taking cocaine, passing around a palm sized bag, and taking turns to snort the powder in the toilets.

Laura leans across to whisper to me.

'Isn't that Zara Westleton?'

She indicates this group of people, but subtly, keeping her finger close to her body.

'What?'

'You know. The soap actress.'

I peer down towards them.

'I'm not sure.'

'Go and look.'

'No you.'

'But I want to represent her. Just go and see.'

'Just wait outside for her afterwards.'

'She's too famous, she's bound to leave early.'

We both squinted, staring down at the seated people.

'She does look familiar.'

Just then one of the party, passing us on his return journey to his seat, stopped at the end of our aisle and leaned towards us.

'Sorry mate, but are you Josh Haddon?'

'Yes.'

Laura nudged me.

'We were just talking about it, and the others didn't believe me. They all had to have a look.'

'Well you're right.'

'Is that Zara Westleton with you?' Laura asked him.

'No. Sorry. Do you think she looks like her?'

'We were wondering.'

'Nah. You're a good actor mate. Take care.'

'Cheers then.'

He put his hands in the pockets of his body-warmer and walked back down to his seat.

'Weird,' I said.

Laura nodded and returned to watching the film. By the time all the thump and thunder had ended I was feeling tired and was ready to go home. Laura kissed me goodbye outside, and climbed into the taxi that, inevitably, pulled up at the same moment we stepped out into the city air, onto the pavement. Standing there, listening to the passing car engines, and the heavier rumble of the buses, I felt a familiar sensory overload. This occurs when background sounds begin to gather in volume, growing suddenly loud and intrusive. It comes on after a whole day in town, and is accompanied by a mild dizziness or the first twinges of a headache; sometimes there is a sense of faintness. The feet of passers-by are suddenly clattering along; previously unnoticed conservations are a clamour of discordant voices, the buildings in the street become sheer and forbidding; the lighting in the shop windows and on the ceiling of the tube station flares in intolerable brightness.

In these moments the idea of home is very attractive, the thought of the orderly hygiene of the kitchen and the comforting sprawl of the lounge, the whole ensemble viewed smoothly at eye level first and then from low down, spot lit and undisturbed, very much a furniture catalogue or showroom image in the mind. The thought of quiet music, the merging and coalescing lights of the night-time city visible through the windows, the gentle onset of drowsiness in front of the television, this is what I desired. It as if there are degrees of privacy, and home is where it is most concentrated, and the streets are where it is most dispersed. And the journey back involves a passing through these, and a sense of privacy increasing at each stage.

First there is the jolting taxi, lurching forward between interruptions, with its mimicking of the rushing pedestrians on the pavement, both alike in their searching for lines of unimpeded progress, both forced to

201

attention by the continual necessity of minute adjustments, under the threat of collisions, making nothing more than erratic progress.

The taxi with its apartness that is only flimsy, with its partition that is an invitation to talk. And then there is the radio that is so often on, and a Beatles song playing, a popular song that must be forty years old. A song that is perhaps one of the country's favourite, one that I've heard so very much, that in its existence must have passed into the ears and through the minds of millions, and that has lost a little of itself each time, as if with each listening it has leached a minute quantity of its substance, as if it has been repeatedly diluted in increments.

This song that has been in the raucous soundtrack of so many of my drunken nights, of so many hopeful summer evenings, of so many celebrations and reunions and discos, that it seems more suitable for it to pass into memory with them. The song whose persistence, whose popularity, now seems a little obscene, as if it has somehow discarded those who first loved it and sang along to it, as if it now dominates and eclipses the feelings it was written to encourage and engender. A song that, it occurs to me, has become like a parasite on youth and good times. One that grows ever more mechanical and charmless, like a bell or an alarm whose ringing recurs periodically, and is never less than distracting and unsettling.

Then the taxi arrives at the entrance to my block of flats, and I linger for a while in the foyer, sitting down on the easy chairs and fiddling with my phone, as if I am waiting for an appointment. Stan is at the reception desk, is typing at a keyboard, his features immobile in the blue light of the monitor screen. There are other residents apparent: the violinist who lives on the floor below, the Russian couple who can't speak English; emerging out of the lifts or entering the doors and crossing the lobby, heading towards the stairs or the lifts. The sounds are the tapping fingers on the keyboard, and the click of shoes on the gleaming tiles of the lobby floor. These sounds are more orderly than those in the street; there are rhythms in the people passing by, the same number each minute, perhaps even spaced the same distance apart, separate enough to be examinable and thought about; so different from the melee outside, with its perpetual churn and chaotic rush, with its continual pressure on the senses. At times this criss-crossing of the lobby brings to mind the mechanism of a town square clock, the medieval Austrian kind, where the hour is signaled by the emergence of painted figurines from tiny doors, which rotate in tandem with the sounding chimes. There is a sense of the manifestation of schedules, of the correct observance of punctuality, of a collective harmony caused by the keeping of contractual attendances and appointments and dinner reservations and agreements.

And, as usual, the impression is that those going by are repeating themselves. Sitting here before, I've noticed that the residents come by at roughly the same time each day, following their usual path across the tiled door and then up the stairs. Usually they, like now, hardly ever speak, or acknowledge each other, and it appears that their only meeting or touch is between the dim outlines of their shadows, when two pass close by. And the imagination suggests that there is little difference between the people and their reflections in the windows, as if the lobby and the window are alternate dimensions placed side by side, and the occupants of the window are the least manifest, and the ones of lobby are more real; and as if there is elsewhere, further on and undetected, another dimension, whose inhabitants are more fully and wholly present.

Then, once this scene is absorbed, there is the quiet pleasure of ascending in the lift, made enjoyable by the anticipation of arriving home, by the sense of being able to relax in that full way that is only possible when alone, when none of the usual social facilities need to be engaged. Those moments when the person we live with has gone away, when we are sure they won't talk to us; and so unknowingly impose on us their demands for attention, which would require our energy to answer, which we resent. One of those moments when the usual housework requirements can be ignored, when the washing up is left until morning and the papers and the other detritus of a working life don't need to be cleared from the table. An evening when a pleasurable habit can be indulged, one that the restless and conflicting demands of a shared life usually make impossible: for instance a newspaper web-site can be read at length, or a glass of wine can be tasted and savoured.

And so the front door is opened with no particular hurry, and a bag is dropped on the floor or placed on a chair, and a snack is assembled from the cupboards and the fridge, and the interior of the kitchen and the lounge appear as static and benign. Eventually, after a leisurely sorting through of the mail, a meal is cooked, but quite slowly, without any of the usual rush. Then, after all these delays, the television is turned on, the television that is the final destination, the prize of this solitude, the personal reward that has been anticipated all day.

So I got home and lay on the sofa, and ate a meal from a tray, and started watching TV. This was a conventional viewing at first, confined to the terrestrial channels, involving the news and a documentary or two. Then as the evening drew on, there were forays into the satellite channels, adventurous little sorties that skimmed through the programs as quickly as possible. I was poised in consideration, flicking between a film starring Vin Diesel, one documentary on an American prison, and another on sexual practices, when there was a knocking sound.

I dismissed it as an inconsequential noise at first, only looking around to see what had fallen over, or slipped off the counter. Then the rapping was repeated, and so I muted the television.

Jeff was standing outside, arms folded, feet shoulder-width apart. He was wearing sun glasses despite the subdued lighting in the corridor.

'Jeff.'

'So I guess you were expecting someone else.'

'What, Suzie?'

'I expect so.'

'No, not especially.'

'So what, you guys aren't married yet?'

His chin was raised, and his tone was somewhere between neutral and skeptical.

'You're back early.'

'Oh yeah. I wonder why that is.'

'There's nothing going on with Suzie and I.'

'I saw that thing on YouTube, and I lost the fucking match.'

'Suzie just came over here for dinner.'

'I don't believe you. Is she here?'

'No.'

'All her stuff's next door.'

He pointed down the corridor, arm outstretched.

'She's been living there for a week. I had to confront the reporters outside.'

'Yeah I saw that too. And you haven't fucked her?'

'No.'

'Have you wanted to?'

'No.'

He maintained his gaze for a moment, before taking off his glasses.

'You're a bad liar, Josh. Now, you got any coffee for me?'

I went over to the kitchen, and put on the kettle. Jeff walked across the living area and sat down at the kitchen table. He put his head in his hands and rubbed his eye sockets with the balls of his thumbs.

'Just because I'm in here man, it doesn't mean we're straight. I need to talk to her too.'

'Well call her.'

'I've been trying all afternoon.'

'I'm sure she'll be back soon.'

'Has she been fucking someone though?'

'I don't know.'

He leant over and began massaging his calves.

'I made it to the quarters man, but that's all.'

'Really? How do you feel?'

'Fine. No fine. My sponsors wanted me to make the quarters. I get a bonus for the semis.'

'You were in the sports news here.'

'Yeah? I'll remind them about that.'

I handed him a mug of coffee.

'Anyway cheers. Welcome back to London.'

'Cheers Josh.'

Then he leaned across and picked up a magazine from the table, shook it open, and began scanning the back pages.

'Any shit happen?'

He stopped in the pages and started reading intently.

'So has Suzie been around much?'

'She was here two nights ago.'

'Oh.'

'Has she been reading the tabloids?'

'I doubt it. She's been working a lot.'

He looked hard at his hands, turning them over as if inspecting the calluses, sighed, and then made a clenching movement with his jaw.

'She's a lively girl,' he said, looking into the other room.

'Are you OK Jeff?'

'Jet-lagged. Why? Do I look pale?'

'No. I'm just surprised you haven't tried any violence on me. It's not like you.'

He stared at me, for a moment, before answering.

'Listen I fucked this girl, one of those goddamn blondes, and some of the paparazzi picked up on it.'

'Really? Oh shit.'

Suddenly, he looked tired over his glass of wine, and older, his face momentarily having the character of an abandoned or fossilised structure, of a building or reef say, that has been vacated by what created and renewed it, as if its formative and revitalising energies have departed. His face suddenly had this look, like a cast or an impression that has replaced the real, original face. This expression is usually only glimpsed accidentally by another, the kind of despairing expression that one reserves for the bathroom mirror, or is permitted to form only in unlit rooms, or out of the line of sight of windows.

It's one that I associate with bad lighting, the kind of expression that is only seen in public late at night, perhaps when everybody is drunk. Then it occurs in a kitchen or a pub toilet or on a tube train; places that have fluorescent lighting, lighting that is never flattering, and that always darkens and petrifies a face. It's an expression that always reveals the unpleasant feelings of the wearer: regret, anxiety, boredom, self-doubt, paranoia, impatience and exhaustion.

More, this expression only truly belongs on a man's face when he has reached a mature age, thirty say, as if there is a struggle between old age and youth which old age begins to win. A mature age by which any excesses of vitality have settled, have stabilised and now rarely flush into and rejuvenate the surface.

An expression that was peculiar to see on Jeff's face, as familiar as it was in its youthful form: from the TV adverts that he's done for the aftershave company, from the magazine campaigns for the sports clothing company and from the billboard portraits for the luxury brand of watches. In these Jeff was presented as a remarkable specimen of cosmopolitan man, athletic and stylish, confident and enviably handsome.

'Where's your phone?'

He groped in his jacket pockets.

'It's next door. One second.'

When Jeff came back in Suzie followed behind him carrying a black satchel and wearing a knee length dark coat, not one of the heavy coats common in London, but a garment that was nylon and lighter. Her hair was pushed back, and she seemed exhilarated, in fact not so much exhilarated as uplifted by a successful day at work, as if she had finished more than she expected to and enjoyed herself more than she expected to. In that moment it was easy to imagine her giving instructions, easy to imagine her deft and practised solving of some professional issue, or her confident manner as she applied her experience.

'Look who was outside.'

'Hi Josh.'

She came over and kissed me, and squeezed my hand.

'Hello.'

We both turned and stared at Jeff.

'Doesn't he look tanned?'

'I know.'

She placed her bag down, and tugged some strands of hair out from under the rear of the collar of her coat.

'Have you eaten, Josh?'

'Yeah.'

I waved my left hand towards the smeared plate.

Jeff sat down again, and crossed his right foot onto his knee.

'How jet-lagged are you?'

'I'm holding up.'

'I've booked a table. It's at your favourite place.'

'Josh just explained the whole misunderstanding to me.'

'Oh did he?'

She gave me a questioning, quizzical, smile.

'I mean what was I thinking?'

It occurred to me then that he knew we were lying to him, and that his approach would be to see how determined we were to further the lie; and that Suzie had expected this, and had entered the flat anticipating this tactic. Perhaps this was why she had arrived in such buoyant spirits, with such a momentum of capability carried over from her working day; so that nothing that Jeff said would have a chance of flustering her or threatening her composure.

A composure that was one of her principal qualities, a trait that must have been built up bit by bit over time, a quality that, doubtless, had in the process of its construction suffered numerous reversals and collapses. A quality that had been reassembled again and again, which each time had involved much gathering of scattered pieces, many private sessions of tears and crying; requiring multiple reappearances to those that had opposed her and done their best to thwart and dismiss her.

Jeff nodded, in a dazed way, as if he was trying to both listen to her and remember something that he had meant to say, as if there was something he had been meaning to tell her; or as if there was some urgent errand he had just remembered he needed to attend to.

'You know I had death by chat-show down there.'

'Did you get me a present?'

'Baby, I had to buy new luggage to get them back here.'

He looked up and smiled at her, and it was as if the corner of his mouth was an arm that swept away all the preoccupations, all the doubtful and introspective thoughts, which had crowded onto his face, pushing them behind and away from his shoulder.

'Will I like them?'

'That depends, it depends on how much you like shoes and, I dunno, what are those things? Handbags?'

And the impression was of Jeff, with his suddenly smiling face turned up towards us, soaring up and away from his jet-lag and suspicion and guilt and regret, of him at the last second escaping the black tentacles of his mood. Here he was, back on familiar ground, being flirted with, and the everyday Jeff, the celebrity Jeff, was suddenly present and interested and attentive.

After a while they left for their dinner reservation, him murmuring into her ear, the rear view of them silhouetted for a moment in my doorway, her recoiling a fraction from what he was saying, perhaps delighted and almost disgusted. Then I fell to speculating over what he'd been thinking, or even despairing, about.

Perhaps he'd been comparing this girl in Australia to his former wife, reflecting how alike they were, both blondes in the neo Californian style: with their soft and mellow tans, their bleached blonde fringes that sway and can be flicked back when climbing in and out of sports cars and SUVs. Girls in beach wear and party dresses; girls long accustomed to swimming pools and endless sun and idle weekends in spacious houses, to electronic security gates and boutique shopping. Girls with beautiful friends, possessing the bounty of other friends who are even more beautiful, all of whom are thriving on the careless liberty of the wealthy.

And then perhaps it occurred to him he'd had a lucky escape, and that he'd done well to leave Australia when he did. He was thinking surely, about the circumstances of his break up with his first wife, about the way she had seemed to be his rightful trophy, as much a mark of his success as his income or the number of homes he owned. And how much, at the time, she had seemed to be something awarded to him from the world of the super rich; a prize from its entrenched and imperious guardians.

I suspect he was remembering the process of their marriage souring, when she began to criticise his performance on the courts, when he began to realise the scale of her expectations. And finally, of course, he wasn't famous enough for her, and so she left him for a Formula One driver. A rare defeat that had, like his disappointing performance in Australia, been part of what was expressed in that sullen look on his face; a weary look that eventually comes to be familiar to everyone, which no-one ever lives entirely free of, no matter how headlong their success and no matter how guaranteed their life-long happiness appears to be.

And there were other ingredients in that withdrawn look; one of them perhaps being a grudging acknowledgement of his good fortune at having escaped, or even of cautious appraisal of how close he had come to being re-entangled. I felt that Jeff was realising how lucky he was, that the smile which had seemed to carry him up so swiftly was one of relief and an all pervading, planet encompassing, gratitude.

Chapter Twelve

I even saw this withdrawn look cross Morton Greaves's face, in those early weeks in Scotland when we began to shoot the *The End of the Ocean*. Despite the changing season the days were still shorter in the highlands, and so we rose before dawn each morning to be made up and quickly begin the filming. The scenes we were shooting weren't the opening ones, but were near the beginning. In them, Morton's character, the late eighteenth century soldier of fortune, has returned home to Scotland from America, where he'd been fighting the English. He has arrived suffering from wounds and malaria, and my character, as his younger cousin, provides shelter and nurses him back to health.

It was these scenes that the director was so keen to commit to celluloid; it was in them that the director intended to develop the visual style of the film; it was here that he planned to experiment with camera angles and matters of light and shade, and degrees of soft focus and close up.

So Morton and I spent days in the low-ceilinged cottage which, in the story, was in the grounds of my estate. Morton's sick bed was in the main room, and he lay there for weeks, being attended to by nurses and examined by a dour and whiskered doctor. The room had a stone tiled floor, a crucifix and a bible, beams with hooks on which lanterns were hung, and a coal fire where an iron kettle was heated. The earliest scenes were of my character on a three legged stool, dabbing at Morton's brow with a white cloth, as he muttered and turned his head from side to side.

And here, of course, it was easier to inhabit the characters, to imagine and conjure them in the mind. It was easy when feeling the same reliance on the warmth of the same meagre fire, when chilled by the draught through the chinks in the window pane, when feeling the strain in the eyes where candle light is the only illumination. Here, where cold water was all that there was for washing, and cotton thread was used to clean the teeth, and shaving was an ordeal, it was easy to lose oneself in the cruder habits of a life that is almost forgotten. And besides all this there was the landscape; the fields behind and the lane with its stunted hedgerow, and the rutted lane with its wooden gate that had to be lifted off its post to be opened; scenery which reminded me of modern watercolours that have a solitary man in the foreground, sketchy paintings in diluted colours of deer stalking or grouse shooting.

A simpler life now only revealed to the hardened seeker or the lucky and casual seeker; a life whose realities can't be sensed by standing on the cliff edge and gazing down and along at the beach, and thinking and listening and breathing; as if its clamour was recently audible, as if its traces are still visible on the sand. A past life that is unreceptive to tourism, to momentary and fleeting and uncommitted and partial inquiries. A past life that stirs at the distant boundaries of the imagination, one that is better known through the feeling of a common discomfort; through the pain of a tooth being jerked out with string, or a cut being stitched without anaesthetic.

The withdrawn look in Morton's face, the sullen look, appeared mainly while we spoke together, when we negotiated over how to act a scene. The look never manifested to the extent that it did on Jeff that night, more it threatened to affect Morton's composure. I realised early on that this suggestion of his disappointment during a conversation, this subtle dimming of his colour and the cloying of his features, was a psychological tactic.

What Morton was asking for was an emphasis on facial close-ups, as he felt he could express each stage of the recovery best by altering the signs of relief in his eyes and by varying the severity of his grimaces. He wanted all this supported by changes in the tone of the background light, to provide the sense of a winter illness and a springtime recovery. However, I argued that these scenes were about the growing friendship between our two characters, about showing the audience a forming bond.

And so we bickered, and Morton loomed over me and frowned a little, in his polite American way, and seemed to be dry-mouthed with frustration at times; and was probably surprised that he was being so much disagreed with and that he wasn't getting his own way easily. My impression was that he was testing the extent to which he could dictate his own terms, that he was interested in how strong the director would be in enforcing the script, and also how forceful I would be in contesting the precious territory that faces the camera lens.

During our talks there were these transitory expressions, these noting and evaluating expressions, which formed on and then passed from his face, as if he was examining me and drawing conclusions, like a psychologist or an interrogator. These were talks that almost always took place away from the camera crew and the director and anyone else.

'Just give us a couple of minutes guys,' Morton would say.

Sometimes we would go and stand behind the cottage, as if we were off to smoke cigarettes, or we would walk up the muddy track towards the road, and talk and nod and look earnest; in our white shirts and waistcoats and breeches we must have resembled a pair of gentlemen naturalists, discussing some once fashionable theory of nineteenth century science.

In those couple of weeks I had the sense that Jakub was avoiding me. He was present on set, as he was preparing some actors for and choreographing a later scene. This one really established the story; in it a band of men from the New World raid the Scottish estate in order to murder Morton's character. He, with my character's help, survives, and decides to return to North America to 'conclude his affairs'. Naturally, my character accompanies him. But, despite this presence, Jakub rarely spoke to me during the working day, or in any of the more relaxed situations where I might have expected us to chat: the shared evening meals of the cast and crew, the occasional game of football, the script read throughs, the games of poker; he was always leaving as I was arriving, or would suddenly receive some intensely private telephone call that he would hurry outside to answer, slightly hunched over and holding the phone up to the side of his head, as if he were shielding himself from recognition.

When we did speak he only ever asked me about Hannah.

'How is she? Is she any better? Nobody here knows.'

'No. She's still unconscious. I visited the hospital last weekend.'

'It's tough for you man.'

And he'd either put his hand on my shoulder or he'd hug me, and then leave a little too quickly, as if I had an infectious illness or as if I were someone he had been warned to avoid. Then I wondered if Jakub was affected by superstition, if he was someone that sees misfortune as contagious, a man that wouldn't give money to a beggar for fear of a transference of bad luck. One of those men that suppress a shudder in the presence of the very old, and that speaks only reluctantly to the obese or to those that are obviously poor and disadvantaged. The kind of man that hesitates to enter a post office or a bus station, and that flinches at the closeness of others in the doctor's waiting room.

When we did start to work together Jakub's manner was business-like and professional; there was scant difference between the way he treated Morton and the way he was with me. The first scene he choreographed with us both was a fight on a stairwell in the main house. Here I defended myself with a broadsword while backing up the stairs, blocking the lunges of an opponent's spear. Meanwhile Morton was on the landing above me, trying to knock a dagger from his assailant's grasp. The fight concludes by Morton and his attacker tumbling down the stairs, distracting the spearman enough for me to thrust into his neck.

The sequence of combat moves in each of our fights was broken down into detailed parts. In mine, Jakub was preoccupied with my foot movements as I evaded and fended off the spear: the kicks, the stamps, the shuffles, and the skips. So he was alongside my opponent and I for more than an hour, instructing us in combinations of offence and defence and watching us repeat them. In mid-morning, during a break, he and I spoke by the table of refreshments.

'You never called me the other week in London,' he said.

'No. You're right. I was really busy.'

He looked at me in a way that was reproachful, an expression which had regret in it, which also contained resignation and was wary; as if there was some matter that I might admonish him over. Then, I wondered if there was money involved, that perhaps he had charged the production company more to train me than he could justify, or that possibly he felt I was disappointed with the training, and that he was expecting me to confront him over it.

'We need to find a moment to talk.'

'Do we?'

'Mmm. There's something we have to discuss together.'

He was filling his plastic cup from the water fountain so his eyes were averted.

'The evenings are a good time,'

'After dinner?'

He sipped some water.

'Yes.'

'Ok. I'll find you.'

He smiled, and patted the upper side of my left arm as he walked on past. And then we didn't speak privately for a few days; our conversations were confined to the practical matters of fight choreography and sparring: of cut and thrust, of turns and parries, of the breaching of guards, of swivels and downward slices to the thighs and knees. Those evenings there were a difficult time as I was so exhausted by the pre-dawn rises and the daytime schedule that I went to bed early. By nine o'clock I was sluggish, and I was in my room, reading the script or watching TV quietly, by ten.

And the daytime schedule wasn't only gruelling because of the early start and the physical activity required. Equally there were the all the usual demands of any workplace or professional environment. All those strains which come from the exertions of self control, the effort involved in not offending anyone or of imposing oneself too much. The demands of workplaces where there are so many boundaries, so many thresholds of hierarchy that a person feels obliged to respect.

There were the meetings, when the director would sit at the head of a table, or at the front of a room, and ask questions, and encourage us to voice our thoughts on the script, or about the previous day's shoot. These sessions, always with Morton there, invariably generated a preoccupied aftermath in me, a reflective personal debrief, in which my remarks, those sallies into the conversational fray, were deliberated over and reconsidered and more often than not regretted. There were a few cameraman and actors and one producer who didn't speak, who seemed determined never to express anything, presumably to avoid exposing themselves to judgement.

The others, including me, felt compelled to make hasty statements, to offer roughly formed opinions that required amending before being finished. Most of these rambling contributions created wary silences, and caused outbreaks of cautious tolerance among those present.

'Obviously it's clear that we need these early starts but can't we have some kind of shift system so that we get to sleep normally on some of the days of the week?'

'The long term weather forecast is really clear about this and I think that if the wind does shift around to the North then the whistling sound in the chimney is going to be a real problem.'

And then there was the atmosphere of the shoot itself, and the murmuring conversations that occurred between the director and the more influential actors and producers. For all of us on set that were relatively unproven, or at least new to acting in Hollywood productions, these inaudible chats were the likely occasions of our appraisal.

So in the evenings I was glad to close the door of my room behind me, and later feel soothed by the shower's wash; as if I was seeking more than recovery by inclining my head and neck beneath its pummelling spray, pressing the palms of my hands against the facing tiles, resting with eyes closed in this posture of deference.

And after a week or so, when Jakub and I did talk, it wasn't in the evening at all, but was instead in the middle of a problematic morning's work. The director had become exasperated during the scene we were trying to shoot; frustrated with my acting, he was saying so with growing conviction and ferocity.

'If you can't find the tone for this now, how can you hope to deal with what's coming later on?'

In the scene my character was arguing with Morton's, trying to persuade him to take me with him to America. We were walking down cliff side steps leading to a tiny stone harbour; here there was a quay and posts for hanging fishing nets, as well as a couple of moored boats bobbing in the swell. Morton had a crate of supplies, with a rope looped around his right shoulder, and I was following, holding a scabbard with a sword in it.

'Here isn't safe for me now.'

'It's more secure than where I'm going.'

'In God's name, you can't do this alone.'

'No maybe. But I shall not do it with you.'

Then the director, who was in the hut on the quay, watching us on the various camera screens, rushed out and waved his arms above his head, a signal for us to stop.

'Again, again,' he shouted up.

Morton and I stood in silence for a moment, staring at each other.

'Okay. Give me five minutes.'

I trudged up to the top of the steps, and when I reached the top, Jakub was there. He had a cutlass in his belt and was pale, as if hung-over or ill.

'Oh hello.'

'Josh.'

'They're all down at the base of cliff.'

'I haven't come to talk to them.'

'Really?'

He nodded, almost to himself.

'Josh I have to leave for a week, and before I should explain I never wanted to burn anything down.'

He spoke loudly and deliberately, across the breeze and the distance. He sounded as if he was repeating something he had memorized; or as if he was talking to someone that was hard of hearing, perhaps an older relative, and his voice had a tone appropriate to this; a tone that was anticipating repetition and drawn out explanation.

'What?'

He breathed in fully, and his eyes wandered before meeting my gaze.

'I put the fire in your house. The idea was to make it little, to scare you, and to help me make you into a stronger man. I'm sorry.'

'What are you talking about?'

'I started that fire. And now, now that your wife is so ill, I can see that the fire was unnecessary. I'm sorry.'

Jakub smiled and shrugged his shoulders, and glanced away to the right, at the horizon. He appeared braced for and resigned to my response, as if he'd been considering the best way to have this conversation for weeks, and had now given up his deliberations as futile and decided to express himself in this direct way.

Next there was what I didn't do, like not swearing at him or rushing at him or even raising my sword and edging forward like a duellist. Nor did I offer up some halfway comment, some postponing comment that might have satisfied him, something like:

'We'll talk next week.'

Or:

'Are you mad?'

Comments that would have cast me in the role of a rational man or an aggrieved man, roles Jakub would easily have been able to respond to; which would have granted him an opposing part to play and led us to resolve the situation.

'I know you're angry,' he might have said.

Or:

'Please forgive me.'

Knowing him, he might even have suggested he yield to a painful revenge; he might even have suggested an honour and vengeance ritual, in which I cut him, or sliced off one of his fingers, or branded him.

'This is something from the traditions in the mountains.'

Possibly he was hoping I would threaten to call the police, and that he would have to beg me not to prosecute.

'Please, think of my future.'

And that then I would feel satiated, and that the matter would be considered over.

Or even if Jakub had approached me there to fight, when we were both armed, in the hope that I challenge him; and that during the duel he might be able to hiss words of encouragement to me when our faces were close behind our parrying blades.

'This is it, this is how you need to be; this passion is what the director wants.'

And that after the fight I would have returned and acted superbly in the scene, and then I might have even felt a twinge of gratitude to Jakub, for everything he'd done. And then the situation would have been finished.

So I didn't speak. This was a situation that language would have been unwelcome in, where it would have been a reminder of the everyday and the casual and the easily forgotten; an intrusion of words that are almost always common and taken for granted and unexamined, so much so that something spoken is like something discarded.

This situation on the cliff top made clear the limitations of everyday speech: the inadequacy of habitual responses, the exhausted quality of all the usually relied upon answers and replies. For a moment Jakub and I were in an eerie and lonely place, in which we were rendered powerless, where our standard repertoire of usual reactions was ineffective.

All I did was frown at him, before turning away and going down the steps. An action intended to take this displaced moment and make it expand and encompass us both, to fix it into being and set its boundaries at cosmological distances. And as Jakub himself turned and walked away, no doubt confused, perhaps the terrain his troubled eyes glanced over seemed changed, more turbulent and restlessly volatile; a world less infiltrated by his powers of mastery than he had supposed.

Chapter Thirteen

When I entered the restaurant Jeff and Suzie didn't notice me at first. They were seated somewhere behind and beyond the closer tables, in the dimmer, less visible areas. The black table surfaces made a hovering symmetry across the floor space, an impression of repetition, of mirrors reflecting in mirrors; which was intensified by the diners and the lighting. These customers resembled each other, many of them older couples, the men in dark jackets, the glittering straps of women's dresses or handbags prominent in the specialised, conical light. This descended from the tinted black canopies of woven cable shades; a personalised, discriminating illumination making each pair seem lit up in a targeted glare better suited to figures on display in a waxwork diorama.

The manager was in his fifties with a pink, heavily furrowed face; together these features made him seem aged but also vigorous. It was a face that appeared almost swollen, as if by drinking hard spirits or exposure to severe weather; one whose features had become fractionally distended and blurred. Standing behind that hybrid of desk and lectern commonly found fronting restaurants, he seemed a technician behind a console of flashing lights, dials, buttons and switches.

'Welcome sir.'

'Hi.'

'Reservations?'

'No, I'm just dropping in on some friends.'

'Of course, now then, Mr Haddon, isn't it? Would you like a table?'

He had one of those inflected, flexible voices; the kind of voice whose tone was a promise to understand all understandings, that suggested deep, gently lapping reservoirs of empathy and discretion. Its qualities included firmness, moral versatility and a respect for the sanctity of money, a reassuring voice that promised to respectfully consider any request made by the very wealthy.

'No. I just want to chat.'

I smiled in a compromised, grimacing way.

'Is it Mr Brazer you've come to see?'

'That's right.'

'Well, this way, sir.'

So we entered the dining area, following broad curves behind the backs of the chairs, passing the diners on their circular tables, so selectively lit. Two passing staff members noticed me, and their peering faces, disembodied above their black uniforms, leant closer. Their features, distorted by the multiplicity of the light sources, and the harsh impulse of celebrity fascination, were each a collision of faceted angles and abnormal divisions of shadow.

Jeff and Suzie were at a circular table near the back, and on my approach, Jeff wiped his mouth with the corner of his napkin, and rose to shake my hand. The light affected his appearance too, accentuating his tan, making his features darker, rigid and more immobile. At that moment he seemed hardened by sun; a person that had become permanently altered, that had passed a point of no return.

'Look who's still hungry.'

Behind him Suzie was startled, straightening herself up, and so I focused on Jeff. Nearby the manager was speedily laying out cutlery on a slightly larger table; his professional urgency was that of a man hurriedly spelling out a warning.

'I think we'll need that other table,' Jeff said.

Suzie was putting her hand to her hair and then rubbing her nails; these movements were of a hunted animal disturbed amongst foliage, abandoning any reliance on camouflage.

'No we won't.'

We stared at each other for a moment.

'What's up Josh?'

He tilted his head, smiled, and put his hands in his pockets, still looking at me. I tried to think who Jeff reminded me of and realised he reminded me of himself.

'I'm sleeping with Suzie. We've been fucking.'

This line was adapted from a stage play I was in once. I tried my best to be deadpan; using the line to neutralise some of the immediacy and reality of the situation.

Jeff nodded, gazing down at the floor; then he stared up at the ceiling, half coughed, coughed more heavily, and put his hand to his mouth.

'OK,' he struggled to say.

Then he turned to the fuller, busier side of the restaurant. Some of the people seated there were watching us already. A couple of them were filming the scene on mobile phones.

'Excuse me ladies and gentleman.'

Almost all of the customers within view looked. And the effect of this was a strange and disturbing one, as if Jeff and I were in a television drama, actors acting, and a field of visibility had suddenly opened up, and the audience, all those uncountable television audiences, all those families and couples spread across the world and through recent time, were suddenly visible to us. And it was as if this audience was, in front of our eyes, behaving differently, as if the usually passive and docile viewers were reacting as if everything was real. A response that seems unimaginable, people reacting to the dramas on their televisions as if real events were being shown: people flinching at every televised gunshot, crying over every actor's death, standing and shouting in horror at every moment of impending danger and doom.

Jeff raised a hand and pointed at me.

'This man is an asshole. Once he was my best friend, but now, he's an asshole.'

There were one or two bemused grins in the audience, a few others leant across to listen to or speak to another at their table, probably for explanations or translations. Personally, I was trying to remember in which TV or film I'd seen an actor do something similar; one with Michael Keaton perhaps.

'Jeff sit down,' Suzie said. She was straining out of her seat, smiling and frowning.

'He's fucked my girl.'

Enjoyably, there was at least one, old-fashioned, gasp of surprise.

An athletic looking man, tall and black, stood up from his table. He was wearing a baggy suit, and he stood so quickly, as if to attention, that its fabric took a moment to resettle onto his frame. He then leaned forward and rested his outstretched hands onto the table, where his long fingers seemed to fix in, to entrench. A moment later he spoke, using a tone of resonant calm, one that suggested a rare composure, perhaps one of martial origins.

'Everybody, ignore this.'

Jeff's arm dropped to his side.

'He has, man.'

'No I've seen this, I know about this. It's in the magazines. They're just messing about. These two are famous for it. They're just fooling.'

People looked from the tall man to us. And some of them, perhaps, were thinking how peculiar it was that this stranger's voice was more imposing than Jeff's, considering how recognisable and powerful Jeff's voice usually is. An audience who were so accustomed to hearing Jeff's voice amplified on television sound systems, or on the radio stereo system; an audience who were surprised to hear Jeff's voice apparently so diminished in the restaurant, and so easily superseded in natural authority by this customer's voice. An audience that was hearing Jeff in the absence of his usual context and that was being reminded of his inherent powerlessness.

And it was as if Jeff was crumpling, realising that he was in the midst of a collapse of the usual illusions, and was becoming more disoriented by this every moment. He turned to me, disappointment appearing to compress his face, the slant of his jaw suddenly prominent.

'Christ Josh, what is all this?'

The manager was suddenly at my shoulder.

'Please, Mr Haddon, Mr Brazer, this is not a film set. You can't do this here.'

'OK, OK,' Jeff said.

'This isn't a public space,' the manager said.

'This is real,' I said.

'God. Look at all these people.'

By now, everyone was staring at me.

'Oh fucking hell,' I said, and rushed into the kitchen, hoping to find an exit, and not be waylaid by chefs trained in karate, rushing and somersaulting towards me; or find myself tripping on dropped bananas, or crashing headlong into waiters carrying serving platters. I feared collisions with heavily laden cheese or desert trolleys, or with waitresses carrying trays of carefully arranged and fizzing glasses of champagne.

I reached my flat sometime around eleven. It was almost midnight when Suzie came in. She'd been crying, and as we stood just inside, I hugged her in a smothering way, with one hand behind her head and the other between her shoulder-blades.

'We just had the biggest scene.'

'Was he really upset?'

'No, he was trying to find out how long it'd been going on.'

We were having a very close-up conversation, a vertical equivalent of her lying on my chest in bed.

'Is that all he was worried about?'

'He's just shaken up. I walked out of the bar we were in. He's probably still there.'

She walked over to the table and began taking off her rings and bracelets, and setting them down on the surface. Then she bent her head to unhook an earring.

'I've got to fly to Cork tomorrow.'

'It's maybe best if you're going away.'

'What are you going to do?'

'I'll try to talk to him tomorrow. My agent's biking over two invitations in the morning. They're for a party for this lifetime achievement award that Morton's been nominated for. I could push a note and a ticket under Jeff's door.'

'You're gorgeous.'

Suzie walked past me into the bedroom, and as she walked past she slipped her hand under my t-shirt, and brushed her fingertips there. She smiled over her shoulder, then sat on the bed and began wriggling out of her dress.

'Can you undo me?'

Later, after the sex, the sudden, athletic sex, the kind that was over too soon, in which, at each wilder stage of intensity, I removed another garment of Suzie's, I lay awake. The curtains were slightly ajar, and the city light, its fluctuating electrical glow, fell across my face and an exposed arm and leg of Suzie's. This distinctive, urban, phosphorescence made us, and the wall opposite the window, shine, but dimly, like a low-wattage light bulb or the fading screen of a turned-off TV. To darken the room I went to close the curtains, a movement which stirred Suzie, so she pushed the upper part of the duvet down and behind her. Staring at her naked body I noted the sparseness of it, the barrenness and smallness of her thin limbs and uncovered back; in that moment they were as absent of qualities as under-decorated rooms or deserted streets emptied by the time of day or a season. After a few moments I closed the curtain and felt my way to my side of the bed. But, despite the darkness and the exhausting events of the day, I didn't sleep. Gradually my eyes began to adjust. Somehow, enough light was present to reveal the outlines of the foot of the bed, and the hazier recess where the mirror was. The room's murk seemed to be denser close to the mirror, as if it was the pulsing origin of the shadows that now enveloped and interred the bed, the wardrobe, and us. After an hour I fell asleep, turned on my side, all the while facing this obscured grey rectangle.

The following evening, in a limo, a chauffeur and I made our way to one of London's most impressive houses. It was a place that I'd seen once or twice in aerial photos, usually in the property sections of Sunday newspapers, often accompanied by a photo of the current celebrity owner, an international rock star. It has ornate chimneys and an eighteenth century facade and a baronial entrance like a church porch and a gravel area in front large enough to host a circus. It's a mansion that taxi drivers point out to their passengers; a residence that estate agents salivate and fantasize over and dream of possessing in their Friday night lager sessions; the kind of residence that can make a postman's job feel worthwhile, which can make him feel a twinge of servile gratitude that he instantly notices in himself and resents, as he drives up the drive. It is a landmark for anyone living remotely nearby, and is endlessly speculated on and gossiped about in the borough paper.

When the limousine arrived at the mansion we were directed to take a side road inside the grounds. This followed the interior of the boundary wall and passed alongside a paved-over plaza, which extended on three sides into a circular concrete amphitheatre. The limousine dropped me off on the paving stones, in the performance area; and then drove off, following the side road, presumably towards an exit.

At the base of the tiers of seats, in the centre at the foot of the steps that led upwards and divided the concrete seating, there was a stall manned by two event employees. These girls were in matching red T-shirts, and stood behind an array of gift bags and laminated maps and gilt edged orders of ceremony.

Jeff was waiting for me there, sitting on the first row of the concrete steps, smoking a cigarette. I raised my hand as I walked over, and he called out,

'I don't want to get photographed smoking up there.'

I walked closer, so the two employees wouldn't overhear.

'Sorry about last night. We should talk some more about Suzie.'

'I thought we'd done that.'

'I know.'

He frowned.

'What do you mean you know?'

'She stayed the night at mine, Jeff.'

He tilted his head, and his frown deepened.

'OK. I'm disappointed, but OK.'

'You travel too much, and you make too many phone calls.'

He shook his head.

'Not always.'

He stood up, dropped the cigarette and ground it under the toe of his left shoe, and walked to the stall. One of the girls handed him a gift bag from the table, and the other gave him an order of ceremony.

From above, on the lawn that the steps led to, a band was playing recent chart hits, and flurries of laughter and conversation drifted down. Spotlights and lasers were beaming upwards and sideways; the familiar, gently restless light of the stars was obscured by the glare of these, apparently wayward, projections diffusing through the higher branches of the trees.

Jeff paused for a moment, reading from his order of ceremony.

'Morton Greaves: Twenty Years of Cinema,' he read aloud.

'What a night.'

I began climbing the steps.

'Josh, we should talk some more.'

'In a second, Jeff.'

'No, not in a second, now; will you turn around?'

'I just want to see what's up here.'

As I ascended the final steps, I saw billboard posters for Morton's films, erected on scaffolds, spaced at intervals along the perimeter of the lawn and opposite the rear of the mansion. The poster for *The End of the Ocean* was there; Morton and I and the others were in our muscular poses; my character looking stoic and resolute. My concerns over Jeff, and all my plans for talking to him, persuading, reassuring him, evaporated. I began to run towards this image of our characters, these ennobled representations, eager to mingle with and join the crowds gathered beneath them.

'Captivity' is Lander Hawes' first published novel. He has previously read short stories at Foyles, the UEA late shift, the National Short Story festival and on BBC Radio Norfolk. His stories have appeared in the 2007 Workshop UEA anthology, the Scarecrow e-zine and in the Unthology 2 collection by Unthank Books. He's been writing to various degrees of intensity for the last ten years, and is hoping to complete a short story collection by the end of 2012.

I'd like to thank Ashley Stokes, Dan Nyman and Robin Jones at Unthank Books for all their editing, advice, hard work and general resourcefulness and ingenuity. Also I'd like to say a thank you to Chris Gribble, Sam, Leila and Katy at Writers Centre Norwich for organising so many of the workshops and other events at the centre of the local arts scene here. Equally I'd like to thank Henry Layte for the treasure that is the Book Hive. I also owe a decade old debt of gratitude to Dennis Kah Swee Ngo for his patience towards a particularly erratic and mystifying student. Lastly I'd like to thank my wife Sarah for her constant love and support, without which I'd be elsewhere and unhappy.

Lander Hawes

Lightning Source UK Ltd.
Milton Keynes UK
UKOW050701040412

190144UK00001B/5/P